Andrew James Symington

Thomas Moore

The Poet. His Life and Works.

Andrew James Symington

Thomas Moore
The Poet. His Life and Works.

ISBN/EAN: 9783337057886

Printed in Europe, USA, Canada, Australia, Japan

Cover: Foto ©Raphael Reischuk / pixelio.de

More available books at **www.hansebooks.com**

THOMAS MOORE.

THOMAS MOORE

The Poet

HIS LIFE AND WORKS

BY

ANDREW JAMES SYMINGTON, F.R.S.N.A.

NEW YORK

HARPER & BROTHERS, FRANKLIN SQUARE

1880

TO

MARY HOWITT,

WHOSE SWEET POEMS ARE HOUSEHOLD WORDS
TREASURED BY OLD AND YOUNG,

THIS VOLUME IS INSCRIBED,

WITH AFFECTION AND ESTEEM,

BY ONE WHO,
DURING SIX-AND-THIRTY CHANGEFUL YEARS,
HAS FOUND, IN HER,
AN UNCHANGING FRIEND.

A. J. S.

Langside, Glasgow, 1880.

PREFACE.

THE aim of the writer, throughout the following pages, has been to present a true picture of the poet MOORE— the man, his life, and works. The facts have been carefully culled from reliable sources; and various opinions regarding the poet and his writings, although formed from different points of view, have neverthe- less, in accordance with this aim, been duly recorded. Copious extracts from his Poems and from his Diary are also given, so as to enable the reader, while making use of the information, criticism, and guidance herein afforded, also, independently, to judge of and enjoy for himself what we set before him.

A. J. S.

LANGSIDE, GLASGOW,
1879.

CONTENTS.

CHAPTER I.

Page

EARLY AND COLLEGE DAYS IN DUBLIN, ... 9

CHAPTER II.

IN LONDON SOCIETY—ODES OF ANACREON—LITTLE'S POEMS, 12

CHAPTER III.

BERMUDA AND AMERICA, ... 23

CHAPTER IV.

RETURN TO ENGLAND—A DUEL—HIS MARRIAGE—JEFFREY—
    ROGERS, ... 34

CHAPTER V.

MAYFIELD COTTAGE—INDEPENDENT SPIRIT—SATIRES,   ... 38

CHAPTER VI.

LALLA ROOKH, ... 55

CHAPTER VII.

NATIONAL AIRS AND SACRED MELODIES—VISIT TO PARIS—
    THE FUDGE FAMILY—SLOPERTON—TRUE CHARITY,   ... 98

CHAPTER VIII.

BERMUDA TROUBLES—CONTINENTAL VISIT—PARIS SOJOURN, 108

CHAPTER IX.

Page

RETURN FROM THE CONTINENT—RHYMES FOR THE ROAD—
FABLES FOR THE HOLY ALLIANCE — LOVES OF THE
ANGELS, ... 118

CHAPTER X.

THE IRISH MELODIES—SELECTIONS—MOORE AS A LYRIC
POET, ... 132

CHAPTER XI.

MOORE'S BEARING IN SOCIETY—PERSONAL APPEARANCE—THE
BURNING OF BYRON'S AUTOBIOGRAPHY—THE EPICUREAN, 161

CHAPTER XII.

POLITICAL ODES—LIFE OF BYRON—SUMMER FETE—PENSION
—LATTER WORKS, ... 179

CHAPTER XIII.

LATTER YEARS AND DEATH, ... 222

CHAPTER XIV.

MOORE'S MEMOIRS—OPINIONS AS TO HIS CHARACTER—MRS.
MOORE, ... 227

CHAPTER XV.

MOORE'S POPULARITY—HIS CENTENARY—ORATION AND ODES
ON THAT OCCASION, ... 234

SELECTIONS

FROM MOORE'S POEMS AND SONGS.

The pieces distinguished by an asterisk (*) are given in full.

	Page
*ODES OF ANACREON XXXV. XXIV. XV. XXIX. XLI. XLVI.,	13–17
Lines to his Mother,	20
My Birth-day,	21
To Lord Viscount Strangford,	25
To the Marchioness Dowager of Donegall. From Bermuda,	26
To George Morgan, Esq. From Bermuda,	27
Bermuda,	28
To the Hon. W. R. Spencer, from Buffalo, upon Lake Erie,	29
To the Lady Charlotte Rawdon. From the Banks of the St. Lawrence,	32
*Canadian Boat-song,	33
Byron on Jeffrey and Moore,	36
*Susan (Young Love liv'd once in a Humble Shed),	38
From THE TWOPENNY POST-BAG.—*Letter I.,	42
Do. do. *Letter V., with Inclosure,	44
Lines addressed to Leigh Hunt and his Brother,	46
*Dialogue between a Sovereign and a One Pound Note,	47
*The Irish Slave,	49
*A Vision—in Imitation of Coleridge,	50
From LALLA ROOKH.—	
From I. The Veiled Prophet:	
Zelica's Love,	63
From II. Paradise and the Peri:	
Introduction,	63
Syria,	65
The Tears of Penitence,	66

Page

From LALLA ROOKH.—
   From III. The Fire-worshippers, • • • • 70
        Hinda's Love, • • • • • 89
        *The Peri's Song, - • • • • 94
   From IV. From the Light of the Harem:
        Cashmere, • • • • • 95
        Light Causes may create Dissension, • 96
        *Song of the Arab Maid, • • • 97
NATIONAL AIRS.—*Hark! the Vesper Hymn is Stealing—Russian, 99
   Do.   *Reason, Folly, and Beauty—Italian, - 99
   Do.   *Oh, Come to Me when Daylight Sets—
        Venetian, • • • • 100
   Do.   *All that's Bright must Fade—Indian, - 101
   Do.   *Oft in the Stilly Night—Scotch, - • 102
SACRED MELODIES.—*Miriam's Song—Sound the Loud Timbrel, 103
   Do.   *This World is all a Fleeting Show, - 103
THE FUDGE FAMILY IN PARIS.—*Miss Biddy's Last Epistle, 104
RHYMES ON THE ROAD.—Different Attitudes in which
        Authors Compose, • • 119
   Do.   *Extract I., - • • • 120
   Do.   *Extract IX., - • • • 122
   Do.   *Extract X., - • • • 124
FABLES FROM THE HOLY ALLIANCE.—A Dream, • • 125
LOVES OF THE ANGELS.—Song of Lilis, from the Second
        Angel's Story, • • • 127
   Do.   Nama and Zaraph's Love, from
        the Third Angel's Story, • 128
Moore's Verse Described by Himself, in Lalla Rookh, • 133
Evening Described by Milton and Moore, - • • - 133–4
IRISH MELODIES.—*Sublime was the Warning, • • 140
   Do.   *Go where Glory waits thee, • • 141
   Do.   *Oh! Breathe not his Name, • • 142
   Do.   *When He who Adores Thee, • • 142
   Do.   *At the Mid Hour of Night, • • 143
   Do.   *Oh the Shamrock, - • • • 143
   Do.   *The Young May Moon, - • • 144
   Do.   *The Harp that Once through Tara's Halls, 145
   Do.   *The Meeting of the Waters, • • 145

Page

IRISH MELODIES.—*The Origin of the Harp, - - - 146
   Do.   *Sing Sweet Harp, - - - - 146
   Do.   *Love's Young Dream, - - - 147
   Do.   *Oh Arranmore, loved Arranmore, - 148
   Do.   *Sweet Innisfallen, - - - - 149
   Do.   *Oh, Could we Do with this World of Ours, 150
   Do.   *I Saw thy Form in Youthful Prime, - 151
   Do.   *She is Far from the Land, - - 152
   Do.   *'Tis the Last Rose of Summer, - - 152
   Do.   *The Minstrel Boy, - - - - 153
   Do.   *I Saw from the Beach, - - - 153
   Do.   *Come Rest in this Bosom, - - - 154
   Do.   *As Slow our Ship, - - - - 154
   Do.   *Dear Harp of my Country, - - 155
BALLADS. SONGS, &c.—*When Midst the Gay I Meet, - 156
   Do.   *When Twilight Dews, - - - 157
   Do.   *The Dream of Home, - - - 157
   Do.   *They tell me Thou'rt the Favoured
           Guest, - - - - 158
   Do.   *The Fancy Fair, - - - - 158
   Do.   *Beauty and Song, - - - 159
   Do.   *Oh, do not Look so Bright and Blest, 160
FROM EVENINGS IN GREECE.—*Song, - - - - 166
The Temple of the Moon (Prose extract), from THE EPICUREAN, 169
ALCIPHRON, - - - - - - - - - 173
*THE PERIWINKLES AND THE LOCUSTS, A SALMAGUNDIAN
   HYMN, - - - - - - - - 179
THE SUMMER FETE—Descriptive, - - - - 186
   Do.   *Song—Bring hither, bring thy Lute,
           while Day is Dying, - - - 188
   Do.   *Song—Who'll Buy? 'tis Folly's Shop,
           Who'll Buy? - - - - 188
*Thoughts on Editors: a Squib, - - - - - 193
*Epigram, - - - - - - - - - 197
*Translation from the Gull Language: a Political Squib, - 198
From THE FUDGES IN ENGLAND.—*Larry O'Branigan's Letter, 203
*Letter in Rhyme to Sydney Smith, - - - - 219
*There was a Little Man: a Ballad, - - - - 234

POETICAL TRIBUTES TO THE MEMORY OF MOORE.

	Page
T. D. Sullivan's Moore Centenary Ode,	242
*Stoddard's Tribute to Moore,	243
*Dr. Oliver Wendell Holmes on Thomas Moore,	244
*Denis Florence Mac Carthy's Ode to Moore,	246

THOMAS MOORE:

HIS LIFE AND WRITINGS.

CHAPTER I

EARLY AND COLLEGE DAYS IN DUBLIN.

THOMAS MOORE was born in Dublin, in the year 1780, of humble but respectable parents, both of whom were Roman Catholics. His father, John Moore, was a grocer and keeper of a small wine store in Aungier Street, where his dwelling-house was over the shop. The usual date assigned for Moore's birth is 1779; but, although the latter date appears upon his tomb-stone, the baptismal register, which has been published by Earl Russell, is still in existence, and proves that he was born in 1780. To his mother's judicious home-training, Moore was indebted for his future success in society.

He was first sent to school, at a very early age, to a Mr. Malone, in the same street—"a wild, odd fellow," he says, "of whose cocked hat I have still a clear remembrance, and who used to pass the greater part of his nights in drinking at public-houses, and was hardly ever able to make his appearance in the school before noon. He would then generally whip the boys all round for disturbing his slumbers."

He afterwards attended the grammar-school of Mr. Samuel White, eminent as an elocutionist, but more widely known as the teacher of Richard Brinsley Sheridan, and Thomas Moore.

His youth was spent in a troubled political period. The French Revolution was regarded as a hopeful event by the Ultramontane party in Ireland, and the poet used to tell how he remembered, at a great public dinner, sitting on the chairman's knee, while the toast, "May the breezes from France fan the Irish oak into verdure," went round amidst triumphant cheering.

In 1794 Moore entered Trinity College, Dublin, with a view to study for law. His career there was more than an ordinary success, although, hating Latin hexameters, he often substituted English for Latin verse, when he conveniently could do so. From his childhood he had exhibited a genius for lyric verse and music; and two of his productions, dropped into the letter-box of a Dublin magazine called *The Anthologia*, appeared in its pages, bearing the initials "T. M.," when he was only fourteen years of age. He was fond of recitation, and was Mr. White's favourite *show*-scholar. "I attained the honour," says Moore, "of being singled out by him on days of public examination as one of his most successful and popular exhibitors—to the no small jealousy, as may be supposed, of all other mammas, and the great glory of my own. As I looked particularly infantine for my age, the wonder was, of course, still more wonderful. 'Oh, he's an old little crab,' said one of the rival Cornelias, on an occasion of this kind; 'he can't be less than eleven or twelve years of age.' 'Then, madam,' said a gentleman sitting next to her, who was slightly acquainted with our family, 'if that is the case he must have been four years old before he was born.' This answer, which was reported to my mother, won her warm heart towards that gentleman for ever after."

In one of his prefaces, he says, "So far back in childhood lies the epoch, that I am really unable to say at what age I first began to act, sing, and rhyme." There is a playbill, still extant, of a performance at Lady Barrowes' private theatre, where one of the attractions set forth is "An Epilogue, 'A Squeeze to St. Paul's,' Master Moore." The bill is dated 1790, and Master Moore was then ten years old. Referring to his happy home life and to the fostering care of his parents, he gratefully adds:—"To these different talents, such as they were, the gay and social habits prevailing in Dublin afforded frequent opportunities of display; while, at home, a most amiable father, and a mother such as, in heart and head, has rarely been equalled, furnished me with that purest stimulus to exertion—the desire to please those whom we at once most love and most respect. It was, I think, a year or two after my entrance into college, that a masque written by myself, and of which I had adapted one of the songs to the air of Haydn's 'Spirit Song,' was acted, under our own humble roof in Aungier Street, by my eldest sister, myself, and one or two other young persons. The little drawing-room over the shop was our grand place of representation, and young ——, now an eminent professor of music in Dublin, enacted for us the part of orchestra at the pianoforte."

He continued to write verses for *The Anthologia*, and, afterwards, for other publications. His sister's music-teacher taught him to play on the pianoforte; he learned Italian from Father Ennis a priest; and picked up French, from La Fosse an emigrant acquaintance.

In 1798 Moore narrowly escaped being involved with Emmet and others in a charge of sedition. He, without doubt, sympathized with their cause, and anonymously wrote two articles, one a poem and the other a fiery

2

letter, in favour of the movement, for *The Press*—a revolutionary paper started towards the end of 1797 by Arthur O'Connor, Robert Emmet, and other chiefs of the United Irish conspiracy. His mother, coming to know of it, bound him by a solemn promise never again to contribute to *The Press*, so that, afterwards, when he was hauled up and examined before Fitzgibbon, the vicechancellor, he owed his escape from danger to his having given heed to her warning voice.

His father, having saved a little money, now resolved to send his son to London to prosecute his law studies. In the same year—1798—which saw so many of his companions exiled or dead, Thomas Moore graduated as B.A., and, bidding adieu to his native city, set out for London, where, early in 1799, he entered as a student at the Middle Temple.

His mother, we are told, gave him no trouble in carrying bank-cheques to the metropolis, but in good housewifely fashion carefully sewed up the gold guineas with a blessed scapular in the waistband of his pantaloons.

CHAPTER II.

IN LONDON SOCIETY—ODES OF ANACREON—LITTLE'S POEMS.

Moore had already translated the *Odes of Anacreon*, and shortly after settling in London he fortunately was able to arrange, through Dr. Hume, one of his earliest friends, with Stockdale of Piccadilly, for their publication in a quarto volume.

The young student and Bachelor of Arts, now returned home to Dublin. On his next visit to England, through another early and kind friend, Joe Atkinson, he was introduced to Lord Moira; for he well knew that, in the then transition state of literature, the success of any publishing venture was largely dependent on the obtaining of a good name for patron; and, so far, the poet was still, in common with others, a dependent; although, later on in life, he was in a position successfully to dictate to, and, independently, arrange with his publishers, on his own acknowledged merits.

Lord Moira, the Duke of Bedford, the Marquis of Lansdowne, and the Prince of Wales became subscribers for this work. To Lord Moira he owed his introduction to this select circle; and the Prince of Wales permitted the dedication of the *Odes* to himself. The volume was published in 1800, when the poet was just of age. He at once became the fashion. Those were the days of supper parties, and even then wit was rare and valued accordingly. Lord Moira, Lord Holland, and Lord Lansdowne were his friends.

Moore's star was rising, and the literary world was full of the praise of the young poet. The authorities of his college, however, did not subscribe for his work. Moore retaliated by calling them "a corporation of boobies, without even sense enough to thank heaven for anything like an effort of literature coming out of their leaden body."

From this volume of translations we select the following—

ODES OF ANACREON.

ODE XXXV.

Cupid once upon a bed
Of roses laid his weary head;
Luckless urchin, not to see
Within the leaves a slumbering bee;
The bee awak'd—with anger wild

The bee awak'd, and stung the child.
Loud and piteous are his cries;
To Venus quick he runs, he flies;
"Oh mother!—I am wounded through—
I die with pain—in sooth I do!
Stung by some little angry thing,
Some serpent on a tiny wing—
A bee it was—for once, I know,
I heard a rustic call it so."
Thus he spoke, and she the while
Heard him with a soothing smile;
Then said, " My infant, if so much
Thou feel the little wild-bee's touch,
How must the heart, ah, Cupid! be,
The hapless heart that's stung by thee!"

ODE XXIV.

To all that breathe the air of heaven,
Some boon of strength has Nature given.
In forming the majestic bull,
She fenced with wreathed horns his skull;
A hoof of strength she lent the steed,
And wing'd the timorous hare with speed.
She gave the lion fangs of terror,
And, o'er the ocean's crystal mirror
Taught the unnumber'd scaly throng
To trace their liquid path along;
While for the umbrage of the grove,
She plum'd the warbling world of love.

To man she gave, in that proud hour,
The boon of intellectual power.
Then what, oh woman, what, for thee,
Was left in Nature's treasury?
She gave thee beauty—mightier far
Than all the pomp and power of war.
Nor steel, nor fire itself hath power
Like woman in her conquering hour.

Be thou but fair, mankind adore thee,
Smile, and a world is weak before thee!

ODE XV.

Tell me why, my sweetest dove,
Thus your humid pinions move,
Shedding through the air in showers
Essence of the balmiest flowers?
Tell me whither, whence you rove,
Tell me all, my sweetest dove.

Curious stranger, I belong
To the bard of Teian song;
With his mandate now I fly
To the nymph of azure eye;—
She, whose eye has madden'd many,
But the poet more than any.
Venus, for a hymn of love,
Warbled in her votive grove,
('Twas in sooth a gentle lay,)
Gave me to the bard away.
See me now his faithful minion.—
Thus with softly-gliding pinion,
To his lovely girl I bear
Songs of passion through the air.
Oft he blandly whispers me,
"Soon, my bird, I'll set you free."
But in vain he'll bid me fly,
I shall serve him till I die.
Never could my plumes sustain
Ruffling winds and chilling rain,
O'er the plains, or in the dell,
On the mountain's savage swell.
Seeking in the desert wood
Gloomy shelter, rustic food.
Now I lead a life of ease,
Far from rugged haunts like these.
From Anacreon's hand I eat

Food delicious, viands sweet;
Flutter o'er his goblet's brim,
Sip the foamy wine with him.
Then, when I have wanton'd round
To his lyre's beguiling sound;
Or with greatly-moving wings
Fann'd the minstrel while he sings:
On his harp I sink in slumbers,
Dreaming still of dulcet numbers!

This is all—away—away—
You have made me waste the day.
How I've chatter'd! prating crow
Never yet did chatter so.

ODE XXIX.

Yes—loving is a painful thrill,
And, not to love, more painful still;
But oh, it is the worst of pain,
To love and not be lov'd again!
Affection now has fled from earth,
Nor fire of genius, noble birth,
Nor heavenly virtue, can beguile
From beauty's cheek one favouring smile.
Gold is the woman's only theme,
Gold is the woman's only dream.
Oh! never be that wretch forgiven—
Forgive him not, indignant heaven!
Whose grovelling eyes could first adore,
Whose heart could pant for sordid ore.
Since that devoted thirst began,
Man has forgot to feel for man;
The pulse of social life is dead,
And all its fonder feelings fled!
War too has sullied Nature's charms,
For gold provokes the world to arms:
And oh! the worst of all its arts,
It rends asunder loving hearts.

ODE XLI.

When Spring adorns the dewy scene,
How sweet to walk the velvet green,
And hear the west wind's gentle sighs,
As o'er the scented mead it flies!
How sweet to mark the pouting vine;
Ready to burst in tears of wine;
And with some maid, who breathes but love,
To walk, at noontide, through the grove,
Or sit in some cool, green recess—
Oh, is not this true happiness?

ODE XLVI.

Behold, the young, the rosy Spring,
Gives to the breeze her scented wing;
While virgin Graces, warm with May,
Fling roses o'er her dewy way.
The murmuring billows of the deep
Have languish'd into silent sleep;
And mark! the flitting sea-birds lave
Their plumes in the reflecting wave;
While cranes from hoary winter fly
To flutter in a kinder sky.
Now the genial star of day
Dissolves the murky clouds away;
And cultur'd field, and winding stream,
Are freshly glittering in his beam.

Now the earth prolific swells
With leafy buds and flowery bells;
Gemming shoots the olive twine,
Clusters ripe, festoon the vine;
All along the branches creeping,
Through the velvet foliage peeping,
Little infant fruits we see,
Nursing into luxury.

Moore's brilliant conversational powers, with his poetical and musical gifts, rendered him everywhere a welcome

guest, and he was now plunged headlong into the vortex
of London fashionable society.

In aristocratic circles he found that refinement and cul-
tured taste which accorded with his inner cravings; for, as
Lord John Russell observes, "Beyond the mere pleasure
of the encounter, it cannot be disputed that much is to
be learned from the conversation of men of reading and
observation. Mr. Fox declared that he learned more,
from Mr. Burke's conversation, than from all the books
he had ever read. It often happens, indeed, that a short
remark in conversation contains the essence of a quarto
volume."

Here we transcribe a pleasant sprightly letter which he
received from his friend, Miss Godfrey, the sister of
Lady Donegall:—

"Dec. 27, 1801.

"I have this moment received your letter, and *me voici la
plume à la main pour y repondre;* not to tell you what we
can make of you, for God only knows what you are good for,
or whether you are good for anything, but to lament and
groan over your restless disposition. Your talents might fit
you for everything, and your idleness unfits you for anything.
You want to come to town, I know you do, merely to get away
from those country-bred, sentimental ladies, the Muses, and I
pray that you may have no other ladies in view to supply
their place. You really might, if you pleased, study all the
morning and amuse yourself all the evening. I entreat you
to make an effort, and not devote every hour and moment of
your existence to pleasure. You know my sermons make you
laugh—*tant mieux.* I never despair of you when you laugh;
if you yawned I should give up the thing as hopeless. Lady
C. Rawdon has so often regretted, and I have so often forgiven
her not writing, that I have not the least objection to our
going on regretting and forgiving to the end of the chapter.
Abstraction, self-contemplation, etiquette, and, God forgive
me, I *was* going to say *strict morality,* but I retract that, are

not great enliveners of society, and I don't wonder at the
Muses being a little discomposed by such an interruption.
But who was the unfortunate fair one to whom those very
pretty lines which you sent me were addressed? If Nature
had been as kind to me as she has been to you, I would write
you something upon the occasion; but Nature has treated me
abominably ill, for which I shall never forgive her; she has
given me feelings to admire with enthusiasm the talents of
others, and she has denied me even the faintest ray of genius.
I never heard of the *Seven Fountains* before. What sort of
book is it—poetry or prose? If I should happen to read it, I
suppose I must 'give God thanks, and make no boast of it.'
The snow, after which you inquire so kindly, has departed this
life, to my great joy. I never am in good-will, either with
myself or my fellow-creatures, in cold weather; are you? I
did intend writing you to-morrow, for which I had a very
wise reason best known to myself, but when I received your
tragi-comic, or rather your more comic than tragic letter, I
resolved to answer it immediately to encourage you to remain
at your post. Nothing ever was more disinterested than this
advice, and I never shall cease to admire myself for giving it;
for, if I followed my own inclinations—which in general don't
lead me astray like yours—I would say, 'Come up to town, by
all means, and the oftener we see you the better.' I consult
your interest when I say the contrary. But yet if you do
come, if the truth must come out, I shall most heartily rejoice
to see you, and so shall we all. Say pretty things for me to
Lady Charlotte about love and friendship, and writing to each
other. I shall give you a *carte blanche* upon the occasion, for
I suspect she does not care the least in the world for me—it
is all stage trick and fine acting; this is quite *entre nous*. Remember me to Lord Forbes. God bless you, and make a good
man of you (I believe it is almost impossible).—Yours very
sincerely, M. GODFREY."

Amidst gaieties, he preserved unimpaired his strong
home affection for his father, and mother, and sister.

His father was "handsome, full of fun, possessed of

good manners," and, as Moore said, "one of nature's
gentlemen." Moore always treated him with a reverence
which could not have been more profound, if the old
man had boasted the proudest ancestry and the amplest
fortune. To his mother, Anastasia Moore, *née* Codd, his
attachment was, from earliest days, as intense as it was
enduring. She was a woman of mind, retiring, unpre-
tending, and kindly. To her he ever gave intense respect
and devoted affection. In the midst of his labours, his
trials, and his triumphs, he never failed—except when
precluded by his absence in Bermuda—to write to her
twice a week; and he freely told her of everything, great
or small, that interested him, knowing it would therefore
interest her, his own "darling mother"—from his introduction to the Prince of Wales, and his visit to Niagara,
to the acquisition of a pencil-case or the purchase of a
pocket-handkerchief.

He wrote out a volume of his early poems expressly
for her, and prefixed to it a loving monograph preface.
When she died, she left four thousand of his letters.
To her he fondly addressed these sweet verses:—

> "They tell us of an Indian tree,
>   Which—how-soe'er the sun and sky
> May tempt its boughs to wander free
>   And shoot and blossom wide and high—
> Far better loves to bend its arms
>   Downward again to that dear earth
> From which the life that fills and warms
>   Its grateful being first had birth.
> 'Tis thus, though woo'd by flattering friends,
>   And fed with fame, if fame it be,
> This heart, my own dear mother, bends
>   With love's true instinct back to thee!"

His first letter addressed to her, in 1793, ended thus:—

> "Your absence, all but ill endure,
> And none so ill as—THOMAS MOORE."

And in 1835, after her death, when visiting the house,
where his mother had been born and brought up, situated
in the old corn-market of Wexford, he wrote:—"One of
the noblest minded, as well as the most warm-hearted of
all God's creatures, was born under that lowly roof."

His sister Ellen, to whom he was greatly attached,
was a small delicate woman, with an expression sharp-
ened somewhat by continuous bodily ailment; but her
mind and disposition were essentially lovable, and she
sang very sweetly. Moore contrived in 1803, when he
had quite enough to do otherwise, to buy and send her a
present of a pianoforte.

Such were, always, his genuine and enduring home
feelings, both then and afterwards, when he was being
lionized in the first London society.

In 1801 he published a volume of "poems" under the
name of "The Late Thomas Little, Esq." These were
full of indecencies, of which, however, he was afterwards
so much ashamed that he altogether excluded many of
them from the collected edition of his poems.

His friend Rogers states, "So heartily has Moore re-
pented of having published *Little's Poems*, that I have
seen him shed tears—tears of deep contrition—when we
were talking of them." And he himself afterwards thus
wrote, in a poem called—

MY BIRTH-DAY.

> "My birth-day"—what a diff'rent sound
> That word had in my youthful ears!
> And how, each time the day comes round,
> Less and less white, its mark appears!

When first our scanty years are told,
It seems like pastime to grow old;
And, as Youth counts the shining links,
　That time around him binds so fast,
Pleas'd with the task, he little thinks
　How hard that chain will press at last.
Vain was the man, and false as vain,
　Who said—"were he ordain'd to run
His long career of life again,
　He would do all that he *had* done."—
Ah, 'tis not thus the voice, that dwells
　In sober birth-days, speaks to me
Far otherwise—of time it tells,
　Lavish'd unwisely, carelessly;
Of counsel mock'd; of talents, made
　Haply for high and pure designs,
But oft, like Israel's incense, laid
　Upon unholy, earthly shrines;
Of nursing many a wrong desire;
　Of wandering after Love too far,
And taking every meteor fire,
　That cross'd my pathway, for his star.—
All this it tells, and, could I trace
　The imperfect picture o'er again,
With pow'r to add, retouch, efface
　The lights and shades, the joy and pain,
How little of the past would stay!
How quickly all should melt away—
All—but that Freedom of the Mind,
　Which hath been more than wealth to me;
Those friendships, in my boyhood twin'd,
　And kept till now unchangingly;
And that dear home, that saving ark,
　Where Love's true light at last I've found,
Cheering within, when all grows dark.
　And comfortless and stormy round!

"Moore at twenty-one," says a writer in the *Athenæum*,

"had a singularly acute insight into his own character. Pretending to describe the nature of the fictitious Mr. Little, he says, 'He had too much vanity to hide his virtues, and not enough of art to conceal his defects.' This indeed expresses Moore completely, and is the secret of his marvellous personal popularity and of the ease with which his private character has always been assailed. He wore his heart upon his sleeve, and the world grew tired of looking at it."

CHAPTER III.

BERMUDA AND AMERICA.

In 1803 Lord Moira procured him an appointment in the Court of Bermuda as Registrar of the Admiralty. Before sailing he wrote thus to his mother:—

"Portsmouth, Thursday, Sept. 22, 1803.

"Just arrived at Portsmouth, and the wide sea before my eyes, I write my heart's farewell to the dear darlings at home. Heaven send I may return to English ground with pockets *more heavy* and spirits *not less light* than I now leave it with. Everything has been arranged to my satisfaction. I am prepared with every comfort for the voyage, and a fair breeze and a loud yo-yo-ee! are all that's now wanting to set me afloat. My dear father should write to Carpenter and thank him for the very friendly assistance he has given me: without that assistance the breeze would be fair in vain for me, and Bermuda might be sunk in the deep, for any share that *I* could pretend to in it; but now all is smooth for my progress, and Hope sings in the shrouds of the ship that is to carry me. Good-by! God bless you all, dears of my heart! I will write again if our departure is delayed by any circumstance. God

bless you again, and preserve you happy till the return of
your   Tom.

"Urge Stevenson to send Carpenter the songs; I shall write
to him.   Sweet Mother, Father, Kate, and Nell, good-by!"

And again, on October 10th, writing on shipboard,
when a homeward-bound sail was in sight. After describing the progress of the voyage, he says:—

"Keep up your spirits, my sweet mother, there is every
hope, every prospect of happiness for all of us. Love to darling father, to my own Kate and Nell. I am now near two
thousand miles from you, but my *heart* is at *home*. God bless
you. The ship is brought to, and our lieutenant is just going
aboard, so I must stop.—Your own,   Tom."
"I wrote a line to Carpenter by a ship we met off the
Western Islands. I hope he has got it. Here is a *kiss* for
you, my darlings, all the way from the Atlantic."

He sailed on the 25th of September in the *Phaeton*
frigate from Spithead, landing at Norfolk, Virginia,
whence, after a stay of about ten days, he proceeded in
a sloop of war to Bermuda. It was the beginning of
1804 when Moore reached the "still-vexed Bermoothes,"
already consecrated to song by Shakspere, Waller, and
Andrew Marvell.

To his mother, on January 19th, 1804, he writes:—

"These little islands of Bermuda form certainly one of the
prettiest and most romantic spots that I could ever have imagined, and the descriptions, which represent it as like a place
of fairy enchantment, are very little beyond the truth. From
my window now as I write, I can see five or six different
islands, the *most distant* not a mile from the others, and
separated by the clearest, sweetest coloured sea you can conceive; for the water here is so singularly transparent that, in
coming in, we could see the rocks under the ship quite plainly.
These little islands are thickly covered with cedar groves,

through the vistas of which you catch a few pretty white houses, which my poetical short-sightedness always transforms into temples."

In his *Odes and Epistles*, subsequently published, we have a series of poetical notes of his progress from place to place, and from these we shall give some extracts:—

TO LORD VISCOUNT STRANGFORD.

ABOARD THE PHAETON FRIGATE, OFF THE AZORES, BY MOON-LIGHT.

Sweet Moon! if, like Crotona's sage,
  By any spell my hand could dare
To make thy disk its ample page,
  And write my thoughts, my wishes there;
How many a friend, whose careless eye
Now wanders o'er that starry sky,
Should smile, upon thy orb to meet
The recollection, kind and sweet,
The reveries of fond regret,
The promise, never to forget,
And all my heart and soul would send
To many a dear-lov'd, distant friend.

.   .   .   .   .   .

Even now delusive hope will steal
Amid the dark regrets I feel,
Soothing, as yonder placid beam
  Pursues the murmurers of the deep,
And lights them with consoling gleam,
  And smiles them into tranquil sleep.
Oh! such a blessed night as this,
  I often think, if friends were near,
How we should feel, and gaze with bliss
  Upon the moon-bright scenery here!
The sea is like a silvery lake,
  And, o'er its calm the vessel glides
Gently, as if it fear'd to wake

The slumber of the silent tides.
The only envious cloud that lowers
   Hath hung its shade on Pico's height,
Where dimly, 'mid the dusk, he towers,
   And scowling at this heav'n of light,
Exults to see the infant storm
Cling darkly round his giant form!

   .   .   .   .   .   .

But hark!—the boatswain's pipings tell
'Tis time to bid my dream farewell:
Eight bells:—the middle watch is set;
Good night, my Strangford!—ne'er forget
That, far beyond the western sea
Is one, whose heart remembers thee.

TO THE MARCHIONESS DOWAGER OF DONEGALL.

FROM BERMUDA, JANUARY, 1804.

   .   .   .   .   .   .

Say, have you ne'er, in nightly vision, stray'd
To those pure isles of ever-blooming shade,
Which bards of old, with kindly fancy, plac'd
For happy spirits in th' Atlantic waste?
There listening, while, from earth, each breeze that came
Brought echoes of their own undying fame,
In eloquence of eye, and dreams of song,
They charm'd their lapse of nightless hours along:—
Nor yet in song that mortal ear might suit,
For every spirit was itself a lute,
Where Virtue waken'd, with elysian breeze,
Pure tones of thought and mental harmonies.

Believe me, Lady, when the zephyrs bland
Floated our bark to this enchanted land,—
These leafy isles upon the ocean thrown,
Like studs of emerald o'er a silver zone,—
Not all the charm, that ethnic fancy gave
To blessed arbours o'er the western wave,

Could wake a dream, more soothing or sublime,
Of bowers ethereal, and the Spirit's clime.

Bright rose the morning, every wave was still,
When the first perfume of a cedar hill
Sweetly awak'd us, and, with smiling charms,
The fairy harbour woo'd us to its arms.
Gently we stole, before the whisp'ring wind,
Through plantain shades, that round, like awnings twin'd,
And kiss'd on either side the wanton sails,
Breathing our welcome to these vernal vales;
While, far reflected o'er the wave serene,
Each wooded island shed so soft a green
That the enamour'd keel, with whisp'ring play,
Through liquid herbage seem'd to steal its way.

Never did weary bark more gladly glide,
Or rest its anchor in a lovelier tide!
Along the margin, many a shining dome,
White as the palace of a Lapland gnome,
Brighten'd the wave;—in every myrtle grove
Secluded bashful, like a shrine of love,
Some elfin mansion sparkled through the shade;
And while the foliage interposing play'd,
Lending the scene an ever-changing grace,
Fancy would love, in glimpses vague, to trace
The flowery capital, the shaft, the porch,
And dream of temples, till her kindling torch
Lighted me back to all the glorious days
Of Attic genius; and I seem'd to gaze
On marble, from the rich Pentelic mount,
Gracing the umbrage of some Naiad's fount.

．　　　．　　　．　　　．　　　．　　　．

TO GEORGE MORGAN, ESQ.
FROM BERMUDA, JANUARY, 1804.

．　　　．　　　．　　　．　　　．　　　．

But, bless the little fairy isle!
How sweetly after all our ills,
We saw the sunny morning smile
3

Serenely o'er its fragrant hills;
And felt the pure, delicious flow
Of airs, that round this Eden blow
Freshly as ev'n the gales that come
O'er our own healthy hills at home.

Could you but view the scenery fair,
   That now beneath my window lies,
You'd think, that nature lavish'd there
   Her purest wave, her softest skies,
To make a heaven for love to sigh in,
For bards to live and saints to die in.
Close to my wooded bank below,
   In glassy calm the waters sleep,
And to the sunbeam proudly show
   The coral rocks they love to steep.
The fainting breeze of morning fails;
   The drowsy boat moves slowly past,
And I can almost touch its sails
   As loose they flap around the mast.
The noontide sun a splendour pours
That lights up all these leafy shores;
While his own heav'n, its clouds and beams,
   So pictur'd in the waters lie,
That each small bark, in passing, seems
   To float along a burning sky.

BERMUDA.

.   .   .   .   .   .

Farewell to Bermuda, and long may the bloom
Of the lemon and myrtle its valleys perfume;
May spring to eternity hallow the shade,
Where Ariel has warbled and Waller has stray'd.
And thou—when at dawn, thou shalt happen to roam,
Through the lime-covered alley that leads to thy home,
Where oft, when the dance and the revel were done,
And the stars were beginning to fade in the sun,
I have led thee along, and have told by the way
What my heart all the night had been burning to say—

> Oh ! think of the past—give a sigh to those times,
> And a blessing for me to that alley of limes.

Knowing that it was an uncongenial post, Moore only remained there for a few months while arranging to have his duties performed by deputy.   In his letters he described the scenery as beautiful, but his occupation, in examining witnesses in regard to captured vessels, &c., as not very poetical.   He left Bermuda in April, resolved to see something of America before his return to England, and sailed to New York; from thence, after a short stay, he revisited Norfolk in Virginia, where Mr. Merry, the English minister, introduced him to President Jefferson—the man who drew up the Declaration of American Independence.   From Norfolk he proceeded on a pleasure tour through the States.

At Philadelphia he formed some agreeable friendships. In lines addressed "To the Honourable W. R. Spencer, from Buffalo, upon Lake Erie," after severely animadverting on the half polished, half barbarous life, then common in the States, and incident to a newly-settled country,

> "Without one breath of soul, divinely strong
> One ray of mind to thaw them into song;"

by way of contrast, he goes on to speak of many pleasant hours spent in the society of Mr. Dennie and his friends there:—

> "Yet, yet forgive me, oh ye sacred few,
> Whom late by Delaware's green banks I knew;
> Whom, known and lov'd through many a social eve,
> 'Twas bliss to live with, and 'twas pain to leave.
> Not with more joy the lonely exile scann'd
> The writing trac'd upon the desert's sand,
> Where his lone heart but little hop'd to find
> One trace of life, one stamp of human kind,

Than did I hail the pure, th' enlighten'd zeal,
The strength to reason and the warmth to feel,
The manly polish and the illumin'd taste,
Which,—'mid the melancholy, heartless waste
My foot has travers'd,—oh you sacred few!
I found by Delaware's green banks with you."

 .   .   .   .

"Believe me, Spencer, while I wing'd the hours
Where Schuylkill winds his way through banks of
    flowers,
Though few the days, the happy evenings few,
So warm with heart, so rich with mind they flew
That my charm'd soul forgot its wish to roam,
And rested there, as in a dream of home.
And looks I met, like looks I'd lov'd before,
And voices too, which as they trembled o'er
The chord of memory, found full many a tone
Of kindness there in concord with their own.
Yes,—we had nights of that communion free,
That flow of heart, which I have known with thee
So oft, so warmly; nights of mirth and mind,
Of whims that taught, and follies that refin'd,
When shall we both renew them? when, restor'd
To the gay feast and intellectual board,
Shall I once more enjoy with thee and thine
Those whims that teach, those follies that refine?
Even now, as wand'ring upon Erie's shore,
I hear Niagara's distant cataract roar,
I sigh for home,—alas! these weary feet
Have many a mile to journey, ere we meet."

Recording his journey by the Mohawk river, he writes:—
"There is a holy magnificence in the immense bank of
woods that overhang it, which does not permit the heart
to rest merely in the admiration of nature, but carries it
to that something less vague than nature—that satisfactory
source of all these exquisite wonders—a divinity."

Visiting Canada, Moore mentions that the captain of the packet in which he crossed "the fresh-water ocean," Lake Ontario, in addition to the other marks of courtesy, begged, on parting with him, to be allowed to decline payment for his passage.

After seeing Niagara Falls, he sailed down the St. Lawrence to Montreal and Quebec, staying for a short time at each of these places.

The visit to Niagara he considered as an era in his life; and the first glimpse he caught of that wonderful cataract gave him a feeling which nothing in this world could ever awaken again. "It was," said he, when writing of it long afterwards, "through an opening among the trees, as we approached the spot where the full view of the Falls was to burst upon us, that I caught this glimpse of the mighty mass of waters folding smoothly over the edge of the precipice; and so overwhelming was the notion it gave me of the awful spectacle I was approaching, that, during the short interval that followed, imagination had far outrun the reality. . . . I retain in my memory but one other dream—for such do events so long past appear—which can in any respect be associated with the grand vision I have just been describing; and, however different the nature of their appeals to the imagination, I should find it difficult to say on which occasion I felt most deeply affected, when looking on the Falls of Niagara, or when standing by moonlight among the ruins of the Colosseum." And, again, of Niagara, he writes:—"My whole heart and soul ascended towards the Divinity in a swell of devout admiration which I never before experienced. Oh! bring the atheist here, and he cannot return an atheist. I pity the man who can coldly sit down to write a description of these ineffable wonders. Much more do I pity him

who can submit them to the admeasurement of gallons
and yards.   It is impossible, by pen or pencil, to convey
even a faint idea of their magnificence.   Painting is
lifeless; and the most burning words of poetry have been
lavished upon inferior and ordinary subjects.   We must
have new combinations of language to describe the Falls
of Niagara."

Of it, too, in his POEMS RELATING TO AMERICA, he
wrote:—

TO THE LADY CHARLOTTE RAWDON.

FROM THE BANKS OF THE ST. LAWRENCE.

.   .   .   .

I dreamt not then, that, e'er the rolling year
Had fill'd its circle, I should wander here
In musing awe; should tread this wondrous world,
See all its store of inland waters hurl'd
In one vast volume down Niagara's steep,
Or calm behold them, in transparent sleep,
Where the blue hills of old Toronto shed
Their evening shadows o'er Ontario's bed;
Should trace the grand Cadaraqui, and glide
Down the white rapids of his lordly tide
Through massy woods, 'mid islets flowering fair,
And blooming glades, where the first sinful pair
For consolation might have weeping trod,
When banish'd from the garden of their God.
Oh, Lady! these are miracles, which man,
Cag'd in the bounds of Europe's pigmy span,
Can scarcely dream of,—which his eye must see
To know how wonderful this world can be!

But lo,—the last tints of the west decline,
And night falls dewy o'er these banks of pine.
Among the reeds, in which our idle boat
Is rock'd to rest, the wind's complaining note
Dies like a half-breath'd whispering of flutes;

Along the wave the gleaming porpoise shoots,
And I can trace him like a watery star
Down the steep current, till he fades afar
Amid the foaming breakers' silvery light,
Where yon rough rapids sparkle through the night,
Here, as along this shadowy bank I stray,
And the smooth glass-snake, gliding o'er my way,
Shows the dim moonlight through his scaly form,
Fancy, with all the scene's enchantment warm,
Hears in the murmur of the nightly breeze
Some Indian Spirit warble words like these:—

> From the land beyond the sea,
> Whither happy spirits flee;
> Where, transform'd to sacred doves,
> Many a blessed Indian roves
> Through the air on wing, as white
> As those wondrous stones of light,
> Which the eye of morning counts
> On the Apallachian mounts,—
> Hither oft my flight I take
> Over Huron's lucid lake,
> Where the wave, as clear as dew,
> Sleeps beneath the light canoe,
> Which, reflected, floating there,
> Looks as if it hung in air.

His *Odes and Epistles* contain descriptive sketches of scenery as remarkable for their fidelity to nature as for their poetical beauty; and of all his poetical records of this tour, none are so exquisitely lovely as the—

CANADIAN BOAT-SONG.

WRITTEN ON THE RIVER ST. LAWRENCE.

Faintly as tolls the evening chime
Our voices keep tune and our oars keep time.
Soon as the woods on shore look dim,
We'll sing at St. Ann's our parting hymn.

Row, brothers, row, the stream runs fast,
The Rapids are near and the daylight's past.

Why should we yet our sail unfurl?
There is not a breath the blue wave to curl;
But, when the wind blows off the shore,
Oh! sweetly we'll rest our weary oar.
Blow, breezes, blow, the stream runs fast,
The Rapids are near and the daylight's past.

Utawas' tide! this trembling moon   .
Shall see us float over thy surges soon.
Saint of this green isle! hear our prayers,
Oh, grant us cool heavens and favouring airs.
Blow, breezes, blow, the stream runs fast,
The Rapids are near and the daylight's past.

CHAPTER IV.

RETURN TO ENGLAND—DUEL—HIS MARRIAGE—JEFFREY— ROGERS.

Moore's whole absence from England was only a period of fourteen months, and from what he saw in the West, or rather from what he could not find there, of refinement in social life and the aroma of society, his previous ideas of republican government were considerably modified.

Through Lord Moira, in 1806, after his return, he obtained for his father the appointment of a barrack-mastership in Dublin, so that his parent was now enabled to leave the counter.

This year, anticipating a home visit to Ireland, he wrote to his mother—

"I think in about a fortnight I shall take flight for the bogs.

Darling mother! how happy I shall be to see you!—it will put a new spur on the heel of my heart, which will make life trot, for the time at least, sixteen miles an hour. I trust in heaven that you are recovering, and that I shall find you as you ought to be.—Ever your own, ꞌ Tom."

Moore's *Odes and Epistles*, from which we have already given quotations, appeared in 1806. Capt. Basil Hall vouches for the accuracy of Moore's description of Bermuda, saying that it is "the most pleasing and exact" he knows. However, the volume was very severely handled by Jeffrey in *The Edinburgh Review*, on the score of its occasional questionable morality; and Moore, irritated, foolishly sent him a challenge. The combatants met at Chalk Farm; but just as they were about to fire, the police, who had got information of the affair, stepped in and put a stop to further proceedings. A few days after this the mutual friends of the poet and the critic contrived a meeting between them as if by accident. An explanation took place; Jeffrey acknowledging that he was too severe, and Moore that he was too hot. Moore, afterwards, boasted that, in the most severe of all his critics, he had found the most cordial of his friends; and, in later years, Jeffrey wrote thus of Moore:—"He has long ago redeemed his error; in all his latter works he appears as the eloquent champion of purity, fidelity, and delicacy, not less than of justice, liberty, and honour."

On the ground, where the duel was to have been fought, it was found by the seconds that one of the pistols had no bullet. A report got abroad that Moore and Jeffrey fought with pistols that were unloaded; and Byron sarcastically commemorated the event in his *English Bards and Scotch Reviewers*, aiming at Jeffrey, to whom he owed a deep grudge, rather than at Moore. Byron's lines are these:—

> "Health to great Jeffrey! Heaven preserve his life
> To flourish on the fertile shores of Fife,
> And guard it secret in his future wars
> Since authors sometimes seek the field of Mars.
> Can none remember that eventful day
> That ever glorious almost fatal fray,
> When Little's leadless pistol met his eye,
> And Bow-street myrmidons stood laughing by?"

However, one folly begets another, and Moore, stung by this biting sarcasm, in hot blood sent Byron a challenge; but, fortunately, matters were adjusted by mutual friends without a hostile meeting, and between the would-be combatants there was formed a friendship that was severed only by death.

In 1807 Moore began to publish *The Irish Melodies*, which were not, however, completed till 1834. He furnished words and adapted the airs, while Sir John A. Stevenson was to provide the accompaniments. In 1808 he published anonymously two poems, *Intolerance*, and *Corruption;* and, in 1809, *The Sceptic*—none of which were very successful. "A Letter to the Roman Catholics of Dublin" appeared in 1810.

Of authorship he wrote to Lady Donegall, on January 3, 1810:—"How a poor author is puzzled now-a-days between quantity and quality! The booksellers won't buy him if the former be not great, and the critics won't let him be read if the latter be not good. Now, there are no two perfections more difficult to attain together, for they are generally (as we little men would wish to establish) in inverse proportion to each other. However, I must do my best."

On Lady-day, in March, 1811, he was so fortunate as to marry Miss Bessie Dyke, a native of Kilkenny, a charming and amiable young actress of considerable ability. Their house was at York Place, Queen's Elm, Brompton. The terrace was isolated, and opposite nursery gardens. Mrs. Moore was very domestic in her tastes, and possessed much energy of character, tact, and a sound judgment; while her personal appearance was such as to draw from Rogers the appellation of "the Psyche," by which name he continued to designate her.

To her, Lord John Russell pays the following well-deserved tribute:—"The excellence of his wife's moral character, her energy and courage, her persevering economy, made her a better, and even a richer partner to Moore than an heiress of ten thousand a year would have been, with less devotion to her duty, and less steadiness of conduct." He also adds, that, "from the year of his marriage to the year of his death, his excellent and beautiful wife received from him the homage of a lover."

Of her personal appearance at a later period Mrs. Hall says:—"Her figure and carriage were perfect; every movement was graceful. Her head and throat were exquisitely moulded; and her voice, when she spoke, was soft and clear, . . . soft brown eyes, . . . features really beautiful; the delicate nose; the sweet and expressive mouth; the dimples, now here, now there; the chin so soft and rounded; the face a perfect oval. Even at that time, no one could have entered a room without murmuring, 'What a lovely woman!'"

With this lovely and gentle wife, Moore, to quote his own words, enjoyed "perfect happiness;" and the story of their lives, through sunshine and gloom, reads like a charming idyll.

In the autumn of 1811, *M.P., or the Blue Stocking*, a comic opera, was produced on the stage. It was a failure, as a whole; but contained some beautiful songs, such as "Young Love Liv'd Once in a Humble Shed,"

"Spirit of Joy, Thy Altar Lies," and "Though Sacred the Tie." We give the first of these:—

SUSAN.

Young Love liv'd once in a humble shed,
    Where roses breathing,
    And woodbines wreathing
Around the lattice their tendrils spread,
As wild and sweet as the life he led.
    His garden flourish'd,
    For young Hope nourish'd
The infant buds with beams and showers;
But lips, though blooming, must still be fed,
And not even Love can live on flowers.

Alas! that Poverty's evil eye
    Should e'er come hither,
    Such sweets to wither!
The flowers laid down their heads to die,
And Hope fell sick as the witch drew nigh.
    She came one morning,
    Ere Love had warning,
And rais'd the latch, where the young god lay;
"Oh ho!" said Love—"is it you? good-bye;"
So he oped the window, and flew away!

CHAPTER V.

MAYFIELD COTTAGE—INDEPENDENT SPIRIT—SATIRES.

For a time after his marriage he had been residing chiefly with Lord Moira, but, in the spring of 1812, he took a cottage at Kegworth, so as still to be near his friend's residence, and yet not quite dependent on him for a home; but, on Lord Moira going to India, he, shortly afterwards in the summer of 1813, left it for Mayfield Cottage, near Ashbourne, in Derbyshire.

His exchequer sometimes got very low.

On November 12, 1812, he writes to Mr. Power, the publisher of the *Irish Melodies*—

"My Dear Sir,—I have but just got your letter, and have only time to say that if you can let me have but three or four pounds by return of post, you will oblige me. I would not have made this hasty and importunate demand on you, but I have foolishly let myself run dry without trying my other resources, and I have been the week past literally without one sixpence. Ever, with most sincere good-will, the penniless

"T. M."

Mr. Power at once sent ten pounds, on which, Moore gives him the following explanation of why he had to be so ungracious as send "such a hurried and begging scrawl." "The truth is, we have been kept on a visit at a house where we have been much longer than I wished or intended, and simply from not having a shilling in our pockets to give the servants on going away. So I know you will forgive my teasing you. . . . You may laugh at my ridiculous distress in being kept to turtle eating and claret-drinking longer than I wish, and merely *because* I have not a shilling in my pocket—but however paradoxical it sounds, it is true."

Travelling from a scene of aristocratic grandeur, of which they had become weary, they longed for the utmost simplicity, retirement, and repose; and determined to take the very first suitable place of the kind they found vacant; and they fixed upon Mayfield Cottage. "It was a poor place," said Moore to William Howitt, "little better than a barn, but we at once took it, and set about making it habitable." The rent he paid for it was £20 a year. In front there is a small flower-garden, slightly terraced, and a path leading up to the front door which has a simple trellised porch. The front of the cottage is partly covered with greenery; it is surrounded by trees; and there is a small arbour where the poet used to sit and write.

The right-hand front window is pointed out as belonging to Moore's little parlour; the window at the side belonged to his little library. Out of doors, in the orchard, when the weather admitted of it, was his favourite study.

The immediate neighbourhood is not striking; but Mayfield lies in a fine country, and within a short distance of it are Dovedale—rendered classic by old Izaak Walton and Cotton—where he used often to ramble with Bessie his wife, and many other beautiful scenes in Derbyshire and Staffordshire. There were many persons of taste and refinement living in the neighbourhood, from whom he and his family received every cordial attention. It was then "within twenty-four hours' drive of town," *i.e.* London. Near Mayfield is laid the scene of that striking modern novel *Adam Bede.*

Moore was much courted by the great, and mingled with them on equal terms; for he possessed, through natural gifts and culture, "a richness of intellectual accomplishment, a capacity of mental toil, a variety of curious learning, a brilliancy of wit, and power of sarcasm which bears comparison with the best of his contemporaries." Of independent spirit, when in serious difficulties, he often set aside frankly proffered aid, and preferred to help himself—and so also to extend aid to others.

In a letter written to Lady Donegall, in 1808, he wisely and quaintly says of Mayfield—"I have here a home where I can live at but little expense, and I have a summer's leisure before me to prepare something for the next campaign, which may enable me to look down upon my enemies without entirely looking up to my friends; for, let one say what one will, looking up too long is tiresome, let the subject be ever so grand or lovely— whether the statue of Venus or the cupola of St. Paul's."

His personal friends all regarded him as lovable, generous, honourable, manly and true.

In 1812 appeared *The Intercepted Letters, or the Two-penny Post Bag, by Thomas Brown, the Younger.*

Hazlitt, after slashing at some of his better and more enduring works, says, "But he has wit at will, and of the first quality. His satirical and burlesque poetry is his best; it is first-rate. His light, agreeable, and polished style pierces through the body of the court, hits off the faded graces of an Adonis of fifty, weighs the vanity of fashion in tremulous scales, mimics the grimace of affectation and folly, shows up the littleness of the great, and spears a phalanx of statesmen with its glittering point as with a diamond." "In *The Twopenny Post Bag*, his light laughing satire attains its most delicate piquancy." Of it Byron wrote, "By-the-bye, what humour—what— everything in the *Post Bag!*"

The wit, pungency, and playfulness of these satires, chiefly aimed at the Prince Regent and his ministers, made them immensely popular, and fourteen editions were called for in the course of one year.

Having been accused of ingratitude for quizzing royalty, he himself has been careful to leave on record the actual amount of *royal* patronage which he had received. The passage referred to occurs in the preface to his third volume, and is to the following effect:—"Luckily, the list of the benefits showered upon me from that high quarter may be despatched in a few sentences. At the request of the Earl of Moira, one of my earliest and best friends,

His Royal Highness graciously permitted me to dedicate to him my Translation of the Odes of Anacreon. I was twice, I think, admitted to the honour of dining at Carlton House; and when the Prince, on his being made Regent in 1811, gave his memorable fête, I was one of the crowd—about 1500, I believe, in number—who enjoyed the privilege of being his guests on the occasion. . . . But, whatever may be thought of the taste or prudence of some of these satires, there exists no longer, I apprehend, much difference of opinion respecting the character of the royal personage against whom they were aimed. Already, indeed, has the stern verdict which the voice of History cannot but pronounce upon him been in some degree anticipated."

"The obligation," it has been remarked, "was certainly not overpowering, especially when the country had to pay for it."

From *The Twopenny Post Bag*, we give the following extracts, which, relating to the current topics of that day, were then well understood:—

LETTER I.

FROM THE PR—NC—SS CH—RL—E OF W—L—S TO THE LADY B—RB—A ASHL—Y.

My dear Lady Bab, you'll be shock'd, I'm afraid,
When you hear the sad rumpus your Ponies have made;
Since the time of horse-consuls (now long out of date),
No nags ever made such a stir in the state.
Lord Eld—n first heard—and as instantly pray'd he
To "God and his King"—that a Popish young Lady
(For though you've bright eyes and twelve thousand a year,
It is still but too true you're a Papist, my dear,)
Had insidiously sent, by a tall Irish groom,
Two priest-ridden Ponies, just landed from Rome,

And so full, little rogues, of pontifical tricks,
That the dome of St. Paul's was scarce safe from their kicks.

the Regent

Off at once to Papa, in a flurry he flies—
For Papa always does what these statesmen advise,
On condition that they'll be, in turn, so polite
As in no case whate'er to advise him *too right*—
" Pretty doings are here, sir," (he angrily cries,
While by dint of dark eyebrows he strives to look wise)—
" 'Tis a scheme of the Romanists, so help me God!
To ride over your *most* Royal Highness roughshod—
Excuse, sir, my tears—they're from loyalty's source—
Bad enough 'twas for Troy to be sack'd by a *Horse*,
But for us to be ruin'd by *Ponies* still worse !"
Quick a Council is call'd—the whole Cabinet sits—
The Archbishops declare, frighten'd out of their wits,
That if once Popish Ponies should eat at my manger,
From that awful moment the Church is in danger!
As, give them but stabling, and shortly no stalls
Will suit their proud stomachs but those at St. Paul's.

The Doctor, and he, the devout man of Leather,
V—ns—tt—t, now laying their Saint-heads together,
Declare that these skittish young *a*-bominations
Are clearly foretold in Chap. vi. Revelations—
Nay, they verily think they could point out the one
Which the Doctor's friend Death was to canter upon.
Lord H—rr—by, hoping that no one imputes
To the Court any fancy to persecute brutes,
Protests, on the word of himself and his cronies,
That had these said creatures been Asses, not Ponies,
The Court would have started no sort of objection,
As Asses were, *there*, always sure of protection.

" If the Pr—nc—ss *will* keep them (says Lord C—stl—
    r—gh),
To make them quite harmless, the only true way
Is (as certain Chief Justices do with their wives)
To flog them within half an inch of their lives.
4

If they've any bad Irish blood lurking about,
This (he knew by experience) would soon draw it out."
Should this be thought cruel, his Lordship proposes
"The new *Veto* snaffle to bind down their noses—
A pretty contrivance, made out of old chains,
Which appears to indulge, while it doubly restrains;
Which, however high-mettled, their gamesomeness checks
(Adds his Lordship humanely) or else breaks their necks!"

   This proposal receiv'd pretty general applause
From the statesmen around—and the neck-breaking clause
Had a vigour about it, which soon reconcil'd
Even Eld—n himself to a measure so mild.
So the snaffles, my dear, were agreed to, *nem. con.,*
And my Lord C—stl—r—gh, having so often shone
In the *fettering* line, is to buckle them on.

   I shall drive to your door in these *Vetos* some day,
But, at present, adieu!—I must hurry away
To go see my Mamma, as I'm suffer'd to meet her
For just half an hour by the Qu—n's best repeater.
CH—RL—TTE.

LETTER V.

My dear Lady ——! I've been just sending out
About five hundred cards for a snug little Rout—
(By-the-bye, you've seen Rokeby?—this moment got mine—
The Mail-Coach Edition—prodigiously fine;)
But I can't conceive how, in this very cold weather,
I'm ever to bring my five hundred together;
As, unless the thermometer's near boiling heat,
One can never get half of one's hundreds to meet.
(Apropos—you'd have laugh'd to see Townsend last night,
Escort to their chair, with his staff, so polite,
The "three maiden Miseries," all in a fright;
Poor Townsend, like Mercury, filling two posts,
Supervisor of *thieves*, and chief-usher of *ghosts!*)

But, my dear Lady ——, can't you hit on some notion,
At least for one night to set London in motion?—
As to having the R—g—nt, *that* show is gone by—
Besides, I've remark'd that (between you and I)
The Marchesa and he, inconvenient in more ways,
Have taken much lately to whispering in doorways;
Which—consid'ring, you know, dear, the *size* of the two—
Makes a block that one's company *cannot* get through;
And a house such as mine is, with doorways so small,
Has no room for such cumbersome love-work at all.—
(Apropos, though, of love-work—you've heard it, I hope,
That Napoleon's old mother's to marry the Pope,—
What a comical pair!)—but, to stick to my Rout,
'Twill be hard if some novelty can't be struck out.
Is there no Algerine, or Kamchatkan arriv'd?
No Plenipo Pacha, three-tail'd and ten-wiv'd?
No Russian, whose dissonant consonant name
Almost rattles to fragments the trumpet of fame?

I remember the time, three or four winters back,
When—provided their wigs were but decently black—
A few Patriot monsters, from Spain, were a sight
That would people one's house for one, night after night.
But—whether the Ministers *paw'd* them too much—
(And you know how they spoil whatsoever they touch)
Or whether Lord G—rge (the young man about town)
Has, by dint of bad poetry, written them down,
One has certainly lost one's *peninsular* rage;
And the only stray Patriot seen for an age
Has been at such places (think, how the fit cools!)
As old Mrs. V—gh—n's or Lord L—v—rp—l's.

But, in short, my dear, names like Wintztschitstopschin-
    zoudhoff
Are the only things now make an ev'ning go smooth off;
So, get me a Russian—till death I'm your debtor—
If he brings the whole Alphabet, so much the better.
And—Lord! if he would but, *in character*, sup
Off his fish-oil and candles, he'd quite set me up!

Au revoir, my sweet girl—I must leave you in haste—
Little Gunter has brought me the Liqueurs to taste.

POSTSCRIPT.

By-the-bye, have you found any friend that can construe
That Latin account, t'other day, of a Monster?
If we can't get a Russian, and *that thing* in Latin
Be not *too* improper, I think I'll bring that in.

INCLOSURE

IN LETTER FROM ABDALLAH, IN LONDON, TO MOHASSAN, IN ISPAHAN.

The tender Gazel I inclose
Is for my love, my Syrian Rose—
Take it when night begins to fall,
And throw it o'er her mother's wall.

GAZEL.

Rememberest thou the hour we past,—
That hour the happiest and the last?
Oh! not so sweet the Siha thorn
To summer bees, at break of morn,
Not half so sweet, through dale and dell,
To Camels' ears the tinkling bell,
As is the soothing memory
Of that one precious hour to me.

How can we live, so far apart?
Oh! why not rather, heart to heart,
United live and die—
Like those sweet birds, that fly together.

As of permanent and more general interest now-a-days,
than old almanack squibs, we quote, from the same source,
Moore's "Lines addressed to Leigh Hunt and his
Brother," who were tried and imprisoned for speaking
somewhat too truthfully regarding the Prince Regent:—

"Go to your prisons—though the air of Spring
No mountain coolness to your cheeks shall bring;

Though Summer flowers shall pass unseen away,
And all your portion of the glorious day
May be some solitary beam that falls,
At morn or eve, upon your dreary walls—
Some beam that enters, trembling as if aw'd,
To tell how gay the young world laughs abroad!
Yet go—for thoughts as blessed as the air
Of Spring or Summer flowers await you there;
Thoughts, such as He, who feasts his courtly crew
In rich conservatories, *never* knew ;
Pure self-esteem—the smiles that light within—
The Zeal, whose circling charities begin
With the few lov'd ones Heaven has plac'd it near,
And spread, till all Mankind are in its sphere;
The Pride, that suffers without vaunt or plea,
And the fresh Spirit, that can warble free,
Through prison-bars, its hymn to Liberty!"

"The course of politics," says Lord John Russell, "led him into the composition of political squibs of various merit. The 'Vision in the Court of Chancery,' 'The Slave,' the 'Breadfruit Tree,' and many more are replete with sense and feeling as well as wit."

Moore's satirical and humorous productions are, admittedly, equal to anything of the kind in the language, and in them his peculiar abilities are exhibited to the best advantage. From the remainder of these we select the following:—

DIALOGUE BETWEEN A SOVEREIGN AND A ONE POUND NOTE.

Said a Sov'reign to a Note,
In the pocket of my coat,
Where they met in a neat purse of leather,
"How happens it, I prithee,
That, though I'm wedded *with* thee,
Fair Pound, we can never live together?

" Like your sex, fond of *change*,
　　With silver you can range,
And of lots of young sixpences be mother;
　　While with *me*—upon my word,
　　Not my Lady and my Lord
Of W—stm—th see so little of each other ! "

　　The indignant Note replied
　　(Lying crumpled by his side),
" Shame, shame, it is *yourself* that roam, sir—
　　One cannot look askance,
　　But, whip ! you're off to France,
Leaving nothing but old rags at home, sir.

　　" Your scampering began
　　From the moment Parson Van,
Poor man, made us *one* in Love's fetter;
　　' For better or for worse'
　　Is the usual marriage curse,
But ours is all ' worse' and no ' better.'

　　" In vain are laws pass'd,
　　There's nothing holds you fast,
Tho' you know, sweet Sovereign, I adore you—
　　At the smallest hint in life,
　　You forsake your lawful wife,
As other Sovereigns did before you.

　　" I flirt with Silver, true—
　　But what can ladies do,
When disown'd by their natural protectors?
　　And as to falsehood, stuff !
　　I shall soon be *false* enough,
When I get among those wicked Bank Directors."

　　The Sovereign, smiling on her,
　　Now swore, upon his honour,
To be henceforth domestic and loyal;
　　But within an hour or two,
　　Why—I sold him to a Jew,
And he's now at No. 10 Palais Royal.

THE IRISH SLAVE.

I heard, as I lay, a wailing sound,
  "He is dead—he is dead," the rumour flew;
And I rais'd my chain, and turn'd me round,
  And ask'd, through the dungeon-window, "Who?"

I saw my livid tormentors pass;
  Their grief 'twas bliss to hear and see!
For, never came joy to them, alas!
  That didn't bring deadly bane to me.

Eager I look'd through the mist of night,
  And ask'd, "What foe of my race hath died?
Is it he—that Doubter of law and right,
  Whom nothing but wrong could e'er decide—

Who, long as he sees but wealth to win,
  Hath never yet felt a qualm or doubt
What suitors for justice he'd keep in,
  Or what suitors for freedom he'd shut out—

"Who, a clog for ever on Truth's advance,
  Hangs round her (like the Old Man of the Sea
Round Sinbad's neck), nor leaves a chance
  Of shaking him off—is't he? is't he?"

Ghastly my grim tormentors smil'd,
  And thrusting me back to my den of woe,
With a laughter even more fierce and wild
  Than their funeral howling, answer'd "No."

But the cry still pierced my prison-gate,
  And again I ask'd, "What scourge is gone?
Is it he—that Chief, so coldly great,
  Whom Fame unwillingly shines upon—

"Whose name is one of the ill-omen'd words,
  They link with hate, on his native plains;
And why?—they lent him hearts and swords,
  And he in return gave scoffs and chains!

"Is it he? is it he?" I loud inquir'd,
    When hark!—there sounded a Royal knell;
And I knew what spirit had just expir'd,
    And, slave as I was, my triumph fell.

He had pledg'd a hate unto me and mine,
    He had left to the future nor hope nor choice,
But seal'd that hate with a Name Divine,
    And he now was dead, and—I *couldn't* rejoice!

He had fann'd afresh the burning brands
    Of a bigotry waxing cold and dim;
He had arm'd anew my torturers' hands,
    And *them* did I curse—but sigh'd for him;

For *his* was the error of head, not heart;
    And—oh, how beyond the ambushed foe,
Who to enmity adds the traitor's part,
    And carries a smile, with a curse below!

If ever a heart made bright amends
    For the fatal fault of an erring head—
Go, learn *his* fame from the lips of friends,
    In the orphan's tear be his glory read!

A Prince without pride, a man without guile,
    To the last unchanging, warm, sincere,
For Worth he had ever a hand and smile,
    And for Misery ever his purse and tear.

Touch'd to the heart by that solemn toll,
    I calmly sunk in my chains again;
While, still as I said, "Heaven rest his soul!"
    My mates of the dungeon sigh'd "Amen!"

A VISION.

BY THE AUTHOR OF CHRISTABEL.

"Up!" said the Spirit, and, ere I could pray
One hasty orison, whirl'd me away
To a Limbo, lying—I wist not where—

Above or below, in earth or air;
For it glimmer'd o'er with a *doubtful* ..ght,
One couldn't say whether 'twas day or night;
And 'twas crost by many a mazy track,
One didn't know how to get on or back;
And I felt like a needle that's going astray
(With its *one* eye out) through a bundle of hay;
When the Spirit he grinn'd, and whisper'd me,
"Thou'rt now in the Court of Chancery!"

Around me flitted unnumber'd swarms
Of shapeless, bodiless, tailless forms;
(Like bottled-up babes, that grace the room
Of that worthy knight, Sir Everard Home)—
All of them, things half-kill'd in rearing;
Some were lame—some wanted *hearing;*
Some had through half a century run,
Though they hadn't a leg to stand upon.
Others, more merry, as just beginning,
Around on a *point of law* were spinning;
Or balanc'd aloft, 'twixt *Bill* and *Answer,*
Lead at each end, like a tight-rope dancer.
Some were so *cross* that nothing could please 'em;—
Some gulph'd down *affidavits* to ease 'em;—
All were in motion, yet never a one,
Let it *move* as it might, could ever move *on.*
"These," said the Spirit, "you plainly see,
Are what they call suits in Chancery!"
I heard a loud screaming of old and young,
Like a chorus by fifty Vellutis sung;
Or an Irish Dump ("the words by Moore")
At an amateur concert scream'd in score;
So harsh on my ears that wailing fell
Of the wretches who in this Limbo dwell!
It seem'd like the dismal symphony
Of the shapes Æneas in hell did see;
Or those frogs, whose legs a barbarous cook
Cut off, and left the frogs in the brook,

To cry all night, till life's last dregs,
"Give us our legs!—give us our legs!"
Touch'd with the sad and sorrowful scene,
I ask'd what all this yell might mean,
When the Spirit replied, with a grin of glee,
"'Tis the cry of the Suitors in Chancery!"

I look'd, and I saw a wizard rise,
With a wig like a cloud before men's eyes.
In his aged hand he held a wand,
Wherewith he beckon'd his embryo band,
And they mov'd and mov'd, as he wav'd it o'er
But they never got on one inch the more.
And still they kept limping to and fro,
Like Ariels round old Prospero—
Saying, "Dear master, let us go,"
But still old Prospero answer'd "No."
And I heard, the while, that wizard elf
Muttering, muttering spells to himself,
While o'er as many old papers he turn'd,
As Hume e'er mov'd for, or Omar burn'd.
He talk'd of his virtue—"though some, less nice,
(He own'd with a sigh) preferr'd his *Vice*"—
And he said, "I think"—"I doubt"—"I hope,"
Call'd God to witness, and damn'd the Pope;
With many more sleights of tongue and hand
I couldn't, for the soul of me, understand.
Amaz'd and pos'd, I was just about
To ask his name, when the screams without,
The merciless clack of the imps within,
And that conjuror's mutterings, made such a din,
That, startled, I woke—leap'd up in my bed—
Found the Spirit, the imps, and the conjuror fled,
And bless'd my stars, right pleas'd to see,
That I wasn't, as yet, in Chancery.

In 1814 Jeffrey wrote Rogers to ask Moore to contribute to the *Edinburgh Review*, stating that the usual

terms were twenty guineas a printed sheet of sixteen pages, but that he would not in this case think of offering less than thirty, and probably a good deal more. All this matter he left entirely to Roger's delicacy and discretion, and Moore felt flattered by the proposal, and reciprocated the friendly feeling by becoming a contributor. Shortly afterwards, Jeffrey wrote Moore—

"Tell me, too, that you will come for a fortnight to Edinburgh early next winter and see our primitive society here. It is but thirty hours' travelling, and will at least be something to laugh at in London, and to describe at Mayfield. We shall treat you very honourably, and let you do whatever you please. Ever most truly yours, F. JEFFREY."

The following letter from Samuel Rogers, belonging to this period, is well worthy of preservation:—

"Venice, October 17, 1814.

"My Dear Moore,—Last night in my gondola I made a vow I would write you a letter if it was only to beg you would write to me at Rome. Like the great Marco Polo, however, whose tomb I saw to-day, I have a sacred wish to astonish you with my travels, and would take you with me, as you would not go willingly, from London to Paris, and from Paris to the Lake of Geneva, and so on to this city of romantic adventure, the place from which he started. I set out in August last with my sister and Mackintosh. He parted with us in Switzerland, since which time we have travelled on together; and happy should we have been could you and Psyche have made a quartette of it. I hope all her predictions have long ago been fulfilled to your mind, and that she and you and the bambini are all as snug and as happy as you can wish to be. By the way, I forgot one of your family who, I hope, is still under your roof. I mean one of nine sisters—the one I have more than once made love to. With another of them, too, all the world knows your *good fortune.* . . . But to proceed to business:—

"Chamouni and the Mer de Glace, Voltaire's chamber at Ferney, Gibbon's terrace at Lausanne, Rousseau's Isle of St. Pierre, the Lake of Lucerne, and the little cantons, the passage over the Alps, the Lago Maggiore, Milan, Verona, Padua, Venice,—what shall I begin with? But I believe I must refer you to my three quartos on the subject whenever they choose to appear. The most wonderful thing we have seen is Bonaparte's road over the Alps—as smooth as that in Hyde Park, and not steeper than St. James's Street. We left Savoy at seven in the morning, and slept at Domo d'Ossola, in Italy, that night. For twenty miles we descended through a mountain-pass, as rocky, and often narrower, than the *narrowest* part of Dovedale; the road being sometimes cut out of the mountain, and three times carried through it, leaving the torrent (and such a torrent!) to work its way by itself. The passages, or galleries, as I believe the French engineers call them, were so long as to require large openings here and there for light; and the roof was hung with icicles, which the carriage shattered as it passed along, and which fell to the ground with a shrill sound. We were eight hours in climbing to the top, and only three in descending. Our wheel was never locked, and our horses were almost always in a gallop. But I must talk to you a little about Venice. I cannot tell you what I felt when the postillion turned gaily round, and, pointing with his whip, cried out 'Venezia!' For there it was, sure enough, with its long line of domes and turrets glittering in the sun. I walk about here all day long in a dream. Is that the Rialto? I say to myself. Is this St. Mark's Place? Do I see the Adriatic? I think if you and I were together here, my dear Moore, we might manufacture something from the ponte dei sospiri, the scala dei giganti, the piombi, the pozzi, and the thousand ingredients of mystery and terror that are here at every turn.

"Nothing can be more luxurious than a gondola and its little black cabin, in which you can fly about unseen, the gondoliers so silent all the while. They dip their oars as if they were afraid of disturbing you; yet you fly. As you are rowed through one of the narrow streets, often do you catch the notes of a guitar, accompanied by a female voice, through some open window; and at night, on the Grand Canal, how amusing it is to observe the moving lights (every gondola has its light), one now and then shooting across at a little distance, and vanishing into a smaller canal. . . . This is indeed a fairy land, and Venice particularly so. If at Naples you see most with the eye, and at Rome with the memory, surely at Venice you see most with the imagination. But enough of Venice. To-morrow we bid adieu to it,—most probably I shall never see it again. We shall pass through Ferrara to Bologna, then cross the Apennines to Florence, and so on to Rome, where I shall look for a line from you. . . .

"Tell Lady D. I passed the little Lake of Lowertz, and saw the melancholy effects of the downfall. It is now a scene of desolation, and the little town of Goldau is buried many fathoms deep. It is a sad story, and you shall have it when we meet. I received a very kind letter from her at Tunbridge, and mean to answer it. I hope to meet you in London-town, when you visit it next; at least I shall endeavour to do so. My sister unites with me in kindest remembrance to Mrs. Moore; and pray, pray believe me to be, Yours ever, S. R."

CHAPTER VI.

LALLA ROOKH.

Moore, in the preface to the twentieth edition of Lalla Rookh, gives the following interesting account of its origin and progress:—"It was about the year 1812 that, impelled far more by the encouraging suggestions of friends than impelled by any promptings of my own ambition, I was induced to attempt a poem upon some oriental subject, and of those quarto dimensions which Scott's late triumphs in that form had then rendered the regular poetical standard. A negotiation on the subject was opened with the Messrs. Longman in the same year, but, from some causes which have now escaped my recollection, led to no decisive result; nor was it till a year or two after, that any further steps were taken in the matter—their house being the only one, it is right to add, with which, from first to last, I held any communication on the subject.

"On this last occasion an old friend of mine, Mr. Perry, kindly offered to lend me the aid of his advice and presence in the interview which I was about to hold with the Messrs. Longman, for the arrangement of our mutual terms; and what, with the friendly zeal of my negotiator on the one side, and the prompt and liberal spirit with which he was met on the other, there has seldom occurred any transaction in which trade and poesy have shone out so advantageously in each other's eyes. The short discussion that then took place between the two parties may be compressed into a very few sentences. 'I am of opinion,' said Mr. Perry—enforcing his view of the case by argu ments which it is not for me to cite—'that Mr. Moore ought to receive for his poem the largest price that has been given in our day for such a work.' 'That was,' answered the Messrs. Longman, 'three thousand guineas.' 'Exactly so,' replied Mr. Perry, 'and no less a sum ought he to receive.'

"It was then objected, and very reasonably, on the part of the firm, that they had never yet seen a single line of the poem, and that a perusal of the work ought to be sent to them before they embarked on so large a sum in the purchase. But no;—the romantic view which my friend, Mr. Perry, took of the matter was that this price should be given as a tribute to reputation already acquired, without any condition for a previous perusal of the new work. This high tone, I must confess, not a little startled and alarmed me; but, to the honour and glory of Romance—as well on the publisher's side as the poet's—this very generous view of the transaction was, without any difficulty, acceded to, and the firm agreed, before we separated, that I was to receive three thousand guineas for my poem."

The Messrs. Longman having thus arranged to give him three thousand guineas for a poetical work of which they had not seen a single line, Moore determined not to disappoint the trust placed in him. The following letters fixed the matter:—

"To Messrs. Longman & Co. London, Dec. 17, 1814.

"Dear Sirs,—I have taken our conversation of yesterday into consideration, and the following are the terms which I propose : —'Upon my giving into your hands a poem of the length of Rokeby, I am to receive from you the sum of £3000. If you agree to this proposal, I am perfectly ready to close with you definitely, and have the honour to be, gentlemen, your very obliged and humble servant, THOMAS MOORE.'

"I beg to stipulate that the few songs which I may introduce in this work shall be considered as reserved for my own setting."

Copy of terms written to Mr. Moore:—

"That upon your giving into our hands a poem of yours of the length of Rokeby, you shall receive from us the sum of £3000. We also agree to the stipulation, that the few songs which you may introduce into the work shall be considered as reserved for your own setting."

After a time he again wrote to Mr. Longman as follows :—

"Mayfield Cottage, April 25, 1815.

"My dear Sir,—I hope to see you in town the beginning of next week. I had copied out fairly about 4000 lines of my work, for the purpose of submitting them to your perusal, as I promised ; but, upon further consideration, I have changed my intention; for it has occurred to me that if you should happen not to be quite as much pleased with what I have done as I could wish, it might have the effect of disheartening me for the execution of the remaining and most interesting part, so I shall take the liberty of withholding it from your perusal till it is finished ; and *then*, I repeat, it shall be perfectly in your power to cancel our agreement, if the merits of the work should not meet your expectation. It will consist altogether of at least 6000 lines ; and as into *every one* of these I am throwing as much mind and polish as I am master of, the task is no trifling one."

The firm, ever honourable in all its transactions, at once expressed its entire confidence in Moore, and its intention to abide by its agreement.

In his cottage at Mayfield, in Derbyshire, he studied Oriental literature summer and winter; and, in four years after his arrangement with the firm, *Lalla Rookh* was completed.

Of this undertaking he himself afterwards said :—"It was, indeed, to the secluded life I led during the years 1813–1816, in a lone cottage among the fields, in Derbyshire, that I owed the inspiration, whatever may have been its value, of some of the best and most popular portions of *Lalla Rookh*. It was amidst the snows of two or three Derbyshire winters that I found myself enabled, by that concentration of thought which retirement alone gives, to call up around me some of the sunniest of those eastern scenes which have since been welcomed in India itself, as almost native to its clime."

Of Mayfield he writes to E. T. Dalton, Esq., in 1815 :— "Tell Sir John (Stevenson) that he *must positively* pass the next summer at this cottage with us. If he loves a beautiful country, where every step opens valleys, woods, parks, and all kinds of rural glories upon the eye, this is the Paradise for him, and (to descend lower in the scale) he shall have as good *brown soup* as we gave him in Kegworth."

In 1816 he removed to Hornsey, near London, in order to see *Lalla Rookh* through the press. It was published—a quarto volume—in 1817, and, striking a new key-note, was a splendid success, dazzling the readers of the day with its gorgeous eastern illustration and imagery. Within a fortnight of its issue the first edition was sold out; and, within six months, it had reached a sixth edition. Parts of the work were rendered into Persian; and Mr. Luttrell, writing to Moore, said :—

> "I'm told, dear Moore, your lays are sung,
> (Can it be true, you lucky man?)
> By moonlight, in the Persian tongue,
> Along the streets of Ispahan."

And Lord Strangford wrote :—

"Clifton, June 20, 1817.

"My dear Moore,— .... I plucked up courage, two days ago, and called on Rogers, who was quite delightful. We *got on* famously together, and I have lost so much of my *terror* that I shall assault him with frequent visitations on my return to town.

"My mother is a bit of a saint; she is reading your book at the other end of the room. The following dialogue has just passed between us :—

"' *Sinner*—I am writing Moore.'

"' *Saint*—I am reading Moore.'

"' *Sinner*—What shall I say to Moore?'

"' *Saint*—That I am shocked at my own wickedness in admiring anything in THIS *world* so much as I do his poem !'

"God bless you. Ever most affectionately yours,

5   "STRANGFORD."

Lalla Rookh,—signifying *tulip cheek,*—is Moore's most elaborate poem. It is an oriental romance, with its dazzling wealth of gorgeous illustration and imagery, presenting a brilliant picture of eastern life and thought. It consists of four tales connected by a slight narrative in prose.

"Lalla Rookh, famed for her beauty, was the youngest daughter of the Emperor Aurungzebe, who reigned in Delhi in India. A marriage having been arranged between this princess and the reigning prince of Lesser Bucharia, which was to be celebrated in Cashmere, Lalla Rookh departed on her journey thither accompanied by a suitable train of attendants, among whom was a young poet noted for his ability in reciting the Stories of the East. To while away the tedium of the journey the services of this young poet were called into requisition, and he charmed the princess by reciting in her hearing four tales, 'The Veiled Prophet of Khorassan,' 'Paradise and the Peri,' 'The Fire-worshippers,' and the 'Light of the Harem.' Arrived at Cashmere Lalla Rookh was overjoyed to recognize in her bridegroom the poet who, by his graceful appearance, gentle mien, and delightful verses, had already completely captivated her affections."[1]

Its illustrations are so accurate, that Col. Wilks, the historian of British India, thought Moore must have travelled in the East. But the lay-figures introduced lack character; there is, throughout, a marked deficiency of dramatic power and completeness; and, from the very excess of ornament and exuberant fancy, its sweetness and sparkle pall on the senses.

The reader sympathizes with the French gentleman who said that "he admired the pastorals of M. de Florian

---

[1] From Blackie's School Classics, *The Fire-worshippers.*

very much, but that he considered a wolf would improve them."

Full of glittering fancy, "it lacks passion, pathos, and the shaping spirit of imagination." Professor Morley quaintly says, that "beside poems that rank with the powers of Nature, it looks like an oriental sugar-candy temple of such confectioner's work as was also fashionable in the days when *Lalla Rookh* was read."

Hazlitt wrote of Moore, "His fancy is for ever on the wing, flutters in the gale, glitters in the sun. Everything lives, moves, and sparkles in his poetry; while, over all, Love waves his purple light. His variety cloys, his rapidity dazzles and distracts the sight. He wants intensity, strength, and grandeur. . . . If *Lalla Rookh* be not a great poem it is a marvellous work of art, and contains paintings of local scenery and manners unsurpassed for fidelity and picturesque effect. The poet was a diligent student, and his oriental reading was as good as riding on the back of a camel."

"I have read *Lalla Rookh* (says Byron), but not with sufficient attention yet, for I ride about, and lounge, and ponder, and two or three other things, so that my reading is very desultory, and not so attentive as it used to be. I am very glad to hear of its popularity, for Moore is a very noble fellow in all respects, and will enjoy it without any of the bad feelings which success—good or evil—sometimes engenders in men of rhyme. Of the poem itself I will tell you my opinion when I have mastered it. I say of the poem, for I don't like the prose at all; in the meantime, the 'Fire-worshippers' is the best, and the 'Veiled Prophet' the worst of the volume."

Lord John Russell says "Crabbe preferred the 'Veiled Prophet;' Byron, the 'Fire-worshippers.' Of these, the 'Veiled Prophet' displays the greater power; the 'Fire-worshippers' the more natural and genuine passion." Scott spoke very highly of the "Fire-worshippers." Stopford A. Brooke adds that "the tales in *Lalla Rookh* are chiefly flash and glitter, but they are pleasant reading."

Some of the lyrics which are found in its pages are very melodious and beautiful; and, while admitting the abstract justice of many of the adverse criticisms we have quoted, we submit that there are times, seasons, and moods, when it is very pleasant to be half smothered in roses!

In the metrical structure of the verse, and in its mellifluous musical rhythm, there are passages of *Lalla Rookh* which are superior to any of his other poems, except the Irish "Melodies." We are about to quote passages from each of the four Tales, and would call attention to the opening passage of "The Light of the Harem," especially to the ten lines beginning,

"Here the music of pray'r from a minaret swells;"

of which it has been well said, "To deny the music of such verses as these would be sheer fatuity. The art with which the broad vowels, with their deep, bell-like sound, are distributed through the first four lines is simply masterly; and the rest, if not quite so good, is still excellent in the impression it preserves of the odorous languor of a silent tropical night." But Moore "rarely reaches, and can never in his narrative poems sustain a level flight so musical as that he contrives to attain in the passage we have just quoted."

The poem also contains some passages of wonderful power, and we have very lately seen, as was remarked by Lord O'Hagan, Prince Bismark, "the man of blood and iron," seeking in the "Veiled Prophet" of the Irish minstrel, illustration of his argument before the Reichsrath.

FROM LALLA ROOKH.

I.—From "The Veiled Prophet of Khorassan."

ZELICA'S LOVE.

There's a bower of roses by Bendemeer's stream,
  And the nightingale sings round it all the day long;
In the time of my childhood 'twas like a sweet dream,
  To sit in the roses and hear the bird's song.

That bower and its music I never forget,
  But oft when alone, in the bloom of the year,
I think—is the nightingale singing there yet?
  Are the roses still bright by the calm Bendemeer?

No, the roses soon wither'd that hung o'er the wave,
  But some blossoms were gather'd, while freshly they shone,
And a dew was distill'd from their flowers, that gave
  All the fragrance of summer, when summer was gone.

Thus memory draws from delight, ere it dies,
  An essence that breathes of it many a year;
Thus bright to my soul, as 'twas then to my eyes,
  Is that bower on the banks of the calm Bendemeer!

II.—From "Paradise and the Peri."

INTRODUCTION.

One morn a Peri at the gate
Of Eden stood, disconsolate;
And as she listen'd to the Springs
  Of Life within, like music flowing,
And caught the light upon her wings
  Through the half-open portal glowing,
She wept to think her recreant race
Should e'er have lost that glorious place!

"How happy," exclaim'd this child of air,
"Are the holy Spirits who wander there,
  Mid flowers that never shall fade or fall;
Though mine are the gardens of earth and sea,

And the stars themselves have flowers for me,
One blossom of Heaven out-blooms them all!

"Though sunny the Lake of cool Cashmere,
With its plane-tree Isle reflected clear,
And sweetly the founts of that Valley fall;
Though bright are the waters of Sing-su-hay,
And the golden floods that thitherward stray,
Yet—oh, 'tis only the Blest can say
How the waters of Heaven outshine them all!

"Go, wing thy flight from star to star,
From world to luminous world, as far
As the universe spreads its flaming wall:
Take all the pleasures of all the spheres,
And multiply each through endless years,
One minute of Heaven is worth them all!"

The glorious Angel, who was keeping
The gates of Light, beheld her weeping;
And, as he nearer drew and listen'd
To her sad song, a tear-drop glisten'd
Within her eyelids, like the spray
From Eden's fountain, when it lies
On the blue flow'r, which—Bramins say—
Blooms nowhere but in Paradise.

"Nymph of a fair but erring line!"
Gently he said—"One hope is thine.
'Tis written in the Book of Fate,
The Peri yet may be forgiv'n
Who brings to this Eternal gate
The Gift that is most dear to Heav'n!
Go, seek it, and redeem thy sin—
'Tis sweet to let the pardon'd in."

Rapidly as comets run
To the embraces of the Sun;—
Fleeter than the starry brands
Flung at night from angel hands
At those dark and daring sprites

Who would climb the empyreal heights,
Down the blue vault the Peri flies,
   And, lighted earthward by a glance
That just then broke from morning's eyes,
   Hung hov'ring o'er our world's expanse.

But whither shall the Spirit go
To find this gift for Heav'n?—"I know
The wealth," she cries, "of every urn,
In which unnumber'd rubies burn,
Beneath the pillars of Chilminar;
I know where the Isles of Perfume are,
Many a fathom down in the sea,
To the south of sun-bright Araby;
I know, too, where the Genii hid
The jewell'd cup of their King Jamshid,
With Life's elixir sparkling high—
But gifts like these are not for the sky.
Where was there ever a gem that shone
Like the steps of Alla's wonderful Throne?
And the Drops of Life—oh! what would they be
In the boundless Deep of Eternity?"

SYRIA.

Now, upon Syria's land of roses
Softly the light of Eve reposes,
And, like a glory, the broad sun
Hangs over sainted Lebanon;
Whose head in wintry grandeur tow'rs,
   And whitens with eternal sleet,
While summer, in a vale of flow'rs,
   Is sleeping rosy at his feet.

To one, who look'd from upper air
O'er all the enchanted regions there,
How beauteous must have been the glow,
The life, the sparkling from below!
Fair gardens, shining streams, with ranks
Of golden melons on their banks,

More golden where the sunlight falls;—
Gay lizards, glitt'ring on the walls
Of ruin'd shrines, busy and bright
As they were all alive with light;
And, yet more splendid, numerous flocks
Of pigeons, settling on the rocks,
With their rich restless wings, that gleam
Variously in the crimson beam
Of the warm West,—as if inlaid
With brilliants from the mine, or made
Of tearless rainbows, such a span
The unclouded skies of Peristan.
And then the mingling sounds that come,
Of shepherd's ancient reed, with hum
Of the wild bees of Palestine,
　　Banqueting through the flow'ry vales;
And, Jordan, those sweet banks of thine,
　　And woods, so full of nightingales.

THE TEARS OF PENITENCE.

And how felt *he*, the wretched Man,
Reclining there—while memory ran
O'er many a year of guilt and strife,
Flew o'er the dark flood of his life,
Nor found one sunny resting-place,
Nor brought him back one branch of grace.
"There *was* a time," he said, in mild,
Heart-humbled tones—"thou blessed child!
When, young and haply pure as thou,
I look'd and pray'd like thee—but now—"
He hung his head—each nobler aim,
　　And hope, and feeling, which had slept
From boyhood's hour, that instant came
　　Fresh o'er him, and he wept—he wept!

Blest tears of soul-felt penitence!
　　In whose benign, redeeming flow
Is felt the first, the only sense
　　Of guiltless joy that guilt can know.

"There's a drop," said the Peri, "that down from the
    moon
Falls through the withering airs of June
Upon Egypt's land, of so healing a pow'r,
So balmy a virtue, that ev'n in the hour
That drop descends, contagion dies,
And health reanimates earth and skies!—
Oh, is it not thus, thou man of sin,
    The precious tears of repentance fall?
Though foul thy fiery plagues within,
    One heavenly drop hath dispell'd them all!"

And now—behold him kneeling there
By the child's side, in humble pray'r,
While the same sunbeam shines upon
The guilty and the guiltless one,
And hymns of joy proclaimed through Heav'n
The triumph of a Soul Forgiv'n!

'Twas when the golden orb had set,
While on their knees they linger'd yet,
There fell a light more lovely far
Than ever came from sun or star,
Upon the tear that, warm and meek,
Dew'd that repentant sinner's cheek.
To mortal eye this light might seem
A northern flash or meteor beam—
But well the enraptur'd Peri knew
'Twas a bright smile the Angel threw
From Heaven's gate, to hail that tear
Her harbinger of glory near!

"Joy, joy for ever! my task is done—
The gates are pass'd, and Heav'n is won!"

III.—From "The Fire-worshippers."

"This story is founded on the fierce struggle so long
maintained between the Ghebers, or ancient Fire-worshippers of Persia, and their haughty Moslem masters. The

cause of tolerance is the inspiring theme; and the spirit that speaks in the melodies of Ireland finds itself at home in the East.—The worship of Fire was introduced into Persia by Zoroaster, a great religious reformer, about the twelfth century before Christ. The Persians saluted the rising sun as the symbol of the purest fire; they regarded fire as the protector of states: and in certain temples the sacred fire was never extinguished, but was kept burning night and day. Every detail concerning the ceremonies of this worship is to be found in the *Zend-Avesta*, or Sacred Book of the Ghebers, which is still extant.

"The word Gheber (infidel) was a term of reproach given by Mussulmans to all (except Jews and Christians) who did not profess Mahommedanism; but it applied particularly to the followers of Zoroaster.

"The events alluded to in this poem are supposed to have taken place as early as the seventh century, when Fire-worship was proscribed, and its partisans dispersed.

"The poem opens with an account of the sufferings of the Ghebers under the tyranny of their Arab conquerors. Then follows a description of Hinda, the Emir's daughter, who having accompanied her father to the war had been placed by him in a safe retreat among the mountains.

"A romantic attachment springs up between her and an unknown youth; but one sad day he reveals to her that he belongs to the hated race of Ghebers, and is therefore the sworn enemy of her father. The interview ends with his declaration that Love must give way to Vengeance: and so they part; he to return to the war, she to mourn in her bower.

"The valour of the Ghebers was unavailing against the overwhelming number of Arabs; and at last Hafed the Gheber chief (the hero of our story) was compelled to retire with a few followers to a mountain fastness.

"For seven weary days Hinda watches in vain for the return of her lover. On the eighth day her father, Al Hassan, tells her with fierce glee that the hiding-place of Hafed has been betrayed, and that before sunset he shall be slain. He bids her return to her native land; and for this purpose places her on board a vessel bound for Arabia. This vessel is attacked by Ghebers, and the maiden taken captive. She is blindfolded, and carried on a litter to the fortress of Hafed. On the way she hears a well-known voice which says, 'Tremble not, love, thy Gheber is here. The bandage is then removed from her eyes, and she discovers that the chief whose name she had been taught to fear and hate is none other than her beloved Gheber! She tells him that his secret has been betrayed, and implores him to fly with her that night: but vengeance again conquers love, and Hafed is determined to die in the cause of his country and his faith. He confides the weeping damsel to the care of his most trustworthy veterans, and bids them convey her back to her father, in the hope that the restoration of Al Hassan's daughter will secure their pardon. The brave young chieftain then sounds the war-whoop, and prepares for his death-struggle.

"The Ghebers assemble at the entrance of a narrow glen which is guarded by a deep ravine. A fearful shout soon warns them of the approach of their enemies, who, by the light of their torches, are seen advancing in great numbers.

"The Moslems dash into the ravine: and while many perish in their attempt to cross the torrent, others are hurled back by the swords of the Ghebers. The dead bodies of the slain fill up the ravine, and form a bridge for the remaining host to pass over. Then ensues a terrible struggle, in which all the brave Ghebers are killed, with the exception of two, their chieftain and one follower. These two make their escape in the darkness, and with difficulty climb up the hill to offer their last breath at the altar of their Fire-God. The Gheber warrior dies just as the shrine is reached; but is placed on the burning pile by his gallant chieftain. Hafed then leaps upon the altar, and expires before the flames can reach him.

"From her bark below, the afflicted maiden hears the war-cry on the mountain, and knows that her lover must die in that fight. Suddenly she sees a blaze on the distant altar, and the form of Hafed is revealed in the act of leaping on the funeral-pile. With a fearful shriek she leaps out of the boat, as if to reach her lover; and sinks beneath the waves."[1]

> 'Tis moonlight over Oman's Sea;
>   Her banks of pearl and palmy isles
> Bask in the night-beam beauteously,
>   And her blue waters sleep in smiles.
> 'Tis moonlight in Harmozia's walls,
> And through her Emir's porphyry halls,
> Where, some hours since, was heard the swell
> Of trumpet and the clash of zel,[3]
> Bidding the bright-eyed sun farewell;—
> The peaceful sun, whom better suits
>   The music of the bulbul's[4] nest,
> Or the light touch of lovers' lutes,
>   To sing him to his golden rest.
> All hush'd—there's not a breeze in motion;
> The shore is silent as the ocean.
> If zephyrs come, so light they come,

---

[1] From Blackie's School Classics, *The Fire-worshippers.*
[3] The Persian Gulf, sometimes so called, which separates the shores of Persia and Arabia.
[3] A Moorish instrument of music.   [4] A singing-bird.

Nor leaf is stirr'd nor wave is driven;—
The wind-tower on the Emir's dome[1]
Can hardly win a breath from heaven.

Ev'n he, that tyrant Arab, sleeps
Calm, while a nation round him weeps;
While curses load the air he breathes,
And falchions from unnumber'd sheaths
Are starting to avenge the shame
His race hath brought on Iran's[2] name.
Hard, heartless Chief, unmov'd alike
'Mid eyes that weep and swords that strike;—
One of that saintly murderous brood,
    To carnage and the Koran given,
Who think through unbelievers' blood
    Lies their directest path to heaven;—
One, who will pause and kneel unshod
    In the warm blood his hand hath pour'd,
To mutter o'er some text of God
    Engraven on his reeking sword;—
Nay, who can coolly note the line,
The letter of those words divine,
To which his blade, with searching art,
Had sunk into its victim's heart!

Just Alla![3] what must be thy look,
    When such a wretch before thee stands
Unblushing, with thy sacred Book,—
    Turning the leaves with blood-stain'd hands,
And wresting from its page sublime
His creed of lust, and hate, and crime;—
Ev'n as those bees of Trebizond,
    Which, from the sunniest flowers that glad
With their pure smiles the gardens round,
    Draw venom forth that drives men mad.

[1] At Gombaroon and other places in Persia, they have towers for the purpose of catching the wind, and cooling the houses.—*Le Bruyn.*
[2] Iran is the true general name for the empire of Persia.
[3] The Arabic name of the Supreme Being.

Never did fierce Arabia send
  A satrap forth more direly great;
Never was Iran doom'd to bend
  Beneath a yoke of deadlier weight.
Her throne had fall'n—her pride was crush'd—
Her sons were willing slaves, nor blush'd,
In their own land,—no more their own,—
To crouch beneath a stranger's throne.
Her towers, where Mithra[1] once had burn'd,
To Moslem shrines—oh shame!—were turn'd,
Where slaves, converted by the sword,
Their mean apostate worship pour'd,
And curs'd the faith their sires ador'd.

Yet has she hearts, 'mid all this ill,
O'er all this wreck high buoyant still
With hope and vengeance;—hearts that yet—
  Like gems, in darkness, issuing rays
They've treasur'd from the sun that's set,—
  Beam all the light of long-lost days!
And swords she hath, nor weak nor slow
  To second all such hearts can dare;
As he shall know, well, dearly know,
  Who sleeps in moonlight luxury there,
Tranquil as if his spirit lay
Becalm'd in Heaven's approving ray
Sleep on—for purer eyes than thine
Those waves are hush'd, those planets shine;
Sleep on, and be thy rest unmov'd
  By the white moonbeam's dazzling pow'r;—
None but the loving and the lov'd
  Should be awake at this sweet hour.

And see—where, high above those rocks
  That o'er the deep their shadows fling,
Yon turret stands;—where ebon locks
  As glossy as a heron's wing
Upon the turban of a king,

    [1] The sun was so called by the Ghebers.

Hang from the lattice, long and wild,—
'Tis she, that Emir's blooming child,
All truth and tenderness and grace,
Though born of such ungentle race;—
An image of Youth's radiant Fountain
Springing in a desolate mountain!

Oh what a pure and sacred thing
    Is beauty, curtain'd from the sight
Of the gross world, illumining
    One only mansion with her light!
Unseen by man's disturbing eye,—
    The flower that blooms beneath the sea,
Too deep for sunbeams, doth not lie
    Hid in more chaste obscurity.
So Hinda, have thy face and mind,
Like holy mysteries, lain enshrin'd.
And oh, what transport for a lover
    To lift the veil that shades them o'er!—
Like those who, all at once, discover
    In the lone deep some fairy shore,
    Where mortal never trod before,
And sleep and wake in scented airs
No lip had ever breath'd but theirs.

Beautiful are the maids that glide,
    On summer-eves, through Yemen's[1] dales,
And bright the glancing looks they hide
    Behind their litters' roseate veils:—
And brides, as delicate and fair
As the white jasmine flowers they wear,
Hath Yemen in her blissful clime,
    Who, lull'd in cool kiosk or bower,
Before their mirrors count the time,
    And grow still lovelier every hour.
But never yet hath bride or maid
    In Araby's gay Haram smil'd

---

[1] The south-western portion of Arabia; called also Arabia Felix, the happy
or blessed Arabia.

Whose boasted brightness would not fade
Before Al Hassan's blooming child.

Light as the angel shapes that bless
An infant's dream, yet not the less
Rich in all woman's loveliness;—
With eyes so pure, that from their ray
Dark vice would turn abash'd away,
Blinded like serpents, when they gaze
Upon the emerald's virgin blaze;—
Yet fill'd with all youth's sweet desires,
Mingling the meek and vestal fires
Of other worlds with all the bliss,
The fond, weak tenderness of this:
A soul, too, more than half divine,
   Where, through some shades of earthly feeling,
Religion's softened glories shine,
   Like light through summer foliage stealing,
Shedding a glow of such mild hue,
So warm, and yet so shadowy too,
As makes the very darkness there
More beautiful than light elsewhere.

Such is the maid who, at this hour,
   Hath risen from her restless sleep,
And sits alone in that high bower,
   Watching the still and shining deep.
Ah! 'twas not thus, with tearful eyes
   And beating heart,—she us'd to gaze
On the magnificent earth and skies,
   In her own land, in happier days.
Why looks she now so anxious down
Among those rocks, whose rugged frown
Blackens the mirror of the deep?
Whom waits she all this lonely night?
   Too rough the rocks, too bold the steep,
   For man to scale that turret's height!—

So deem'd at least her thoughtful sire,
   When high, to catch the cool night-air,

After the day-beam's withering fire,
  He built her bower of freshness there,
And had it deck'd with costliest skill,
  And fondly thought it safe as fair;—
Think, reverend dreamer! think so still,
  Nor wake to learn what love can dare;—
Love, all-defying Love, who sees
No charm in trophies won with ease;—
Whose rarest, dearest fruits of bliss
Are pluck'd on Danger's precipice!
Bolder than they, who dare not dive
  For pearls, but when the sea's at rest,
Love, in the tempest most alive,
  Hath ever held that pearl the best
He finds beneath the stormiest water.
Yes—Araby's unrivall'd daughter,
Though high that tower, that rock-way rude,
  There's one who, but to kiss thy cheek,
Would climb the untrodden solitude
  Of Ararat's tremendous peak,
And think its steeps, though dark and dread,
Heaven's pathways, if to thee they led!
Ev'n now thou seest the flashing spray,
That lights his oar's impatient way;—
Ev'n now thou hear'st the sudden shock
Of his swift bark against the rock,
And stretchest down thy arms of snow,
As if to lift him from below!
Like her to whom, at dead of night,
The bridegroom, with his locks of light,
Came, in the flush of love and pride,
And scal'd the terrace of his bride;—
When, as she saw him rashly spring,
And midway up in danger cling,
She flung him down her long black hair,
Exclaiming breathless, "There, love, there!"
And scarce did manlier nerve uphold
  The hero Zal in that fond hour,
G

Than wings the youth who, fleet and bold,
   Now climbs the rocks to Hinda's bower.
See—light as up their granite steeps
   The rock-goats of Arabia clamber,
Fearless from crag to crag he leaps,
   And now is in the maiden's chamber.
She loves—but knows not whom she loves,
   Nor what his race, nor whence he came;—
Like one who meets, in Indian groves,
Some beauteous bird without a name,
Brought by the last ambrosial breeze,
From isles in the undiscover'd seas,
To show his plumage for a day
To wondering eyes, and wing away!
Will *he* thus fly—her nameless lover?
   Alla forbid! 'twas by a moon
As fair as this, while singing over
   Some ditty to her soft Kanoon,[1]
Alone, at this same witching hour,
   She first beheld his radiant eyes
Gleam through the lattice of the bower,
   Where nightly now they mix their sighs;
And thought some spirit of the air
(For what could waft a mortal there?)
Was pausing on his moonlight way
To listen to her lonely lay!
This fancy ne'er hath left her mind:
   And—though, when terror's swoon had past
She saw a youth, of mortal kind,
   Before her in obeisance cast,—
Yet often since, when he hath spoken
Strange, awful words,—and gleams have broken
From his dark eyes, too bright to bear,
   Oh! she hath fear'd her soul was given
To some unhallow'd child of air,
Some erring Spirit cast from heaven,
Like those angelic youths of old,

---

[1] A stringed instrument of music.

Who burn'd for maids of mortal mould,
Bewilder'd left the glorious skies,
And lost their Heaven for woman's eyes.
Fond girl! nor fiend nor angel he
Who woos thy young simplicity;
But one of earth's impassion'd sons,
　　As warm in love, as fierce in ire,
As the best heart whose current runs
　　Full of the Day-god's living fire.

But quench'd to-night that ardour seems,
　　And pale his cheek, and sunk his brow;—
Never before, but in her dreams,
　　Had she beheld him pale as now:
And those were dreams of troubled sleep,
From which 'twas joy to wake and weep;
Visions, that will not be forgot,
　　But sadden every waking scene,
Like warning ghosts, that leave the spot
All wither'd where they once have been.

"How sweetly," said the trembling maid,
Of her own gentle voice afraid,
So long had they in silence stood,
Looking upon that tranquil flood—
"How sweetly does the moonbeam smile
To-night upon yon leafy isle!
Oft, in my fancy's wanderings,
I've wish'd that little isle had wings,
And we, within its fairy bowers,
　　Were wafted off to seas unknown,
Where not a pulse should beat but ours,
　　And we might live, love, die alone!
Far from the cruel and the cold,—
　　Where the bright eyes of angels only
Should come around us, to behold
　　A paradise so pure and lonely.
Would this be world enough for thee?"—
Playful she turn'd, that he might see

The passing smile her cheek put on;
But when she mark'd how mournfully
  His eyes met hers, that smile was gone;
And, bursting into heart-felt tears,
"Yes, yes," she cried, "my hourly fears,
My dreams have boded all too right—
We part—for ever part—to-night!
I knew, I knew it *could* not last—
'Twas bright, 'twas heavenly, but 'tis past!
Oh! ever thus, from childhood's hour,
  I've seen my fondest hopes decay;
I never loved a tree or flower,
  But 'twas the first to fade away.
I never nurs'd a dear gazelle,
  To glad me with its soft black eye,
But when it came to know me well,
  And love me, it was sure to die!
Now too—the joy most like divine
  Of all I ever dreamt or knew,
To see thee, hear thee, call thee mine,—
  Oh, misery! must I lose *that* too?
Yet go—on peril's brink we meet;—
  Those frightful rocks—that treacherous sea—
No, never come again—though sweet,
  Though heaven, it may be death to thee.
Farewell—and blessings on thy way,
  Where'er thou goest, beloved stranger!
Better to sit and watch that ray,
And think thee safe, though far away,
  Than have thee near me, and in danger!"

"Danger!—Oh, tempt me not to boast—"
The youth exclaim'd—"thou little know'st
What he can brave, who, born and nurst
In Danger's paths, has dar'd her worst!
Upon whose ear the signal-word
Of strife and death is hourly breaking;
Who sleeps with head upon the sword
His fever'd hand must grasp in waking!"

. . . . .

   With sudden start he turn'd
 And pointed to the distant wave,
Where lights, like charnel meteors, burn'd
 Bluely, as o'er some seaman's grave:
And fiery darts, at intervals,
 Flew up all sparkling from the main,
As if each star that nightly falls,
 Were shooting back to heaven again.

"My signal-lights!—I must away—
Both, both are ruin'd, if I stay.
Farewell—sweet life! thou cling'st in vain—
Now, Vengeance, I am thine again."
Fiercely he broke away, nor stopp'd,
Nor look'd—but from the lattice dropp'd
Down 'mid the pointed crags beneath,
As if he fled from love to death.
While pale and mute young Hinda stood,
Nor mov'd, till in the silent flood
A momentary plunge below
Startled her from her trance of woe;—
Shrieking she to the lattice flew,
 "I come—I come—if in that tide
Thou sleep'st to-night, I'll sleep there too,
 In death's cold wedlock, by thy side.
Oh! I would ask no happier bed
 Than the chill wave my love lies under:—
Sweeter to rest together dead,
 Far sweeter, than to live asunder!"
But no—their hour is not yet come—
 Again she sees his pinnace fly,
Wafting him fleetly to his home,
 Where'er that ill-starr'd home may lie;
And calm and smooth it seem'd to win
 Its moonlight way before the wind,
As if it bore all peace within,
 Nor left one breaking heart behind!

The morn hath risen clear and calm,
  And o'er the Green Sea[1] palely shines,
Revealing Bahrein's[2] groves of palm,
  And lighting Kishma's[3] amber vines.
Fresh smell the shores of Araby,
While breezes from the Indian sea
Blow round Selama's sainted cape,
  And curl the shining flood beneath,—
Whose waves are rich with many a grape,
  And cocoa-nut and flowery wreath,
Which pious seamen, as they pass'd,
Had tow'rd that holy headland cast—
Oblations to the Genii[4] there
For gentle skies and breezes fair!
The nightingale now bends her flight
From the high trees, where all the night
  She sung so sweet, with none to listen;
And hides her from the morning star
  Where thickets of pomegranate glisten
In the clear dawn,—bespangled o'er
  With dew, whose night-drops would not stain
The best and brightest scimitar
That every youthful Sultan wore
  On the first morning of his reign.

And see—the Sun himself!—on wings
Of glory up the East he springs.
Angel of Light! who from the time
Those heavens began their march sublime,
Hath first of all the starry choir
Trod in his Maker's steps of fire!
  Where are the days, thou wondrous sphere,
When Iran, like a sun-flower, turn'd
To meet that eye where'er it burn'd?—

[1] The Persian Gulf.   [2] An island in the Persian Gulf.
[3] An island in the Persian Gulf.
[4] Good or evil spirits, supposed by the ancients to preside over every person, place, and thing, and especially to preside over a man's destiny from his birth.

When, from the banks of Bendemeer[1]
To the nut-groves of Samarcand,[2]
Thy temples flam'd o'er all the land?
Where are they? ask the shades of them
   Who, on Cadessia's[3] bloody plains,
Saw fierce invaders pluck the gem
From Iran's[4] broken diadem,
   And bind her ancient faith in chains:—
Ask the poor exile, cast alone
On foreign shores, unlov'd, unknown,
Beyond the Caspian's Iron Gates,
   Or on the snowy Mossian mountains,
Far from his beauteous land of dates,
   Her jasmine bowers and sunny fountains:
Yet happier so than if he trod
His own belov'd, but blighted, sod,
Beneath a despot stranger's nod!—
Oh, he would rather houseless roam
   Where Freedom and his God may lead,
Than be the sleekest slave at home
   That crouches to the conqueror's creed !

Is Iran's pride then gone for ever,
   Quench'd with the flame in Mithra's caves?—
No—she has sons, that never—never—
   Will stoop to be the Moslem's slaves,
   While heaven has light or earth has graves;—
Spirits of fire, that brood not long,
But flash resentment back for wrong:
And hearts where, slow but deep, the seeds
Of vengeance ripen into deeds,
Till, in some treacherous hour of calm,
They burst, like Zeilan's giant palm,[5]

---

[1] A river of Persia.
[2] A city of Bokhara, a country of Central Asia. It is situated in a beautiful and fertile valley and is surrounded with gardens.
[3] The place where the Persians were finally defeated by the Arabs, and their ancient monarchy destroyed.
[4] Persia.
[5] The Talpot or Talipot tree, a beautiful palm. The sheath which envelops

Whose buds fly open with a sound
That shakes the pigmy forest round!

Yes, Emir! he, who scal'd that tower—
    And, had he reach'd thy slumbering breast,
Had taught thee, in a Gheber's power
    How safe ev'n tyrant heads may rest—
Is one of many, brave as he,
Who loathe thy haughty race and thee;
Who, though they know the strife is vain,
Who, though they know the riven chain
Snaps but to enter in the heart
Of him who rends its links apart,
Yet dare the issue,—blest to be
Ev'n for one bleeding moment free,
And die in pangs of liberty!
Thou know'st them well—'tis some moons since
    Thy turban'd troops and blood-red flags,
Thou satrap of a bigot prince,
    Have swarm'd among these Green Sea crags;
Yet here, ev'n here, a sacred band,
Ay, in the portal of that land
Thou, Arab, dar'st to call thy own,
Their spears across thy path have thrown;
Here—ere the winds half wing'd thee o'er—
Rebellion brav'd thee from the shore.
Rebellion! foul, dishonouring word,
    Whose wrongful blight so oft has stain'd
The holiest cause that tongue or sword
    Of mortal ever lost or gain'd.
How many a spirit, born to bless,
    Hath sunk beneath that withering name,
Whom but a day's, an hour's success
    Had wafted to eternal fame!
As exhalations, when they burst
From the warm earth, if chill'd at first,

the flower is very large, and when it bursts makes an explosion like the report of a cannon.

If check'd in soaring from the plain,
Darken to fogs and sink again;—
But, if they once triumphant spread
Their wings above the mountain-head,
Become enthron'd in upper air,
And turn to sun-bright glories there!

And who is he, that wields the might
　　Of Freedom on the Green Sea brink,
Before whose sabre's dazzling light
　　The eyes of Yemen's[1] warriors wink?
Who comes, embower'd in the spears
Of Kerman's[2] hardy mountaineers?—
Those mountaineers that truest, last,
　　Cling to their country's ancient rites,
As if that God, whose eyelids cast
　　Their closing gleam on Iran's heights,
Among her snowy mountains threw
The last light of his worship too!

'Tis Hafed—name of fear, whose sound
　　Chills like the muttering of a charm!—
Shout but that awful name around,
　　And palsy shakes the manliest arm.
'Tis Hafed, most accurs'd and dire
(So rank'd by Moslem hate and ire)
Of all the rebel Sons of Fire;
Of whose malign, tremendous power
The Arabs, at their mid-watch hour,
Such tales of fearful wonder tell,
That each affrighted sentinel
Pulls down his cowl upon his eyes,
Lest Hafed in the midst should rise!
A man, they say, of monstrous birth,
A mingled race of flame and earth,
Sprung from those old, enchanted kings,
　　Who in their fairy helms, of yore
A feather from the mystic wings

[1] Arabia Felix.   [2] A province of Persia, lying on the Persian Gulf.

Of the Simoorgh resistless wore;
And gifted by the Fiends of Fire,
Who groan'd to see their shrines expire,
With charms that, all in vain withstood,
Would drown the Koran's light in blood!

Such were the tales that won belief,
    And such the colouring Fancy gave
To a young, warm, and dauntless Chief,—
    One who, no more than mortal brave,
Fought for the land his soul ador'd,
    For happy homes and altars free,—
His only talisman,[1] the sword,
    His only spell-word, Liberty!
One of that ancient hero line,
Along whose glorious current shine
Names that have sanctified their blood ;
As Lebanon's small mountain-flood
Is render'd holy by the ranks
Of sainted cedars on its banks.
'Twas not for him to crouch the knee
Tamely to Moslem tyranny;
'Twas not for him whose soul was cast
In the bright mould of ages past,
Whose melancholy spirit fed
With all the glories of the dead,
Though fram'd for Iran's happiest years,
Was born among her chains and tears!—
'Twas not for him to swell the crowd
Of slavish heads, that shrinking bow'd
Before the Moslem, as he pass'd,
Like shrubs beneath the poison-blast—
No—far he fled—indignant fled
    The pageant of his country's shame;
While every tear her children shed
    Fell on his soul like drops of flame;
And as a lover hails the dawn

---

[1] A charm or spell

Of a first smile, so welcom'd he
The sparkle of the first sword drawn
  For vengeance and for liberty !

But vain was valour—vain the flower
Of Kerman, in that deathful hour,
Against Al Hassan's whelming power,—
In vain they met him, helm to helm,
Upon the threshold of that realm
He came in bigot pomp to sway,
And with their corpses block'd his way—
In vain—for every lance they rais'd,
Thousands around the conqueror blaz'd ;
For every arm that lin'd their shore,
Myriads of slaves were wafted o'er,—
A bloody, bold, and countless crowd,
Before whose swarm as fast they bow'd
As dates beneath the locust cloud.

There stood—but one short league away
From old Harmozia's sultry bay—
A rocky mountain, o'er the Sea
Of Oman beetling awfully;
A last and solitary link
  Of those stupendous chains that reach
From the broad Caspian's reedy brink
  Down winding to the Green Sea beach.
Around its base the bare rocks stood,
Like naked giants, in the flood,
  As if to guard the Gulf across;
While, on its peak, that brav'd the sky,
A ruin'd Temple tower'd, so high
  That oft the sleeping albatross
Struck the wild ruins with her wing,
And from her cloud-rock'd slumbering
Started—to find man's dwelling there
In her own silent fields of air !
Beneath, terrific caverns gave
Dark welcome to each stormy wave

That dash'd, like midnight revellers, in;—
And such the strange, mysterious din
At times throughout those caverns roll'd,—
And such the fearful wonders told
Of restless sprites imprison'd there,
That bold were Moslem, who would dare,
At twilight hour, to steer his skiff
Beneath the Gheber's lonely cliff.

On the land side, those towers sublime,
That seem'd above the grasp of Time,
Were sever'd from the haunts of men
By a wide, deep, and wizard glen,
So fathomless, so full of gloom,
  No eye could pierce the void between:
It seem'd a place where Gholes might come
With their foul banquets from the tomb,
  And in its caverns feed unseen.
Like distant thunder from below,
  The sound of many torrents came,
Too deep for eye or ear to know
If 'twere the sea's imprison'd flow,
  Or floods of ever-restless flame.
For, each ravine, each rocky spire
Of that vast mountain stood on fire;[1]
And, though for ever past the days
When God was worshipp'd in the blaze
That from its lofty altar shone,—
Though fled the priests, the votaries gone,
Still did the mighty flame burn on,[2]
Through chance and change, through good and ill,
Like its own God's eternal will,
Deep, constant, bright, unquenchable!

Thither the vanquish'd Hafed led
  His little army's last remains;—

[1] The Ghebers generally built their temples over subterraneous fires.
[2] The Ghebers assert that the sacred fire in the Temple at Yezd, a city of
Persia, has continued to burn since the days of Zoroaster.

" Welcome, terrific glen !" he said,
" Thy gloom, that Eblis'[1] self might dread,
   Is heav'n to him who flies from chains !"
O'er a dark, narrow bridge-way known
To him and to his Chiefs alone,
They cross'd the chasm and gain'd the towers,—
" This home," he cried, " at least is ours ;
   Here we may bleed, unmock'd by hymns
     Of Moslem triumph o'er our head ;
Here we may fall, nor leave our limbs
     To quiver to the Moslem's tread.
Stretch'd on this rock, while vulture's beaks
Are whetted on our yet warm cheeks,
Here—happy that no tyrant's eye
Gloats on our torments—we may die !

   .   .   .   .   .

   This spot, at least, no foot of slave
Or satrap ever yet profaned ;
   And though but few—though fast the wave
Of life is ebbing from our veins,
Enough for vengeance still remains.
As panthers, after set of sun,
Rush from the roots of Lebanon
Across the dark sea-robber's way,
We'll bound upon our startled prey ;
And when some hearts that proudest swell
Have felt our falchion's last farewell ;
When Hope's expiring throb is o'er,
And ev'n Despair can prompt no more,
This spot shall be the sacred grave
Of the last few who, vainly brave,
Die for the land they cannot save !"

His Chiefs stood round—each shining blade
Upon the broken altar laid—
And though so wild and desolate
Those courts, where once the Mighty sate ;

---

[1] Lucifer, Satan.

No longer on those mouldering towers
Was seen the feast of fruits and flowers,
With which of old the Magi fed [1]
The wandering spirits of their dead;
Though neither priests nor rites were there,
    Nor charmed leaf of pure pomegranate;
Nor hymn, nor censer's fragrant air,
    Nor symbol of their worshipp'd planet;
Yet the same God that heard their sires
Heard *them*, while on that altar's fires
They swore the latest, holiest deed
Of the few hearts, still left to bleed,
Should be, in Iran's injured name,
To die upon that Mount of Flame—
The last of all her patriot line,
Before her last untrampled Shrine!

.   .   .   .   .

'Tis the eighth morn—Al Hassan's brow
    Is brighten'd with unusual joy—
What mighty mischief glads him now,
    Who never smiles but to destroy?
The sparkle upon Herkend's sea,
When toss'd at midnight furiously,
Tells not of wreck and ruin nigh,
More surely than that smiling eye!
" Up, daughter, up—the Kerna's [2] breath
Has blown a blast would waken death,
And yet thou sleep'st—up, child, and see
This blessed day for Heaven and me,
A day more rich in Pagan blood
Than ever flash'd o'er Oman's flood.
Before another dawn shall shine,
His head—heart—limbs—will all be mine;

[1] The Magi were a sect of priests or philosophers in Persia. They used to place upon the top of high towers various kinds of rich viands, upon which it was supposed the Peris and spirits of their departed heroes regaled themselves.

[2] A kind of trumpet,

This very night his blood shall steep
These hands all over ere I sleep !"

" *His* blood !" she faintly scream'd—her mind
Still singling *one* from all mankind—
"Yes—spite of his ravines and towers,
Hafed, my child, this night is ours.
Thanks to all-conquering treachery,
 Without whose aid the links accurst,
That bind these impious slaves, would be
 Too strong for Alla's self to burst !

  .   .   .   .

His bloody boast was all too true;
There lurk'd one wretch among the few
Whom Hafed's eagle eye could count
Around him on that fiery Mount,—
One miscreant, who for gold betray'd
The pathway through the valley's shade
To those high towers, where Freedom stood
In her last hold of flame and blood.
Left on the field last dreadful night,
When, sallying from their sacred height,
The Ghebers fought Hope's farewell fight,
He lay—but died not with the brave;
That sun, which should have gilt his grave,
Saw him a traitor and a slave;—
And, while the few, who thence return'd
To their high rocky fortress, mourn'd
For him among the matchless dead
They left behind on glory's bed,
He liv'd, and, in the face of morn,
Laugh'd them and Faith and Heaven to scorn.

  . . . . . .

HINDA'S LOVE.

With watchfulness the maid attends
His rapid glance, where'er it bends—
Why shoot his eyes such awful beams?

What plans he now? what thinks or dreams?
Alas! why stands he musing here,
When every moment teams with fear?
" Hafed, my own beloved Lord,"
She kneeling cries—" first, last ador'd!
If in that soul thou'st ever felt
    Half what thy lips impassion'd swore,
Here, on my knees that never knelt
    To any but their God before,
'I pray thee, as thou lov'st me, fly—
Now, now—ere yet their blades are nigh.
Oh haste—the bark that bore me hither
    Can waft us o'er yon dark'ning sea,
East—west—alas, I care not whither,
    So thou art safe, and I with thee!
Go where we will, this hand in thine,
    Those eyes before me, smiling thus,
Through good and ill, through storm and shine,
    The world's a world of love for us!
On some calm, blessed shore we'll dwell,
Where 'tis no crime to love too well;—
Where thus to worship tenderly
An erring child of light like thee
Will not be sin—or if it be,
Where we may weep our faults away,
Together kneeling, night and day,
Though, for *my* sake at Alla's shrine,
And I—at *any* God's for thine."

Wildly these passionate words she spoke—
    Then hung her head and wept for shame;
Sobbing, as if a heart-string broke
    With every deep-heaved sob that came.
While he, young, warm—oh! wonder not
    If for a moment pride and fame,
    His oath—his cause—that shrine of flame,
And Iran's self are all forgot
For her whom at his feet he sees

Kneeling in speechless agonies.
No, blame him not, if hope awhile
Dawn'd in his soul, and threw her smile
O'er hours to come—o'er days and nights,
Wing'd with those precious, pure delights
Which she, who bends all beauteous there,
Was born to kindle and to share,
A tear or two, which, as he bow'd
 To raise the suppliant, trembling stole,
First warn'd him of this dang'rous cloud
 Of softness passing o'er his soul.
Starting, he brush'd the drops away,
Unworthy o'er that cheek to stray;—
Like one who, on the morn of fight,
Shakes from his sword the dews of night,
That had but dimm'd, not stain'd its light.
Yet though subdued th' unnerving thrill,
Its warmth, its weakness linger'd still
 So touching in its look and tone,
That the fond, fearing, hoping maid
Half-counted on the flight she pray'd,
 Half thought the hero's soul was grown
 As soft, as yielding as her own,
And smil'd and bless'd him, while he said,—
" Yes—if there be some happier sphere,
Where fadeless truth like ours is dear,—
If there be any land of rest
 For those who love, and ne'er forget,
Oh! comfort thee—for safe and blest
 We'll meet in that calm region yet!"

Scarce had she time to ask her heart
If good or ill these words impart,
When the rous'd youth impatient flew
To the tow'r-wall, where, high in view,
A pond'rous sea-horn hung, and blew
A signal, deep and dread as those
The storm-fiend at his rising, blows.—
 7

Full well his Chieftains, sworn and true
Through life and death, that signal knew;
For 'twas th' appointed warning blast,
Th' alarm, to tell when hope was past,
And the tremendous death-die cast!
And there upon the mould'ring tow'r,
Hath hung this sea-horn many an hour,
Ready to sound o'er land and sea
That dirge-note of the brave and free.

They came—his Chieftains at the call
Came slowly round, and with them all—
Alas how few!—the worn remains
Of those who late o'er Kerman's plains
Went gaily prancing to the clash
   Of Moorish zel and tymbalon,
Catching new hope from every flash
   Of their long lances in the sun.
And as their coursers charg'd the wind,
And the white ox-tails streamed behind,
Looking, as if the steeds they rode,
Were wing'd, and every chief a god!
How fall'n, how alter'd now! how wan
Each scarr'd and faded visage shone
As round the burning shrine they came;—
   How deadly was the glare it cast
As mute they paus'd before the flame
   To light their torches as they pass'd!
'Twas silence all—the youth had plann'd
The duties of his soldier-band;
And each determin'd brow declares
His faithful Chieftains well know theirs.

But minutes speed—night gems the skies—
And oh! how soon, ye blessed eyes,
That look from heaven, ye may behold
Sights that will turn your star-fires cold!
Breathless with awe, impatience, hope,
The maiden sees the veteran group

Her litter silently prepare,
  And lay it at her trembling feet;—
And now the youth, with gentle care,
  Hath placed her in the shelter'd seat,
And press'd her hand, that ling'ring press
  Of hands that for the last time sever;
Of hearts, whose pulse of happiness,
  When that hold breaks, is dead for ever.
And yet to *her* this sad caress
  Gives hope—so fondly hope can err !
'Twas joy, she thought, joy's mute excess—
  Their happy flight's dear harbinger;
'Twas warmth—assurance—tenderness—
  'Twas anything but leaving her.

"Haste, haste," she cried, " the clouds grow dark,
  But still ere night we'll reach the bark;
And by to-morrow's dawn—oh bliss !
  With thee upon the sun-bright deep,
Far off, I'll but remember this,
  As some dark vanish'd dream of sleep ;
And thou——" but ah !—he answers not—
  Good Heav'n !—and does she go alone ?
She now has reach'd that dismal spot,
  Where some hours since, his voice's tone
Had come to soothe her fears and ills,
Sweet as the angel Israfil's,
When every leaf on Eden's tree
Is trembling to his minstrelsy—
Yet now—oh, now, he is not nigh.—
  "Hafed ! my Hafed !—if it be
Thy will, thy doom this night to die;
  Let me but stay to die with thee,
And I will bless thy loved name,
Till the last life-breath leave this frame.
Oh ! let our lips our cheeks be laid
But near each other while they fade;
Let us but mix our parting breaths,

And I can die ten thousand deaths!
You too, who hurry me away
So cruelly, one moment stay—
   Oh! stay—one moment is not much—
He yet may come—for *him* I pray—
Hafed! dear Hafed!"—all the way
   In wild lamentings, that would touch
A heart of stone, she shriek'd his name
To the dark woods—no Hafed came :—
No—hapless pair—you've look'd your last :—
   Your hearts should both have broken then :
The dream is o'er—your doom is cast—
   You'll never meet on earth again!

THE PERI'S SONG.

Farewell—farewell to thee, Araby's daughter!
   (Thus warbled a Peri beneath the dark sea),
No pearl ever lay, under Oman's green water,
   More pure in its shell than thy spirit in thee.

Oh! fair as the sea-flower close to thee growing,
   How light was thy heart till Love's witchery came,
Like the wind of the south o'er a summer lute blowing,
   And hush'd all its music, and wither'd its frame!

But long, upon Araby's green sunny highlands,
   Shall maids and their lovers remember the doom
Of her, who lies sleeping among the Pearl Islands,
   With nought but the sea-star to light up her tomb.

And still, when the merry date-season is burning,
   And calls to the palm-groves the young and the old,
The happiest there, from their pastime returning
   At sunset, will weep when thy story is told.

The young village-maid, when with flow'rs she dresses
   Her dark flowing hair for some festival day,
Will think of thy fate till, neglecting her tresses,
   She mournfully turns from the mirror away.

Nor shall Iran, belov'd of her Hero! forget thee—
  Though tyrants watch over her tears as they start,
Close, close by the side of that Hero she'll set thee,
  Embalm'd in the innermost shrine of her heart.

Farewell—be it ours to embellish thy pillow
  With ev'rything beauteous that grows in the deep;
Each flow'r of the rock and each gem of the billow
  Shall sweeten thy bed and illumine thy sleep.

Around thee shall glisten the loveliest amber
  That ever the sorrowing sea-bird has wept;
With many a shell, in whose hollow-wreath'd chamber,
  We, Peris of Ocean, by moonlight have slept.

We'll dive where the gardens of coral lie darkling,
  And plant all the rosiest stems at thy head;
We'll seek where the sands of the Caspian are sparkling,
  And gather their gold to strew over thy bed.

Farewell—farewell—until Pity's sweet fountain
  Is lost in the hearts of the fair and the brave,
They'll weep for the Chieftain who died on the mountain
  They'll weep for the Maiden who sleeps in this wave.

IV.—FROM "THE LIGHT OF THE HAREM."

CASHMERE.

Who has not heard of the Vale of Cashmere,
  With its roses the brightest that earth ever gave,
Its temples, and grottos, and fountains as clear
  As the love-lighted eyes that hung over their wave?

Oh! to see it at sunset,—when warm o'er the Lake
  Its splendour at parting a summer eve throws,
Like a bride, full of blushes, when ling'ring to take
  A last look of her mirror at night ere she goes!—
When the shrines through the foliage are gleaming half
      shown,
And each hallows the hour by some rites of its own.
Here the music of pray'r from a minaret swells,

Here the Magian his urn, full of perfume, is swinging,
And here, at the altar, a zone of sweet bells
    Round the waist of some fair Indian dancer is ringing.
Or to see it by moonlight,—when mellowly shines   .
The light o'er its palaces, gardens, and shrines;
When the water-falls gleam, like a quick fall of stars,
And the nightingale's hymn from the Isle of Chenars
Is broken by laughs and light echoes of feet
From the cool, shining walks where the young people
    meet.—
Or at morn, when the magic of daylight awakes
A new wonder each minute, as slowly it breaks,
Hills, cupolas, fountains, call'd forth every one
Out of darkness, as if but just born of the Sun:
When the Spirit of Fragance is up with the day,
From his Haram of night-flowers stealing away;
And the wind, full of wantonness, woos like a lover
The young aspen-trees, till they tremble all over;
When the East is as warm as the light of first hopes,
    And Day, with his banner of radiance unfurl'd,
Shines in through the mountainous portal that opes,
    Sublime, from that Valley of bliss to the world!

LIGHT CAUSES MAY CREATE DISSENSION.

Alas!—how light a cause may move ＇
Dissension between hearts that love!
Hearts that the world in vain had tried,
And sorrow but more closely tied;
That stood the storm, when waves were rough,
Yet in a sunny hour fall off,
Like ships that have gone down at sea,
When heaven was all tranquillity!
A something, light as air—a look,
    A word unkind or wrongly taken—
Oh! love, that tempests never shook,
    A breath, a touch like this hath shaken.
And ruder words will soon rush in
To spread the breach that words begin;

And eyes forget the gentle ray
They wore in courtship's smiling day;
And voices lose the tone that shed
A tenderness round all they said;
Till fast declining, one by one,
The sweetnesses of love are gone,
And hearts, so lately mingled, seem
Like broken clouds,—or like the stream,
That smiling left the mountain's brow,
 As though its waters ne'er could sever,
Yet, ere it reach the plain below,
 Breaks into floods, that part for ever.

SONG OF THE ARAB MAID.

Fly to the desert, fly with me,
Our Arab tents are rude for thee;
But, oh! the choice what heart can doubt,
Of tents with love, or thrones without?

Our rocks are rough, but smiling there
The acacia waves her yellow hair,
Lonely and sweet, nor lov'd the less
For flow'ring in a wilderness.

Our sands are bare, but down their slope
The silv'ry-footed antelope
As gracefully and gaily springs
As o'er the marble courts of kings.

Then come—thy Arab maid will be
The lov'd and lone acacia-tree,
The antelope, whose feet shall bless
With their light sound thy loneliness.

Oh! there are looks and tones that dart
An instant sunshine through the heart,—
As if the soul that minute caught
Some treasure it through life had sought;

As if the very lips and eyes,
Predestin'd to have all our sighs,

And never be forgot again,
Sparkled and spoke before us then!

So came thy ev'ry glance and tone
When first on me they breath'd and shone;
New, as if brought from other spheres,
Yet welcome as if lov'd for years.

Then fly with me,—if thou hast known
No other flame, nor falsely thrown
A gem away, that thou hadst sworn
Should ever in thy heart be worn.

Come, if the love thou hast for me,
Is pure and fresh as mine for thee,—
Fresh as the fountain under ground,
When first 'tis by the lapwing found.

But if for me thou dost forsake
Some other maid, and rudely break
Her worshipp'd image from its base,
To give to me the ruin'd place;—

Then, fare thee well—I'd rather make
My bower upon some icy lake
When thawing suns begin to shine,
Than trust to love so false as thine!

CHAPTER VII.

NATIONAL AIRS AND SACRED MELODIES—VISIT TO PARIS—THE
FUDGE FAMILY—SLOPERTON—TRUE CHARITY.

National Airs, a volume of poems, containing "Flow on, thou Shining River," "All that's Bright must Fade," "Those Evening Bells," "Oft in the Stilly Night," and others, was published in 1815.

From it we select the following:—

HARK! THE VESPER HYMN IS STEALING.

RUSSIAN AIR.

Hark! the vesper hymn is stealing
O'er the waters soft and clear;
Nearer yet and nearer pealing,
And now bursts upon the ear:
Jubilate, Amen.
Farther now, now farther stealing,
Soft it fades upon the ear:
Jubilate, Amen.

Now, like moonlight waves retreating
To the shore, it dies along;
Now, like angry surges meeting,
Breaks the mingled tide of song:
Jubilate, Amen.
Hush! again, like waves, retreating
To the shore, it dies along:
Jubilate, Amen.

REASON, FOLLY, AND BEAUTY.

ITALIAN AIR.

Reason, and Folly, and Beauty, they say,
Went on a party of pleasure one day:
Folly play'd
Around the maid,
The bells of his cap rang merrily out;
While Reason took
To his sermon-book—
Oh! which was the pleasanter no one need doubt,
Which was the pleasanter no one need doubt.

Beauty, who likes to be thought very sage,
Turn'd for a moment to Reason's dull page,
Till Folly said,
"Look here, sweet maid!"—
The sight of his cap brought her back to herself;

While Reason read
His leaves of lead,
With no one to mind him, poor sensible elf!
No,—no one to mind him, poor sensible elf!

Then Reason grew jealous of Folly's gay cap;
Had he that on, he her heart might entrap—
"There it is,"
Quoth Folly, "old quiz!"
(Folly was always good-natured, 'tis said,)
"Under the sun
There's no such fun,
As Reason with my cap and bells on his head,
Reason with my cap and bells on his head!"

But Reason the head-dress so awkwardly wore,
That Beauty now lik'd him still less than before;
While Folly took
Old Reason's book,
And twisted the leaves in a cap of such *ton*,
That Beauty vow'd
(Though not aloud),
She lik'd him still better in that than his own,
Yes,—lik'd him still better in that than his own.

OH, COME TO ME WHEN DAYLIGHT SETS.

VENETIAN AIR.

Oh, come to me when daylight sets;
Sweet! then come to me,
When smoothly go our gondolets
O'er the moonlight sea.
When Mirth's awake, and Love begins,
Beneath that glancing ray,
With sound of lutes and mandolins,
To steal young hearts away.
Then, come to me when daylight sets;
Sweet! then come to me,
When smoothly go our gondolets
O'er the moonlight sea.

Oh, then's the hour for those who love,
  Sweet! like thee and me;
When all's so calm below, above.
  In heav'n and o'er the sea.
When maidens sing sweet barcarolles
  And Echo sings again
So sweet, that all with ears and souls
  Should love and listen then.
So, come to me when daylight sets;
  Sweet! then come to me,
When smoothly go our gondolets
  O'er the moonlight sea.

ALL THAT'S BRIGHT MUST FADE.

INDIAN AIR.

All that's bright must fade,—
  The brightest still the fleetest;
All that's sweet was made,
  But to be lost when sweetest.
Stars that shine and fall;—
  The flower that drops in springing;—
These, alas! are types of all
  To which our hearts are clinging.
All that's bright must fade,—
  The brightest still the fleetest;
All that's sweet was made
  But to be lost when sweetest!

Who would seek or prize
  Delights that end in aching?
Who would trust to ties
  That every hour are breaking?
Better far to be
  In utter darkness lying,
Than to be bless'd with light and see
  That light for ever flying.
All that's bright must fade,—
  The brightest still the fleetest;

All that's sweet was made
But to be lost when sweetest!

OFT, IN THE STILLY NIGHT.

SCOTCH AIR.

Oft, in the stilly night,
  Ere Slumber's chain has bound me,
Fond Memory brings the light
  Of other days around me:
    The smiles, the tears,
    Of boyhood's years,
  The words of love then spoken;
    The eyes that shone,
    Now dimm'd and gone,
  The cheerful hearts now broken!
Thus, in the stilly night,
  Ere Slumber's chain hath bound me,
Sad Memory brings the light
  Of other days around me.

When I remember all
  The friends, so link'd together,
I've seen around me fall,
  Like leaves in wintry weather;
    I feel like one,
    Who treads alone
  Some banquet-hall deserted,
    Whose lights are fled,
    Whose garlands dead,
  And all but me departed!
Thus, in the stilly night,
  Ere Slumber's chain has bound me,
Sad Memory brings the light
  Of other days around me.

In 1816 appeared two series of *Sacred Melodies*. From
these, we quote two songs:—

MIRIAM'S SONG.

"And Miriam the Prophetess, the sister of Aaron, took a timbrel in her hand; and all the women went out after her with timbrels and with dances."
—Ex. xv. 20.

Sound the loud Timbrel o'er Egypt's dark sea!
Jehovah has triumph'd—his people are free.
Sing—for the pride of the Tyrant is broken,
   His chariots, his horsemen, all splendid and brave,
How vain was their boast, for the Lord hath but spoken,
   And chariots and horsemen are sunk in the wave.
Sound the loud Timbrel o'er Egypt's dark sea;
Jehovah has triumph'd—his people are free.

Praise to the Conqueror, praise to the Lord!
His word was our arrow, his breath was our sword.—
Who shall return to tell Egypt the story
   Of those she sent forth in the hour of her pride?
For the Lord hath look'd out from his pillar of glory,
   And all her brave thousands are dash'd in the tide.
Sound the loud Timbrel o'er Egypt's dark sea;
Jehovah has triumph'd—his people are free.

THIS WORLD IS ALL A FLEETING SHOW.

This world is all a fleeting show,
   For man's illusion given;
The smiles of Joy, the tears of Woe,
Deceitful shine, deceitful flow—
   There's nothing true, but Heaven!

And false the light on Glory's plume,
   As fading hues of Even;
And Love, and Hope, and Beauty's bloom,
Are blossoms gather'd for the tomb—
   There's nothing bright, but Heaven!

Poor wand'rers of a stormy day!
   From wave to wave we're driven,
And Fancy's flash and Reason's ray,
Serve but to light the troubled way—
   There's nothing calm, but Heaven!

These last lines, Moore himself believed to be the finest of all his compositions; and that opinion, at all events, sincerely indicated the current of his matured thought, and the direction of his aspirations.

After the splendid success of *Lalla Rookh*, in holiday mood, Moore, leaving his wife at Hornsey, accepted from Rogers the offer of a seat in his carriage, and set out, in 1817, for a visit to Paris. The Bourbon dynasty had just been restored; society was in a chaotic state, and Paris swarmed with English, whose ridiculous cockneyism and nonsense furnished him with materials for the letters entitled *The Fudge Family in Paris*, published the following year (in 1818), and consisting of a happy blending of the political squib and the social burlesque.

Of it Moore says, "Making its appearance at such a crisis, the work brought with it that best seasoning of all such *jeux-d'esprit*, the *à-propos* of the moment; and, accordingly, in the race of successive editions Lalla Rookh was, for some time, kept pace with, by Miss Biddy Fudge."

As a specimen, we give Miss Biddy Fudge's last epistle:—

" Four o'clock.

"Oh, Dolly, dear Dolly, I'm ruin'd for ever—
I ne'er shall be happy again, Dolly, never!
To think of the wretch—what a victim was I!
'Tis too much to endure—I shall die, I shall die—
My brain's in a fever—my pulses beat quick—
I shall die, or, at least, be exceedingly sick!
Oh, what do you think? after all my romancing,
My visions of glory, my sighing, my glancing,
This Colonel—I scarce can commit it to paper—
This Colonel's no more than a vile linen-draper!!
'Tis true as I live—I had coax'd brother Bob so,
(You'll hardly make out what I'm writing, I sob so),
For some little gift on my birth-day—September
The thirtieth, dear, I'm eighteen, you remember—

That Bob to a shop kindly order'd the coach,
  (Ah, little I thought who the shopman would prove),
To bespeak me a few of those *mouchŏirs de poche,*
  Which, in happier hours, I have sigh'd for, my love—
(The most beautiful things—two Napoleons the price—
And one's name in the corner embroider'd so nice!)
Well, with heart full of pleasure, I enter'd the shop,
But—ye Gods, what a phantom!—I thought I should
    drop—
There he stood, my dear Dolly—no room for a doubt—
  There, behind the vile counter, these eyes saw him stand,
With a piece of French cambric, before him roll'd out,
  And that horrid yard-measure uprais'd in his hand!
Oh—Papa, all along, knew the secret, 'tis clear—
'Twas *a shopman* he meant by a " Brandenburgh," dear!
The man, whom I fondly had fancied a King,
  And, when *that* too delightful illusion was past,
As a hero who worshipp'd—vile, treacherous thing—
  To turn out but a low linen-draper at last!
My head swam around—the wretch smil'd, I believe,
But his smiling, alas, could no longer deceive—
I fell back on Bob—my whole heart seem'd to wither—
And, pale as a ghost, I was carried back hither!
I only remember that Bob, as I caught him,
  With cruel facetiousness said, ' Curse the Kiddy!
A staunch Revolutionist always I've thought him,
  But now I find out he's a *Counter* one, Biddy!'

"Only think, my dear creature, if this should be known
To that saucy, satirical thing, Miss Malone!
What a story 'twill be at Shandangan for ever!
  What laughs and what quizzing she'll have with the men!
It will spread through the country—and never, oh, never
  Can Biddy be seen at Kilrandy again!
Farewell—I shall do something desp'rate, I fear—
And, ah! if my fate ever reaches your ear,
One tear of compassion my Doll will not grudge
To her poor—broken-hearted—young friend,
                      BIDDY FUDGE.

"*Nota bene*—I am sure you will hear, with delight,
That we're going, all three, to see Brunet to-night,
A laugh will revive me—and kind Mr. Cox
(Do you know him?) has got us the Governor's box."

The Fudge Family was *once* amusing; but it is the natural fate of ephemeral satire to perish with the events which gave rise to it. This work was succeeded, in 1819, by the publication of *Tom Crib's Memorial to Congress.*

On his return from his continental tour, he was urged by the Marquis of Lansdowne, his ever-constant friend, to come and live near him; and he, accordingly, took Sloperton Cottage, near Devizes and contiguous to his friend's beautiful demesne of Bowood, in Wiltshire.

He took possession of it in November, 1817, and it was his only home in England till his death in 1852.

From Sloperton he writes to Corry on December 8th, 1817,—"We have got a very snug little thatched cottage here, which Lord Lansdowne most friendlily volunteered to find out for us. I pay for it, furnished, but forty pounds a year, and yet I think it promises to be by far the most comfortable dwelling we have had. Lord Lansdowne's library is within a moderate walk of me, and as most of my London friends come down to visit him in the course of the year, I shall have just those *glimpses* of society which throw a light over one's solitude, and enliven it."

Subsequently he became its tenant under a repairing lease at £18 annual rent. It was originally a labourer's dwelling standing in the midst of a delightful country half buried among the trees of a wooded lane; yet, from its upper windows, as well as from its garden, obtaining peeps, of retired slopes, woodland hollows, and lovely old English scenes, through between their branches. "It has a small garden and lawn in front, and a kitchen-garden behind; along two sides of this kitchen-garden is a raised bank." It ran the whole length, was bounded by a laurel hedge, and was called by the poet the "terrace walk." There, a small deal table stood through all weathers; for it was his custom to compose as he walked; and, at this table, to pause and write down his thoughts; here, too, he delighted to watch the setting sun—a sight which, Mrs. Moore tells us, he very rarely missed. The poet's study was upstairs. "Views of Sloperton Cottage every one has seen; but it is only when you stand actually before it, see it covered with clematis, its two porches hung with roses, and the lawn and garden which sorrounded it kept in the most exquisite order, and fragrant with every flower of the season, that you are fully sensible of what a genuine poet's nest it is." So wrote William Howitt, of Moore's Cottage; and Moore himself described it as—

> "That dear house, that saving ark
> Where Love's true light at last I found;
> Cheering within when all grows dark,
> And comfortless, and stormy round."

The following letter affords a pleasing glimpse of life in his cottage home, and of Mrs. Moore, who was, as Moore said of her, "independent to the heart's core."

"Sloperton Cottage, Jan. 9, 1818.

"We are getting on here as quietly and comfortably as possible; and the only thing I regret is the want of some near and plain neighbours for Bessy to make intimacy with, and enjoy a little tea-drinking now and then, as she used to do in Derbyshire. She continues, however, to employ herself very well without them; and her favourite task, of cutting out things for the poor people, is here even in greater requisition than we bargained for, as there never was such wretchedness in any place where we have been; and the better class of people (with but one or two exceptions) seem to consider their contributions to the poor-rates as abundantly sufficient, without making any further exertions towards the relief of the poor wretches. It is a pity Bessy has not more means, for she takes the true method of charity,—that of going herself into the cottages, and seeing what they are most in want of. . . . She is, however, very much pleased both with Lord and Lady Lansdowne; who have, indeed, been everything that is kind and amiable to her."

CHAPTER VIII

BERMUDA TROUBLES—CONTINENTAL VISIT—SOJOURN AT PARIS.

Moore had not been long settled in Sloperton Cottage when intelligence reached him that the deputy whom he had appointed at Bermuda had, by embezzlement, involved him in a debt of £6000 for which he was responsible. Friends at once offered Moore pecuniary aid.

He had, unfortunately, neglected the common business precaution of requiring security from his deputy, and had only his pen by which to retrieve himself, so that, trusting to it, he resolved gratefully to decline many pressing offers of assistance, and endeavoured to work out his deliverance entirely by his own efforts. Of this period he writes:—"I was more than consoled for all such embarrassment, were it even ten times as much, by the eager kindness with which friends pressed forward to help to release me from my difficulties. . . . I shall so far lift the veil in which such delicate generosity seeks to shroud itself, as to mention briefly the manner in which one of these kind friends—himself possessing but limited means—proposed to contribute to the object of relieving me from my embarrassments. After adverting in his letter to my misfortunes, and 'the noble way,' as he was pleased to say, 'in which I bore them,' he adds,— 'would it be very impertinent to say that I have £500 entirely at your disposal, to be paid when you like; and as much more that I could advance upon any reasonable security, payable in seven years?' The writer concludes by apologizing anxiously and delicately for 'the liberty which he thus takes,' assuring me that he would not have made the offer if he did not feel that he would most readily accept the same assistance from me."

The writer of this letter was Lord Jeffrey, whom Moore had formerly challenged, and the communication is altogether so creditable to both parties that we here present the whole:—

> "Jordan's, St. James' Street,
> "Tuesday, May 30, 1818.

"My Dear Moore,—What I inclose has been justly owing you, I am ashamed to say, ever since you were so kind as to send me that account of M. de J——, I do not know how long ago; but I did not know your address, and I neglect everything. Will you let me hope for a contribution from you some day soon?

"I cannot from my heart resist adding another word. I have heard of your misfortunes, and of the noble way you bear them. Is it very impertinent to say that I have £500 entirely at your service, which you may repay when you please; and as much more, which I can advance upon any reasonable security of repayment in seven years?

"Perhaps it is very unpardonable in me to say this; but upon my honour I would not *make* you the offer if I did not feel that I would *accept* it without scruple from you.

"At all events, pray don't be angry with me, and don't send me a letter beginning *Sir*. I shall ask your pardon with the truest submission if I have offended you; but I trust I have not. At all events, and however this ends, no living soul shall

ever know of my presumption but yourself.   Believe me, with
great respect and esteem, very faithfully yours,
                                        " F. JEFFREY."

Sir William Napier, the historian, also wrote:—"My
Dear Moore,—Knowing your feelings about pecuniary
affairs, I feel almost afraid to tell you that I have several
hundred pounds at my bankers; that there is not the
slightest chance of my wanting them, for a year at least;
and until your affairs are arranged with Murray, I do
hope that you will not be offended if I say they are at
your service.—Wm. Napier." And this entry occurs in
one of Moore's memorandum-books:—"Without entering into particulars on this subject, I will only say, that
when my embarrassment wore its worst aspect, Lord
Lansdowne came forward to take the whole weight of my
loss, whatever it might be, on himself." Such are fine
examples of the chivalry of · friendship; and Moore's
setting them aside, and resolving to help himself by his
pen, was as chivalrous.

About this period we find the following interesting
memoranda in his diary:—

COMPOSING IN BED.

" Feb. 21, 1819.—Breakfasted in bed for the purpose of hastening the remainder of my 'Crib' work. It is singular the difference that bed makes, not only in the facility, but the *fancy*
of what I write. Whether it be the horizontal position (which
Richeraud, the French physiologist, says is most favourable
to thought), or more probably the removal of all those external
objects that divert the attention, it is certain that the effect
is always the same ; and if I did not find that it relaxed me
exceedingly, I should pass half my days in bed for the purpose
of composition."

A French author, M. de Valois, in a Latin poem asserts,
although on what authority we know not, that Herodotus
and Plato studied in bed.

C. 191

MOORE'S MUSIC—NATIONAL MELODIES.

"9th June, 1819.—Met Bishop by appointment at Power's, in order for him to look over the national melodies I have done, and take my ideas as to their arrangement. This being our first time of working together, I felt rather nervous; but he appears everything I could wish; intelligent, accommodating, and quick at understanding my wishes upon the subject. One thing flattered me a good deal: among the airs I produced to him, I had stolen in one of my own, under the disguise of a Swedish air. It was the last I brought forward, and he had scarcely played two bars of it when he exclaimed, 'Delicious!' and when he finished it, said, 'This is the sweetest air you have selected yet.' I could not help telling him the truth about it; and, indeed, I doubt very much whether I shall go on with the imposture by introducing it into the collection. If I do, I shall call it a *Moorish* air."

"July 14th, 1819.—Dined with Power (Strand) to meet Bishop, who brought two more of the airs he has arranged. He mentioned a good story to prove how a musician's ear requires the extreme seventh to be resolved. Sebastian Bach, one morning, getting out of bed for some purpose, ran his fingers over the keys of the pianoforte as he passed, but when he returned to bed he found he could not sleep. It was in vain he tossed and turned about. At length he recollected that the last chord he struck was that of the seventh; he got up again, resolved it, and then went to bed and slept as comfortably as he could desire."

In Diary, July, 1819, Moore drolly mentions that "George Dyer, in despair of getting any one to listen to him reading his own poetry, at last, when Dr. Graham came into the neighbourhood with his plan of burying people up to the neck in the earth and leaving them there some hours (as a mode of cure for some disease), took advantage of the situation of these patients, and went and read to them all, while they were thus stuck in the earth!!!"

Meanwhile an attachment had issued against Moore from the Court of Admiralty; and as negotiations were about to be opened with the American claimants for a reduction of their large demand on him—a sum supposed at that time to amount to six thousand pounds—it was deemed necessary, that, pending the treaty, in order to avoid arrest, he should sojourn for a time on the Continent. So, in September, 1819, Moore started off, setting out with Lord John Russell, for the Simplon and Italy. Of this tour he writes in his diary:—

"27th Sept., 1819.—Arrived at Brieg, at the foot of the Simplon; an oriental-looking little place, with its spires and towers. Ascended the Simplon, which baffles all description. A road carried up into the very clouds, over torrents and precipices; nothing was ever like it. At the last stage, before we reached the barrier on the summit, walked on by myself, and saw such a scene of sunset as I shall never forget. That mighty panorama of the Alps, whose summits there, indistinctly seen, looked like the top of gigantic waves, following close upon each other; the soft lights falling on those green spots which cultivation has conjured up in the midst of this wild scene; the painted top of the Jungfrau, whose snows were then pink with the setting sun; all was magnificent to a degree that quite overpowered me, and I alternately shuddered and shed tears as I looked upon it. Just, too, as we arrived near the snows on the very summit, the moon rose beautifully over them, and gave a new sort of glory to the scene."

"I shall never forget," says Lord John Russell, "the day when I hurried him on, from a post-house in the Jura mountains, to get a first view of the Alps at sunset, and on coming up to him, found him speechless and in tears, overcome with the sublimity of Mont Blanc."

At Milan they met Lord Kinnaird, thence, Lord John went to Genoa, and Moore proceeded to Venice to meet

Lord Byron. At Rome, the two poets explored the works of ancient and modern art, under the personal guidance of men such as ‚ Canova, Chantrey, Turner, Lawrence, Jackson, and Eastlake.

When in Italy, he entered in his private journal— "Got letters from my sweet Bessy, more precious to me than all the wonders I can see;" and while in Paris, when sending for Bessy and his little ones, he significantly added—"Wherever *they* are will be *home*, and a happy home to me."

On returning from Rome to Paris in January, 1820, he was there joined by his family, and settled down to literary work. During the nearly three years he lived in Paris, his life was precisely the same as when in England, one continued round of visiting amongst the English aristocracy and travellers who came there. At the same time he was busy on *The Life of Sheridan, The Epicurean, Rhymes on the Road, The Loves of the Angels,* &c., which were published at a later period.

To illustrate this portion of his life, we cull the following characteristic entries from his DIARY:—

May, 1820 (in Paris):—"A person meeting a friend running through the rain with an umbrella over him, said, 'Where are you running to in such a hurry, like a mad mushroom?'"

Sept. 11, 1820.—In Paris, visited the Père la Chaise. Afterwards "gave them a dinner at the Cadran Bleu (Bessy, Dumoulin, Miss Wilson, Anastasia, and Dr. Yonge's little girl), and took them afterwards to the Porte St. Martin. Iced punch on our way home. The whole cost me about three Napoleons—just what I ought to have reserved for the *Voyages de Pythagore.* Bessy, however, told me when we came home that she had saved by little pilferings from me, at different times, four

Napoleons, and that I should have them now to buy those books."

On 14th Oct., 1820, in Paris, after going to their new home in the Allée des Veuves, we find the following entry in his diary :—" We dined alone with our little ones, for the first time since the first of July, which was a very great treat to both of us; and Bessy said, in going to bed, ' This is the first rational day we have had for a long time.'" To this entry Lord John Russell appends the following note :—"Mrs. Moore was quite right: in reading over the diary of dinners, balls, and visits to the theatre, I feel some regret in reflecting that I had some hand in persuading Moore to prefer France to Holyrood. His universal popularity was his chief enemy."

15th April, 1821.—"Dawson told a good story of an Irish landlord counting out the change of a guinea :— ' Twelve, thirteen, fourteen '—(a shot heard)—' Bob, go and see who's that that's killed ;' ' fifteen, sixteen, seven-teen '—(enter Bob)—'It's Kelly, sir.' 'Poor Captain Kelly —a very good customer of mine—eighteen, nineteen, twenty—there's your change, sir.'"

9th May, 1821.—"It is said of Madame Talleyrand, that one day her husband having told her that Denon was coming to dinner, bid her read a little of his book upon Egypt, just published, in order that she might be able to say something civil to him upon it, adding that he would leave the volume for her on his own study table. He forgot this, however, and Madame, upon going into the study, found a volume of *Robinson Crusoe* on the table instead, which, having read very attentively, she was not long on opening upon Denon at dinner about the desert island, his manner of living, &c. &c., to the great asto-nishment of poor Denon, who could not make head or tail of what she meant. At last, upon her saying, '*Eh puis, ce cher Vendredi !'* he perceived she took him for no less a person than Robinson Crusoe."

4th June, 1821.—"Kenny said that 'Antony Pasquin' (who was a very dirty fellow) 'died of a cold caught by washing his face.'"

July 3, 1821.—"Before dinner, on my remarking to Luttrel a fine effect of sunshine in the garden, which very soon passed away, he said, 'How often in life we should like to arrest our *beaux momens;* should be so obliged to the *five minutes* if they would only stay ten.'"

5th July, 1821.—"Luttrel told of an Irishman, who, having jumped into the water to save a man from drowning, upon receiving sixpence from the person as a reward for the service, looked first at the sixpence, then at him, and at last exclaimed, 'By Jasus, I'm *over*paid for the job !'"

5th July, 1821.—"By the bye, I yesterday gave Lady Holland Lord Byron's *Memoirs* to read ; and on my telling her I rather feared he had mentioned her name in an unfair manner somewhere, she said, 'Such things give me no uneasiness : I know perfectly well my station in the world ; and I know all that can be said of me. As long as the few friends, that I *really* am sure of, speak kindly of me (and I would not believe the contrary if I saw it in black and white), all, that the rest of the world can say, is a matter of complete indifference to me.'"

26th July, 1821.—"An Irish Story from Lattin.—A man asked another to come and dine off boiled beef and potatoes with him. 'That I will,' says the other ; 'and it's rather odd it should be exactly the same dinner I had at home for myself, *barring* the beef.'"

26th July, 1821.—"Denon told an anecdote of a man who, having been asked repeatedly to dinner by a person whom he knew to be but a shabby Amphitryon, went

at last, and found the dinner so meagre and bad, that
he did not get a bit to eat. When the dishes were re-
moving, the host said, 'Well, now the ice is broken; I
suppose, you will ask me to dine with you, some day.'
'Most willingly.' 'Name your day then.' '*Aujourd'hui
par exemple,*' answered the dinnerless guest."

On same date.—"Luttrel told of a good phrase of an
attorney's, in speaking of a reconciliation that had taken
place between two persons whom he wished to set by the
ears, 'I am sorry to tell you, sir, that a compromise has
broken out between the parties.'"

12th Aug., 1821.—"In talking to Rogers about my
living in Paris, I said, 'One would not enjoy even Paradise, if one was obliged to live in it.' 'No,' says he; 'I
dare say, when Adam and Eve were turned out, they
were very happy.'"

13th Oct., 1821.—"Story of a man asking a servant,
'Is your master at home?' 'No sir, he's out.' 'Your
mistress?' 'No sir, she's out.' 'Well, I'll just go in and
take an air of the fire till they come.' 'Faith, sir, that's
out too!'"

When on a visit to London, *incog.,* on Oct. 22, 1821,
we find the following entry in his diary:—"Letters
from Bess, in which, alluding to what I had communicated to her of Lord Lansdowne's friendship, and the
probability of my being soon liberated from exile, she
says:—'God bless you, my own free, fortunate, happy
bird (what she generally calls me), but remember that
your cage is in Paris, and that your mate longs for
you.'"

June 3d, 1822.—"Harry Erskine said to a man who
found him digging potatoes in his garden, 'This is what
you call *otium cum diggin' a taté!*'"

17th Aug., 1822. — "Received to-day a letter from

Brougham, inclosing one from Barnes (the editor of *The Times*), proposing that, as he is ill, I shall take his place for some time in writing the leading articles of that paper; the pay to be £100 a month.   This is flattering. To be thought capable of wielding so powerful a political machine as *The Times* newspaper is a tribute the more flattering (as is usually the case) from my feeling conscious that I do not deserve it.

18th.—"Wrote to decline the proposal of *The Times.*"

And, on Sept. 1st, 1822, he notes a curious illustration of French liberty.   When dining with the Bryans, "a Frenchman of the party, a Royalist, told of a girl he walked with last year, at the *bal masqué*, being arrested while with him for having a tricolor ribbon on her gown; and (as he since found out) imprisoned six months; no other offence, and it was by chance the poor girl put on the ribbon."

Moore was in seven different lodgings in or near Paris; but the dwelling which he liked best was a cottage belonging to their friends the Villamils, at La Butte Coaslin, near Sevres, which they occupied for some time. It reminded him of Sloperton, and he happily defined it by a quotation from Pope—

> " A little cot with trees a row,
>   And, like its master, very low."

Here he used to wander in the park of St. Cloud, writing verses, planning chapters of the *Epicurean*, and closing the evening by practising duets with the lady of his Spanish friend, or listening to her guitar.   Kenney, the dramatic writer, lived near them, and Washington Irving visited him there.

At length, in September, 1822, he received a letter from Rees, of Longmans, informing him that the Bermuda defalcation had been arranged, and that he might now safely return to England when he pleased.

The claims of the American merchants had been reduced from £6000 to £1000 or £1200. Mr. Sheddon, a merchant in London, and the uncle of the delinquent, contributed £300; and the Marquis of Lansdowne the remainder. There was afterwards a further and final claim of £200, which Lord John Russell advanced. The two latter sums, however, were repaid in full, by Moore, from the balance which was placed to his credit by the Messrs. Longmans during the following summer.

CHAPTER IX.

RETURN FROM THE CONTINENT—RHYMES FOR THE ROAD— FABLES FOR THE HOLY ALLIANCE—LOVES OF THE ANGELS.

In the end of November, 1822, Moore returned to Sloperton Cottage, in Wiltshire; and, in 1823, published *Rhymes for the Road*, with *Fables for the Holy Alliance*, and *Loves of the Angels*, which he had written when in exile. In June of this year, his publishers placed £1000 to his credit from the sale of the last-named work; and £500 from the *Fables for the Holy Alliance*, so that he was able not only to clear himself from debt, but to continue to assist his relatives.

Rhymes on the Road is a series of clever trifles—often graceful and pleasing, but occasionally indelicate—conversational and unstudied, and often "little better," to use Moore's own words, than "prose fringed with rhyme." We select the following four from *Rhymes on the Road:*—

DIFFERENT ATTITUDES IN WHICH AUTHORS COMPOSE.

What various attitudes, and ways,
 And tricks, we authors have in writing!
While some write sitting, some, like BAYES,
 Usually stand, while they're inditing.
Poets there are, who wear the floor out,
 Measuring a line at every stride;
While some, like HENRY STEPHENS, pour out
 Rhymes by the dozen, while they ride.
HERODOTUS wrote most in bed;
 And RICHERAND, a French physician, *t
Declares the clock-work of the head
Goes best in that reclin'd position.
If you consult MONTAIGNE and PLINY on
The subject, 'tis their joint opinion
That Thought its richest harvest yields
Abroad, among the woods and fields;
That bards, who deal in small retail,
 At home may, at their counters, stop;
But that the grove, the hill, the vale,
 Are Poesy's true wholesale shop.
And, verily, I think they're right—
 For, many a time, on summer eves,
Just at that closing hour of light,
 When, like an Eastern Prince, who leaves
For distant war his Harem bow'rs,—
The Sun bids farewell to the flow'rs,
 Whose heads are sunk, whose tears are flowing
Mid all the glory of his going!—
Ev'n *I* have felt, beneath those beams,
 When wand'ring through the fields alone,
Thoughts, fancies, intellectual gleams,
 Which, far too bright to be my own,
Seem'd lent me by the Sunny Pow'r,
That was abroad at that still hour.

If thus I've felt, how must *they* feel,
 The few, whom genuine Genius warms;

Upon whose souls he stamps his seal,
　　Graven with Beauty's countless forms;—
The few upon this earth, who seem
Born to give truth to PLATO's dream,
Since in their thoughts, as in a glass,
　　Shadows of heavenly things appear,
Reflections of bright shapes that pass
　　Through other worlds, above our sphere!

.　　.　　.　　.　　.　　.

Some bards there are who cannot scribble
Without a glove, to tear or nibble;
Or a small twig to whisk about—
　　As if the hidden founts of Fancy,
Like wells of old, were thus found out
　　By mystic tricks of rhabdomancy.
Such was the little feathery wand,
That, held for ever in the hand
Of her, who won and wore the crown
　　Of female genius in this age,
Seem'd the conductor, that drew down
　　Those words of lightning to her page.
As for myself—to come, at last,
　　To the odd way in which *I* write—
Having employ'd these few months past
　　Chiefly in travelling, day and night,
I've got into the easy mode,
Of rhyming thus along the road—
Making a way-bill of my pages,
Counting my stanzas by my stages,
'Twixt lays and *re*-lays no time lost—
In short, in two words, *writing post*.

EXTRACT I.

'Twas late—the sun had almost shone
His last and best, when I ran on,
　Anxious to reach that splendid view,
Before the day-beams quite withdrew;
And feeling as all feel, on first

Approaching scenes, where, they are told,
Such glories on their eyes will burst,
As youthful bards in dreams behold.

'Twas distant yet, and, as I ran,
Full often was my wistful gaze
Turn'd to the sun, who now began
To call in all his outpost rays,
And form a denser march of light,
Such as beseems a hero's flight.
Oh, how I wish'd for JOSHUA's pow'r,
To stay the brightness of that hour!
But no—the sun still less became,
Diminish'd to a speck, as splendid
And small as were those tongues of flame,
That on th' Apostles' heads descended!

'Twas at this instant—while there glow'd
This last, intensest gleam of light—
Suddenly, through the opening road,
The valley burst upon my sight!
That glorious valley, with its Lake,
And Alps on Alps in clusters swelling,
Mighty, and pure, and fit to make
The ramparts of a Godhead's dwelling.

I stood entranc'd—as Rabbins say
This whole assembled, gazing world
Will stand, upon that awful day,
When the Ark's Light, aloft unfurl'd,
Among the opening clouds shall shine,
Divinity's own radiant sign!

Mighty MONT BLANC, thou wert to me,
That minute, with thy brow in heaven,
As sure a sign of Deity
As e'er to mortal gaze was given.
Nor ever, were I destin'd yet
To live my life twice o'er again,
Can I the deep-felt awe forget,

The dream, the trance that rapt me then!
'Twas all that consciousness of pow'r
And life, beyond this mortal hour;—
Those mountings of the soul within
At thoughts of Heav'n—as birds begin
By instinct in the cage to rise,
When near their time for change of skies;—
That proud assurance of our claim
    To rank among the Sons of Light,
Mingled with shame—oh bitter shame!—
    At having risk'd that splendid right,
    For aught that earth through all its range
Of glories, offers in exchange!
'Twas all this, at that instant brought,   .
Like breaking sunshine, o'er my thought—
'Twas all this, kindled to a glow
    Of sacred zeal, which, could it shine
Thus purely ever, man might grow,
    Ev'n upon earth a thing divine,
And be, once more, the creature made
To walk unstain'd th' Elysian shade!

No, never shall I lose the trace
Of what I've felt in this bright place.
And, should my spirit's hope grow weak,
    Should I, oh God, e'er doubt thy pow'r,
This mighty scene again I'll seek,
    At the same calm and glowing hour,
And here, at the sublimest shrine
    That Nature ever rear'd to Thee,
Rekindle all that hope divine,
    And *feel* my immortality!

EXTRACT IX.

And is there then no earthly place,
    Where we can rest, in dream Elysian,
Without some curst, round English face,
    Popping up near, to break the vision?
'Mid northern lakes, 'mid southern vines,

Unholy cits we're doom'd to meet;
Nor highest Alps nor Apennines
  Are sacred from Threadneedle Street!

If up the Simplon's path we wind,
Fancying we leave this world behind,
Such pleasant sounds salute one's ear
As—"Baddish news from 'Change, my dear—
"The Funds—(phew, curse this ugly hill)—
Are low'ring fast—(what, higher still?)
And—(zooks, we're mounting up to heaven!)—
Will soon be down to sixty-seven."

Go where we may—rest where we will,
Eternal London haunts us still.
The trash of Almack's or Fleet Ditch—
And scarce a pin's head difference *which*—
Mixes, though ev'n to Greece we run,
With every rill from Helicon!
And, if this rage for travelling lasts,
If Cockneys, of all sects and castes,
Old maidens, aldermen, and squires,
Will leave their puddings and coal fires,
To gape at things in foreign lands,
No soul among them understands;
If Blues desert their coteries,
To show off 'mong the Wahabees;
If neither sex nor age controls,
  Nor fear of Mamelukes forbids
Young ladies, with pink parasols,
  To glide among the pyramids—
Why, then, farewell all hope to find
A spot that's free from London-kind!
Who knows, if to the West we roam,
But we may find some *Blue* "at home"
Among the *Blacks* of Carolina—
Or, flying to the Eastward, see
Some Mrs. HOPKINS, taking tea
  And toast, upon the Wall of China!
9

EXTRACT X.

They tell me thou'rt the favour'd guest
    Of every fair and brilliant throng;
No wit like thine, to wake the jest,
    No voice like thine, to breathe the song.
And none could guess, so gay thou art,
That thou and I are far apart.
Alas, alas, how diff'rent flows,
    With thee and me the time away.
Not that I wish thee sad, heaven knows—
    Still, if thou canst, be light and gay;
I only know that without thee
The sun himself is dark for me.

Do I put on the jewels rare
Thou'st always lov'd to see me wear?
Do I perfume the locks that thou
So oft hast braided o'er my brow,
Thus deck'd through festive crowds to run,
    And all th' assembled world to see,—
All but the one, the absent one,
    Worth more than present worlds to me!
No, nothing cheers this widow'd heart—
My only joy, from thee apart,
From thee thyself, is sitting, hours
    And days, before thy pictur'd form—
That dream of thee, which Raphael's pow'rs
    Have made with all but life-breath warm!—
And as I smile to it, and say
The words I speak to thee in play,
I fancy from their silent frame,
Those eyes and lips give back the same;
And still I gaze, and still they keep
Smiling thus on me—till I weep!
Our little boy, too, knows it well,
    For there I lead him every day,
And teach his lisping lips to tell

The name of one that's far away.
Forgive me, love, but thus alone
My time is cheer'd, while thou art gone.

From *Fables for the Holy Alliance*, we give a part of
the first fable, on its dissolution. It is under the sem-
blance of

A DREAM.

I've had a dream that bodes no good
Unto the Holy Brotherhood.
I may be wrong, but I confess—
   As far as it is right or lawful
For one, no conjurer, to guess—
   It seems to me extremely awful.

Methought, upon the Neva's flood
A beautiful Ice Palace stood,
A dome of frost-work, on the plan
Of that once built by Empress Anne,
Which shone by moonlight—as the tale is—
Like an Aurora Borealis.

In this said Palace, furnish'd all
   And lighted as the best on land are,
I dreamt there was a splendid Ball,
   Given by the Emperor Alexander,
To entertain with all due zeal,
   Those holy gentlemen, who've shown a
Regard so kind for Europe's weal,
At Troppau, Laybach, and Verona. .

The thought was happy—and design'd
To hint how thus the human Mind
May, like the stream imprison'd there,
Be check'd and chill'd, till it can bear
The heaviest Kings, that ode or sonnet
E'er yet beprais'd, to dance upon it.

And all were pleas'd, and cold, and stately,
   Shivering in grand illumination—

Admir'd the superstructure greatly,
    Nor gave one thought to the foundation.
 Much too the Czar himself exulted,
    To àll plebeian fears a stranger,
For, Madame Krüdener, when consulted,
    Had pledged her word there was no danger.
So, on he caper'd, fearless quite,
    Thinking himself extremely clever,
And waltz'd away with all his might,
    As if the Frost would last for ever.

These humorous and satirical collections appeared from
time to time, and "were all genial things free from spite," for
his playful fancy was "alive to the points suitable for ridi-
cule, rather than to the ebullition of spleen.   The shafts
of his wit were keen, but not poisoned at the point; and
though they pierced thin-skinned people, left no rankling
wound behind . . .   his own personal character and
friendships were never compromised by these sallies.
The wit was too happy to bring hate, even from those on
whom it fell."   The lightness and gaiety of his satiric
touch have often been characterized as unique.   Hazlitt,
while from political motives lampooning the "Melodies,"
was reluctantly forced to eulogize these poems, and described them as "essences" and "nests of spicery."

In contradistinction to Hazlitt's mistaken judgment as
to the "Melodies," it has been well said:—"It is the
misfortune of the writer who mixes up poetry and politics
that his popularity gains for a present generation what it
loses for posterity.   Moore's epistles, satires, despatches,
&c., are printed in his works, but never read; while the
'Irish Melodies' are such gems of lyrical composition that
they rank with the best things, of their kind, the language
possesses."

Of Moore's larger poetical works, the next in im

portance to *Lalla Rookh*, is his *Loves of the Angels*, an allegory founded on the eastern story of the angels Harut and Marut, and the rabbinical fictions of the loves of Uzziel and Shamchazai.

It is a series of three simple stories, arranged so as to shadow out the fall of the soul from its original purity in the pursuit of this world's unsubstantial pleasures; and the punishments, from conscience and Divine justice, which visit those who presumptuously pry into the awful secrets of Heaven.

There is considerable power displayed in the description of that fearful catastrophe which closes the "Second Angel's Story" in a climax of horror. All the three are related with graceful tenderness and passion; but his angels, curiously enough, actually fall, over head and ears, in love with the fairest of earth's daughters.

SONG OF LILIS.

FROM THE SECOND ANGEL'S STORY

Come, pray with me, my seraph love,
  My angel-lord, come pray with me;
In vain to-night my lip hath strove
To send one holy prayer above—
The knee may bend, the lip may move,
  But pray I cannot, without thee!
I've fed the altar in my bower
  With droppings from the incense tree;
I've shelter'd it from wind and shower,
But dim it burns the livelong hour,
As if, like me, it had no power
  Of life or lustre, without thee!

A boat at midnight sent alone
  To drift upon the moonless sea,
A lute, whose leading chord is gone,
A wounded bird, that hath but one

Imperfect wing to soar upon,
  Are like what I am, without thee!

Then ne'er, my spirit-love, divide,
  In life or death, thyself from me;
But when again, in sunny pride,
Thou walk'st through Eden, let me glide,
A prostrate shadow, by thy side—
  Oh happier thus than without thee!

NAMA AND ZARAPH'S LOVE.

FROM THE THIRD ANGEL'S STORY.

Oh Love, Religion, Music—all
  That's left of Eden upon earth—
The only blessings, since the fall ⎰
Of our weak souls, that still recall
  A trace of their high, glorious birth-
How kindred are the dreams you bring;
  How Love, though unto earth so prone,
Delights to take religion's wing,
  When time or grief hath stain'd his own!
How near to Love's beguiling brink, ·
⎰ Too oft, entranc'd Religion lies!
While Music, Music is the link
  They *both* still hold by to the skies,
The language of their native sphere,
Which they had else forgotten here.
·   ·   ·   ·   ·   ·   ·   ·

  To love as her own Seraph lov'd,
With Faith, the same through bliss and woe—
  Faith, that, were even its light remov'd,
Could, like the dial, fix'd remain,
And wait till it shone out again;—
  With Patience that, though often bow'd
  By the rude storm, can rise anew;
And Hope that, even from Evil's cloud,
  Sees sunny Good half breaking through!
This deep, relying Love, worth more

In heaven than all a Cherub's lore—
This Faith, more sure than aught beside,
Was the sole joy, ambition, pride
Of her fond heart—th' unreasoning scope
   Of all its views, above, below—
So true she felt it that to *hope*,
   To *trust*, is happier than to *know*.
And thus in humbleness they trod,
Abash'd, but pure before their God;
Nor e'er did earth behold a sight
   So meekly beautiful as they,
When, with the altar's holy light
   Full on their brows, they knelt to pray,
Hand within hand, and side by side,
Two links of love, awhile untied
From the great chain above, but fast
Holding together to the last!—

.   .   .   .

In what lone region of the earth
These pilgrims now may roam or dwell,
God and his angels, who look forth
To watch their steps, alone can tell.
But should we, in our wanderings,
Meet a young pair whose beauty wants
But the adornment of bright wings
To look like Heaven's inhabitants;
Who shine where'er they tread, and yet
Are humble in their earthly lot,
As is the wayside violet
That shines unseen, and were it not
For its sweet breath, would be forgot;
Whose hearts in every thought are one,
Whose voices utter the same wills,
Answering as echo doth some tone
Of fairy music 'mong the hills—
So like itself we seek in vain
Which is the echo, which the strain;
Whose piety is love, whose love,

Though close as 'twere their soul's embrace,
Is not of earth but from above;
　Like two fair mirrors, face to face,
Whose light, from one to th' other thrown,
Is heaven's reflection, not their own—
Should we e'er meet with aught so pure,
So perfect here, we may be sure
　'Tis ZARAPH and his bride we see;
And call young lovers round, to view
The pilgrim pair, as they pursue
　Their pathway towards eternity.

From the entries made in his DIARY in 1822 and 1823 we extract the following, which speak for themselves:—

Nov. 26th, 1822.—"Shee told me a *bon-mot* of Rogers' the other day. On somebody remarking that Payne Knight had got very deaf, ' 'Tis from want of practice,' says Rogers; Knight being a bad listener."

Dec. 17th, 1822.—"Scroope Davies called some person who had a habit of puffing out his cheeks when he spoke, and was not remarkable for veracity, ' The Æolian Lyre.' "

28th Dec., 1822.—" In talking of cheap living, Jekyll (at Lord Lansdowne's) mentioned a man who told him, his eating cost him almost nothing, for, 'On Sunday,' said he, 'I always dine with my old friend ——, and then eat so much that it lasts until Wednesday, when I buy some tripe, which I hate like . . , and which, accordingly, makes me so sick that I cannot eat any more till Sunday again.' "

The entry on Dec. 22, 1822, tells of a curious mode of communicating sound:—

" Jekyll said that when the great waterworks were established at Chelsea there was a proposal for having there, also, a great organ from which families might be supplied with sacred music, according as they wished, by turning the cock on or off; but one objection he said was, that upon a thaw occurring after a long frost, you might have 'Judas Maccabeus' bursting out at Charing Cross, and there would be no getting him under. He said that it was an undoubted fact that Lord (?), the proprietor of Lansdowne House before the old Lord Lansdowne, had a project of placing seven-and-twenty fiddlers, hermetically sealed, in an apartment underground, from which music might be communicated by tubes to any apartment where it was wanted. Lord L. bore witness to the truth of this (with the exception of its being an organ instead of Jekyll's hermetically sealed fiddlers), and said that the pipes, which had already been laid for this plan, were found during some repairs that took place at Lansdowne House."

7th Jan., 1823.—"At breakfast (at Lord Lansdowne's) Jekyll told of some one remarking on the inaccuracy of the inscription on Lord Kenyon's tomb, *Mors Janua vita;* upon which Lord Ellenborough said, 'Don't you know that *that* was by Kenyon's express desire, as he left it in his will that they should not go to the expense of a diphthong?'"

7th Jan., 1823.—"Rogers told a story of an old gentleman, when sleeping at the fire, being awakened by the clatter of the fire-irons all tumbling down, and saying, 'What! going to bed without one kiss!' taking it for the children."

11th June, 1823.—"Foote once said to a canting sort of lady that asked him, 'Pray, Mr. Foote, do you ever go to church?' 'No, madam; not that I see any harm in it.'"

18th June, 1823.—"Luttrel told about a man from India, who, hearing the House of Commons mentioned, said, 'Oh, is that going on still?'"

21st June, 1823.—"Constable asked me to accept the editorship of the *Edinburgh Review*, and his partner writes him on the subject, 'Moore is out of all sight the best man we could have; his name would revive the reputation of the 'Review;' he would continue to us our connection with the old contributors, and the work would become more literary and more regular; but we must get him gradually into it, and the first step is to persuade him to come to Edinburgh.' The offer was declined."

Aug. 19th and 20th, 1823.—"Called on Samuel Lover, the artist, in Dublin."

CHAPTER X.

THE IRISH MELODIES—SELECTIONS—MOORE AS A LYRIC POET.

At this time (1823) Moore made a favourable arrangement regarding the copyright of *The Irish Melodies*. As early as 1797 his attention had been called to Bunting's collection of Irish Melodies; and, at intervals, Moore had written words for some of them which he was accustomed to sing with great effect. In 1807, as we have stated, he began to publish these, receiving from Mr. Power £50 each, for the first two numbers. The songs were immensely and deservedly popular, and now, in 1823, Mr. Power agreed to pay Moore £500 a year, for a series of years, that he might have the exclusive right of publishing *The Irish Melodies*. The whole ten numbers of these were not completed till 1834, and are likely to prove the most lasting of all his works.

Of all that Moore has written, the best of his *Irish Melodies* and *National Airs*, without doubt, are very perfect, and most likely to live with the language itself, and

so perpetuate his fame.   He wrought at these series of
songs for over a quarter of a century; but, of these, his
earlier melodies are decidedly the best.   In *National Airs*
(1815), *Sacred Songs* (1816), *Evenings in Greece* (1825),
and *The Summer Fête* (1831), as has been remarked, he
simply displayed his growing inability to recover "the
first fine careless rapture" of his song.   In these four
volumes there are only a few gems of any great value,
such as "Oft in the Stilly Night," and "Sound the Loud
Timbrel."   This paucity and deterioration, the anonymous
writer, to whom we refer, attributes to the social stress on
the talents of Moore having prematurely reduced his
powers.   Bright and sparkling at his best, Moore is the
Rossini of musicians and the humming-bird of poets.
His airy verse, with its drawing-room sheen and polish,
may be aptly described in his own words, from *Lalla
Rookh:*—

> " Mine is the lay that lightly floats,
> And mine are the murmuring dying notes
> That fall as soft as snow on the sea,
> And melt in the heart as instantly;
> And the passionate strain that, deeply going,
> Refines the bosom it trembles through,
> As the musk-wind, over the water blowing,
> Ruffles the wave, but sweetens it too."

It has often been said that Moore displays more fancy
than imagination.   To illustrate what is really meant by
those who say so, let the reader compare the two following passages, which describe the coming on of evening:—
Moore writes—

> " 'Twas one of those ambrosial eves
> A day of storm so often leaves,
> At its calm setting, when the West
> Opens her golden bowers of rest,

> And a moist radiance from the skies
> Shoots trembling down, as from the eyes
> Of some meek penitent, whose last
> Bright hours atone for dark ones past;
> And whose sweet tears o'er wrong forgiven,
> Shine as they fall with light from Heaven."   -

And Milton's lines, on nearly the same theme, are—

> "Now came still Evening on, and Twilight grey,
> Had in her sober livery all things clad.
> Silence accompanied; for beast and bird
> Those to their grassy couch, these to their nests
> Were slunk: All but the wakeful nightingale:
> She all night long her amorous descant sung:
> Silence was pleased. Now glowed the firmament
> With living sapphires. Hesperus that led
> The starry host rode brightest, till the moon,
> Rising in clouded majesty, at length
> Apparent Queen, unveiled her peerless light,
> And o'er the dark her silver mantle threw."

No one would go to Moore, expecting to find the robust
vigour, condensed wisdom, and epigrammatic point of a
Shakspere or a Burns; but sentiment, though less deep
and more diffuse, may still be true, and touch our hearts.
How often the cadence of a line recalls some well-nigh
forgotten song, heard long ago, while the phrase of haunt-
ing melody, so sadly sweet, yet sweetly sad, with which
it is inseparably and for ever associated, floats magically
through the soul, wafting us away like the music of a
dream to other days and brighter scenes, when hope was
young:—

> "Sweet air, how every note brings back
>   Some sunny hope, some day-dream bright
> That, shining o'er life's early track,
>   Fill'd even its tears with light!"

Strange to say, Moore, though Irish, is, in a national sense, the least Irish of Irish bards, and does not even approach the natural pathos and humour of Samuel Lover. His songs are characterized more by sprightly fancy and sentiment than by imagination; but he thoroughly understood the requirements of *vocalization*, and his verse is perfectly modulated *for singing*—an art to which very few poets, even of a much higher order, have attained.

Moore speaks admiringly of the marvellous and matchless skill of Burns, in successfully adapting words to music, as encouraging him in his own attempts, and adds :—"I have always felt, in adapting words to an expressive air, that I was but bestowing upon it the gift of articulation, and thus enabling it to speak to others all that was conveyed in its wordless eloquence to myself." Indeed, before Moore's day, Burns alone pre-eminently represented "the singing element in literature;" and so Moore revived the minstrelsy both of Ireland and England.

Moore adds, and every word which he utters on a theme, so peculiarly his own, is intensely interesting and of weight,—"That Burns, however untaught, was yet, in ear and feeling, a musician, is clear from the skill with which he adapts his verse to the structure and character of each different strain. Still more strikingly did he prove his fitness for this peculiar task, by the sort of instinct with which, in more than one instance, he discerned the real and innate sentiment which an air was calculated to convey, though previously associated with words expressing a totally different cast of feeling. Thus the air of a ludicrous old song, "Fee him, Father, fee him," has been made the medium of one of Burns' most pathetic effusions; while still more marvellously "Hey

tuttie tattie" has been elevated by him into that heroic
strain, "Scots wha hae wi' Wallace bled,"—a song which,
in a great national crisis, would be of more avail than all
the eloquence of a Demosthenes. . . . I only know,
that in a strong and inborn feeling for music lies the
source of whatever talent I may have shown for poetical
composition; and that it was the effort to translate into
language the emotions and passions which music appeared
to me to express that first led to my writing any poetry
at all deserving of the name. . . . Accustomed as I
have always been to consider my songs as a sort of
compound creations, in which the music forms no less
essential a part than the verses, it is with a feeling which
I can hardly expect my un-lyrical readers to understand,
that I see such a swarm of songs as crowd these pages
all separated from the beautiful airs which have formed,
hitherto, their chief ornament and strength—their *decus et
tutamen.* But, independently of this uneasy feeling or
fancy, there is yet another inconvenient consequence of the
divorce of the words from the music, which will be more
easily, perhaps, comprehended, and which, in justice to
myself as a metre-monger, ought to be noticed. These
occasional breaches of the laws of rhythm, which the task
of adapting words to airs demands of the poet, though
frequently one of the happiest results of his skill, become
blemishes when the verse is separated from the melody,
and require, to justify them, the presence of the music
to whose wildness or sweetness the sacrifice has been
made."

He also wrote, in the preface to the *Irish Melodies:*—
"With respect to the verses which I have written for
these melodies, as *they are intended rather to be sung than
read,* I can answer for their sound, with somewhat more
confidence than for their sense. Yet it would be affecta-

tion to deny that I have given much attention to the task,
and that, it is not through any want of zeal or industry, if
I unfortunately disgrace the sweet airs of my country by
poetry altogether unworthy of their taste, their energy,
and their tenderness."

The following anecdote illustrates his painstaking
efforts to put the right word in the right place, so that
his work might be as perfect as possible:—Moore was on
a visit to a literary friend in France, and, while there,
wrote a short poem.   One day, while the guest was
engaged in his literary labour, the two took a stroll into
an adjacent wood, and the host soon perceived that his
companion was given up to his own thoughts; he was
silent and abstracted, noticing neither his friend and
entertainer, nor the surrounding beauties of the landscape.
By-and-by he began to gnaw the finger-tips of his glove,
pulling and twitching spasmodically, and when this had
gone on for a long time his friend ventured to ask him
what was the trouble.   "I'll tell you," said Moore.   "I
have left at home, on my table, a poem in which is a word
I do not like.   The line is perfect, save that one word,
and that one word is perfect save its inflection.   Thus it
is," and he repeated the line and asked his friend if he
could help him.   It was a delicate point.   The friend saw
the need—saw where and how the present word jarred,
just the slightest possible bit, upon the exquisite harmony
of the cadence; but he could not supply the want.   The
twain cudgelled their brains, until they reached the house,
on their return, without avail.   The rest of the day was
spent as usual, as was the evening, save that, ever and
anon, Moore would sink into silent fits in pursuit of the
absent word.   And so came on the night, and the poet
went to bed in a deep study.   The following morning
was bright and beautiful, and Moore came down from his

chamber with a bounding step, with a scrap of paper in his hand, and a glorious light in his genial countenance. The word had come to him! He had awakened during the night, and the kind genius of inspiration had visited his pillow, and he had got up and torn a scrap from his note-book, and at the window, by the light of the moon, had made the thought secure. "There," he said, when he had incorporated it into the text, "there it is—only a simple, single word, a word as common as a, b, c, and yet it cost me twelve hours of unflagging labour to find it, and put it where it is."

Moore's intention, then, ought to be borne in mind; and it is not fair to criticise the accent of his songs apart from the music to which they are written; for the one is dependent on, modified by, and quite *inseparable* from the other. In short, as Samuel Lover points out, even "Moore is liable to be falsely read, when the ordinary accent is given to the reading," that is, "when measured syllabically rather than rhythmically." This, Lover amply proves and illustrates by the example of "The Minstrel Boy to the War is Gone," given, marked in longs and shorts, showing that the music is *more* than essential, and absolutely *increases* the power of the lines —the remarkable succession of long sounds in the noble air giving a grandeur of effect to the poem which is otherwise wanting. Thus, as they would be read:—

> ˘ ― ˘ ― ˘ ˘ ― ˘ ―
> The minstrel boy to the war is gone,
> ˘ ˘ ― ˘ ― ˘ ― ˘
> In the ranks of death you'll find him;
> ˘ ― ˘ ― ˘ ˘ ― ˘ ―
> His father's sword he has girded on,
> ˘ ˘ ― ˘ ― ˘ ― ˘
> And his wild harp slung behind him;

while, it is as follows, when accentuated by the music:—

Irish air—*The Moreen.*

The min-strel boy to the war is gone, In the

ranks of death you'll find him; His fa-ther's sword he has

gird - ed on; And his wild harp slung be - hind him.

Lover, who himself, in this respect, was only second in Ireland to Moore, and free from many of Moore's defects, characterized the *Irish Melodies* as " that work, not only the crowning wreath of its author, but among the glories of the land that gave him birth. To the finest national music in the world he wrote the finest lyrics; and if Ireland never .produced, nor should ever produce, another lyric poet, sufficient for her glory is the name of Thomas Moore."

In a letter, addressed to the present writer, Lover said:—"Moore was keenly alive to the *character* of a melody—hence, from those of his own land which are so lovely, he selected judiciously the air suited to the spirit of his lay. Then, as the verses he wrote were meant to be *sung* (not merely read), with what consummate skill he has accommodated every word to be capable of the ' linked sweetness long drawn out.' *In this respect I think* Moore MATCHLESS."

His patriotic songs are the most real in feeling, and therefore the best. With these, Moore permeated society, and, so, created an interest in Irish matters and wrongs.

10

Next to these patriotic songs, are those conveying moral reflections in metaphor.

The following selections are from *The Irish Melodies:*—

SUBLIME WAS THE WARNING.

Sublime was the warning that Liberty spoke,
And grand was the moment when Spaniards awoke
   Into life and revenge from the conqueror's chain. `
Oh, Liberty! let not this spirit have rest,
Till it move, like a breeze, o'er the waves of the west—
Give the light of your look to each sorrowing spot,
Nor, oh, be the Shamrock of Erin forgot
   While you add to your garland the Olive of Spain!

If the fame of our fathers, bequeath'd with their rights,
Give to country its charm, and to home its delights,
   If deceit be a wound, and suspicion a stain,
Then, ye men of Iberia, our cause is the same!
And oh! may his tomb want a tier and a name,
Who would ask for a nobler, a holier death,
Than to turn his last sigh into victory's breath,
   For the Shamrock of Erin and Olive of Spain!

Ye Blakes and O'Donnels, whose fathers resign'd
The green hills of their youth, among strangers to find
   That repose which, at home, they had sigh'd for in vain,
Join, join in our hope that the flame, which you light,
May be felt yet in Erin, as calm, and as bright,
And forgive even Albion while blushing she draws,
Like a truant, her sword, in the long-slighted cause
   Of the Shamrock of Erin and Olive of Spain!

God prosper the cause!—oh, it cannot but thrive,
While the pulse of one patriot heart is alive,
   Its devotion to feel, and its rights to maintain;
Then, how sainted by sorrow, its martyrs will die!
The finger of glory shall point where they lie;
While, far from the footstep of coward or slave,
The young spirit of Freedom shall shelter their grave
   Beneath Shamrocks of Erin and Olives of Spain!

GO WHERE GLORY WAITS THEE.

Go where glory waits thee,
But, while fame elates thee,
  Oh! still remember me.
When the praise thou meetest
To thine ear is sweetest,
  Oh! then remember me.
Other arms may press thee,
Dearer friends caress thee,
All the joys that bless thee,
  Sweeter far may be;
But when friends are nearest,
And when joys are dearest,
  Oh! then remember me!

When, at eve, thou rovest
By the star thou lovest,
  Oh! then remember me.
Think, when home returning,
Bright we've seen it burning,
  Oh! thus remember me.
Oft as summer closes,
When thine eye reposes
On its ling'ring roses,
  Once so lov'd by thee,
Think of her who wove them,
Her who made thee love them,
  Oh! then remember me.

When, around thee dying,
Autumn leaves are lying,
  Oh! then remember me.
And, at night, when gazing
On the gay hearth blazing,
  Oh! still remember me.
Then should music, stealing
All the soul of feeling,
To thy heart appealing,

Draw one tear from thee;
Then let memory bring thee
Strains I us'd to sing thee,—
Oh! then remember me.

OH! BREATHE NOT HIS NAME.

Oh! breathe not his name, let it sleep in the shade,
Where cold and unhonour'd his relics are laid:
Sad, silent, and dark, be the tears that we shed,
As the night-dew that falls on the grass o'er his head.

But the night-dew that falls, though in silence it weeps,
Shall brighten with verdure the grave where he sleeps;
And the tear that we shed, though in secret it rolls,
Shall long keep his memory green in our souls.

WHEN HE, WHO ADORES THEE.

When he, who adores thee, has left but the name
Of his fault and his sorrows behind,
Oh! say wilt thou weep, when they darken the fame
Of a life that for thee was resign'd?
Yes, weep, and however my foes may condemn,
Thy tears shall efface their decree;
For Heaven can witness, though guilty to them,
I have been but too faithful to thee.

With thee, were the dreams of my earliest love;
Every thought of my reason was thine;
In my last humble prayer, to the Spirit above,
Thy name shall be mingled with mine.
Oh! blest are the lovers and friends who shall live
The days of thy glory to see;
But the next dearest blessing that Heaven can give
Is the pride of thus dying for thee.

In the following song, mark—how strangely beautiful
and weirdlike is the flow of the uncommon measure! It
is perfect, but requires the aid of the music fully to interpret and evolve the very peculiar rhythm:—

AT THE MID HOUR OF NIGHT.

At the mid hour of night, when stars are weeping, I fly
To the lone vale we lov'd, when life shone warm in thine eye,
  And I think oft, if spirits can steal from the regions of air,
    To revisit past scenes of delight, thou wilt come to me there,
And tell me our love is remember'd, even in the sky.

Then I sing the wild song 'twas once such pleasure to hear!
When our voices commingling breath'd, like one, on the ear;
  And, as Echo far off through the vale my sad orison rolls,
    I think, oh my love! 'tis thy voice from the Kingdom of
      Souls,
Faintly answering still the notes that once were so dear.

OH THE SHAMROCK.

Through Erin's Isle,
  To sport awhile,
As Love and Valour wander'd,
  With Wit, the sprite,
  Whose quiver bright
A thousand arrows squander'd.
  Where'er they pass,
  A triple grass
Shoots up, with dew-drops streaming,
  As softly green
  As emeralds seen
Through purest crystal gleaming.
Oh the Shamrock, the green, immortal Shamrock!
  Chosen leaf,
  Of Bard and Chief,
Old Erin's native Shamrock!

Says Valour, "See,
  They spring for me,
Those leafy gems of morning!"—
  Says Love, "No, no,
  For *me* they grow,
My fragrant path adorning."

But Wit perceives
The triple leaves,
And cries, "Oh! do not sever
A type, that blends
Three godlike friends,
Love, Valour, Wit, for ever!"
Oh the Shamrock, the green, immortal Shamrock!
Chosen leaf
Of Bard and Chief,
Old Erin's native Shamrock!
So firmly fond
May last the bond
They wove that morn together,
And ne'er may fall
One drop of gall
On Wit's celestial feather.
May Love, as twine
His flowers divine,
Of thorny falsehood weed 'em;
May Valour ne'er
His standard rear
Against the cause of Freedom!
Oh the Shamrock, the green, immortal Shamrock!
Chosen leaf
Of Bard and Chief,
Old Erin's native Shamrock!

THE YOUNG MAY MOON.

The young May moon is beaming, love,
The glow-worm's lamp is gleaming, love,
How sweet to rove
Through Morna's grove,
When the drowsy world is dreaming, love!
Then awake!—the heavens look bright, my dear,
'Tis never too late for delight, my dear,
And the best of all ways
To lengthen our days,
Is to steal a few hours from the night, my dear!

Now all the world is sleeping, love,
But the Sage, his star-watch keeping, love,
    And I, whose star,
    More glorious far,
Is the eye from that casement peeping, love.
Then awake!—till rise of sun, my dear,
The Sage's glass we'll shun, my dear,
    Or, in watching the flight
    Of bodies of light,
He might happen to take thee for one, my dear.

THE HARP THAT ONCE THROUGH TARA'S HALLS.

The harp that once through Tara's halls
    The soul of music shed,
Now hangs as mute on Tara's walls,
    As if that soul were fled.—
So sleeps the pride of former days,
    So glory's thrill is o'er,
And hearts, that once beat high for praise,
    Now feel that pulse no more.

No more to chiefs and ladies bright
    The harp of Tara swells;
The chord alone, that breaks at night,
    Its tale of ruin tells.
Thus Freedom now so seldom wakes,
    The only throb she gives,
Is when some heart indignant breaks,
    To show that still she lives.

THE MEETING OF THE WATERS.

There is not in the wide world a valley so sweet
As that vale in whose bosom the bright waters meet;
Oh! the last rays of feeling and life must depart,
Ere the bloom of that valley shall fade from my heart.

Yet it *was* not that Nature had shed o'er the scene
Her purest of crystal and brightest of green;

'Twas *not* her soft magic of streamlet or hill,
Oh! no,—it was something more exquisite still.

'Twas that friends, the belov'd of my bosom, were near,
Who made every dear scene of enchantment more dear,
And who felt how the best charms of nature improve,
When we see them reflected from looks that we love.

Sweet vale of Avoca! how calm could I rest
In thy bosom of shade, with the friends I love best,
Where the storms that we feel in this cold world should cease,
And our hearts, like thy waters, be mingled in peace.

THE ORIGIN OF THE HARP.

'Tis believ'd that this Harp, which I wake now for thee,
Was a Syren of old, who sung under the sea;
And who often, at eve, thro' the bright waters rov'd,
To meet, on the green shore, a youth whom she lov'd.

But she lov'd him in vain, for he left her to weep,
And in tears, all the night, her gold tresses to steep;
Till heav'n look'd with pity on true love. so warm,
And chang'd to this soft Harp the sea-maiden's form.

Still her bosom rose fair—still her cheeks smil'd the same—
While her sea-beauties gracefully form'd the light frame;
And her hair, as, let loose, o'er her white arm it fell,
Was chang'd to bright chords utt'ring melody's spell.

Hence it came, that this soft Harp so long hath been known
To mingle love's language with sorrow's sad tone;
Till *thou* didst divide them, and teach the fond lay
To speak love when I'm near thee, and grief when away.

SING, SWEET HARP.

Sing, sweet Harp, oh sing to me
    Some song of ancient days,
Whose sounds, in this sad memory,
    Long buried dreams shall raise;—
Some lay that tells of vanish'd fame,
    Whose light once round us shone;

Of noble pride, now turn'd to shame,
  And hopes for ever gone.—
Sing, sad Harp, thus sing to me;
  Alike our doom is cast,
Both lost to all but memory,
  We live but in the past.

How mournfully the midnight air
  Among thy chords doth sigh,
As if it sought some echo there
  Of voices long gone by;—
Of Chieftains, now forgot, who seem'd
  The foremost then in fame;
Of Bards who, once immortal deem'd,
  Now sleep without a name.—
In vain, sad Harp, the midnight air
  Among thy chords doth sigh;
In vain it seeks an echo there
  Of voices long gone by.

Couldst thou but call those spirits round,
  Who once, in bower and hall,
Sat listening to thy magic sound,
  Now mute and mould'ring all;—
But, no; they would but wake to weep
  Their children's slavery;
Then leave them in their dreamless sleep,
  The dead, at least, are free!—
Hush, hush, sad Harp, that dreary tone,
  That knell of Freedom's day;
Or, listening to its death-like moan,
  Let me, too, die away.

LOVE'S YOUNG DREAM.

Oh! the days are gone, when Beauty bright
  My heart's chain wove;
When my dream of life, from morn till night,
  Was love, still love.

New hope may bloom,
And days may come,
Of milder, calmer beam,
But there's nothing half so sweet in life
As love's young dream:
No, there's nothing half so sweet in life
As love's young dream.

Though the bard to purer fame may soar,
When wild youth's past;
Though he win the wise, who frown'd before,
To smile at last;
He'll never meet
A joy so sweet,
In all his noon of fame,
As when first he sung to woman's ear
His soul-felt flame,
And at every close, she blush'd to hear
The one lov'd name.

No,—that hallow'd form is ne'er forgot
Which first love trac'd;
Still it lingering haunts the greenest spot
On memory's waste.
'Twas odour fled
As soon as shed;
'Twas morning's winged dream;
'Twas a light, that ne'er can shine again
On life's dull stream:
Oh! 'twas light that ne'er can shine again
On life's dull stream.

OH! ARRANMORE, LOV'D ARRANMORE.

Oh! Arranmore, lov'd Arranmore,
How oft I dream of thee,
And of those days when, by thy shore,
I wander'd young and free.
Full many a path I've tried, since then,
Through pleasure's flowery maze,

But ne'er could find the bliss again
    I felt in those sweet days.

How blithe upon thy breezy cliffs
    At sunny morn I stood,
With heart as bounding as the skiffs
    That danc'd along thy flood;
Or, when the western wave grew bright
    With daylight's parting wing,
Have sought that Eden in its light
    Which dreaming poets sing;—

That Eden where th' immortal brave
    Dwell in a land serene,—
Whose bow'rs beyond the shining wave,
    At sunset, oft are seen.
Ah dream too full of sadd'ning truth!
    Those mansions o'er the main
Are like the hopes I built in youth,—
    As sunny and as vain!

SWEET INNISFALLEN.

Sweet Innisfallen, fare thee well,
    May calm and sunshine long be thine!
How fair thou art let others tell,—
    To *feel* how fair shall long be mine.

Sweet Innisfallen, long shall dwell
    In memory's dream that sunny smile,
Which o'er thee on that evening fell,
    When first I saw thy fairy isle.

'Twas light, indeed, too blest for one,
    Who had to turn to paths of care—
Through crowded haunts again to run,
    And leave thee bright and silent there;

No more unto thy shores to come,
    But, on the world's rude ocean tost,
Dream of thee sometimes, as a home
    Of sunshine he had seen and lost.

Far better in thy weeping hours
   To part from thee, as I do now,
When mist is o'er thy blooming bowers,
   Like sorrow's veil on beauty's brow.

For, though unrivall'd still thy grace,
   Thou dost not look, as then, *too* blest,
But thus in shadow, seem'st a place
   Where erring man might hope to rest—

Might hope to rest, and find in thee
   A gloom like Eden's, on the day
He left its shade, when every tree,
   Like thine, hung weeping o'er his way.

Weeping or smiling, lovely isle!
   And all the lovelier for thy tears—
For though but rare thy sunny smile,
   'Tis heav'n's own glance when it appears.

Like feeling hearts, whose joys are few,
   But, when *indeed* they come, divine—
The brightest light the sun e'er threw
   Is lifeless to one gleam of thine!

OH, COULD WE DO WITH THIS WORLD OF OURS.

Oh, could we do with this world of ours
As thou dost with thy garden bowers,
Reject the weeds and keep the flowers,
   What a heaven on earth we'd make it!
So bright a dwelling should be our own,
So warranted free from sigh or frown,
That angels soon would be coming down,
   By the week or month to take it.

Like those gay flies that wing through air,
And in themselves a lustre bear,
A stock of light, still ready there,
   Whenever they wish to use it;
So, in this world I'd make for thee,

Our hearts should all like fire-flies be,
And the flash of wit or poesy
    Break forth whenever we choose it.

While ev'ry joy that glads our sphere
Hath still some shadow hov'ring near,
In this new world of ours, my dear,
    Such shadows will all be omitted:—
Unless they're like that graceful one,
Which, when thou'rt dancing in the sun,
Still near thee, leaves a charm upon
    Each spot where it hath flitted!

I SAW THY FORM IN YOUTHFUL PRIME.

I saw thy form in youthful prime,
    Nor thought that pale decay
Would steal before the steps of Time,
    And waste its bloom away, Mary!
Yet still thy features wore that light,
    Which fleets not with the breath;
And life ne'er looked more truly bright
    Than in thy smile of death, Mary!

As streams that run o'er golden mines,
    Yet humbly, calmly glide,
Nor seem to know the wealth that shines
    Within their gentle tide, Mary!
So veil'd beneath the simplest guise,
    Thy radiant genius shone,
And that, which charm'd all other eyes,
    Seem'd worthless in thy own, Mary!

If souls could always dwell above,
    Thou ne'er hadst left that sphere;
Or could we keep the souls we love,
    We ne'er had lost thee here, Mary!
Though many a gifted mind we meet,
    Though fairest forms we see,
To live with them is far less sweet,
    Than to remember thee, Mary!

SHE IS FAR FROM THE LAND.

She is far from the land where her young hero sleeps,
    And lovers are round her, sighing:
But coldly she turns from their gaze, and weeps,
    For her heart in his grave is lying.

She sings the wild songs of her dear native plains,
    Every note which he lov'd awaking;—
Ah! little they think who delight in her strains,
    How the heart of the Minstrel is breaking.

He had liv'd for his love, for his country he died,
    They were all that to life had entwin'd him;
Nor soon shall the tears of his country be dried,
    Nor long will his love stay behind him.

Oh! make her a grave where the sunbeams rest,
    When they promise a glorious morrow;
They'll shine o'er her sleep, like a smile from the West,
    From her own lov'd island of sorrow.

'TIS THE LAST ROSE OF SUMMER.

'Tis the last rose of summer
    Left blooming alone;
All her lovely companions
    Are faded and gone;
No flower of her kindred,
    No rose-bud is nigh,
To reflect back her blushes,
    Or give sigh for sigh.

I'll not leave thee, thou lone one!
    To pine on the stem;
Since the lovely are sleeping,
    Go, sleep thou with them.
Thus kindly I scatter
    Thy leaves o'er the bed,
Where thy mates of the garden
    Lie scentless and dead.

So soon may *I* follow,
  When friendships decay,
And from love's shining circle
  The gems drop away.
When true hearts lie wither'd,
  And fond ones are flown,
Oh! who would inhabit
  This bleak world alone.

THE MINSTREL BOY.

The Minstrel Boy to the war is gone,
  In the ranks of death you'll find him;
His father's sword he has girded on,
  And his wild harp slung behind him.—
"Land of song!" said the warrior-bard,
  "Though all the world betrays thee,
One sword, at least, thy rights shall guard,
  One faithful harp shall praise thee!"

The Minstrel fell!—but the foeman's chain
  Could not bring his proud soul under;
The harp he lov'd ne'er spoke again,
  For he tore its chords asunder;
And said, "No chains shall sully thee,
  Thou soul of love and bravery!
Thy songs were made for the pure and free,
  They shall never sound in slavery."

I SAW FROM THE BEACH.

I saw from the beach, when the morning was shining,
  A bark o'er the waters move gloriously on;
I came when the sun o'er that beach was declining,
  The bark was still there, but the waters were gone.

And such is the fate of our life's early promise,
  So passing the spring-tide of joy we have known,
Each wave that we danc'd on at morning, ebbs from us,
  And leaves us at eve, on the bleak shore alone.

Ne'er tell me of glories, serenely adorning
　　The close of our day, the calm eve of our night;—
Give me back, give me back the wild freshness of Morning,
　　Her clouds and her tears are worth Evening's best light.

Oh, who would not welcome that moment's returning,
　　When passion first wak'd a new life through his frame,
And his soul, like the wood that grows precious in burning,
　　Gave out all its sweets to love's exquisite flame.

COME, REST IN THIS BOSOM.

Come, rest in this bosom, my own stricken deer,
Though the herd have fled from thee, thy home is still here;
Here still is the smile, that no cloud can o'ercast,
And a heart and a hand all thy own to the last.

Oh! what was love made for, if 'tis not the same
Through joy and through torment, through glory and shame?
I know not, I ask not, if guilt's in that heart,
I but know that I love thee, whatever thou art.

Thou hast called me thy Angel in moments of bliss,
And thy Angel I'll be, 'mid the horrors of this,—
Through the furnace, unshrinking, thy steps to pursue,
And shield thee, and save thee,—or perish there too!

AS SLOW OUR SHIP.

　　As slow our ship her foamy track
　　　　Against the wind was cleaving,
　　Her trembling pennant still look'd back
　　　　To that dear Isle 'twas leaving.
　　So loath we part from all we love,
　　　　From all the links that bind us;
　　So turn our hearts as on we rove,
　　　　To those we've left behind us.

　　When round the bowl, of vanish'd years
　　　　We talk, with joyous seeming,—
　　With smiles that might as well be tears,
　　　　So faint, so sad their beaming; •

While mem'ry brings us back again
　　Each early tie that twined us,
Oh, sweet's the cup that circles then
　　To those we've left behind us.

And when, in other climes, we meet
　　Some isle, or vale enchanting,
Where all looks flow'ry, wild, and sweet,
　　And nought but love is wanting;
We think how great had been our bliss,
　　If Heav'n had but assign'd us
To live and die in scenes like this,
　　With some we've left behind us!

As trav'llers oft look back at eve,
　　When eastward darkly going,
To gaze upon that light they leave
　　Still faint behind them glowing,—
So, when the close of pleasure's day
　　To gloom hath near consign'd us,
We turn to catch one fading ray
　　Of joy that's left behind us.

DEAR HARP OF MY COUNTRY.

Dear Harp of my Country! in darkness I found thee,
　　The cold chain of silence had hung o'er thee long,
When proudly, my own Island Harp, I unbound thee,
　　And gave all thy chords to light, freedom, and song!
The warm lay of love and the light note of gladness
　　Have waken'd thy fondest, thy liveliest thrill;
But so oft hast thou echo'd the deep sigh of sadness,
　　That ev'n in thy mirth it will steal from thee still.

Dear Harp of my Country! farewell to thy numbers,
　　This sweet wreath of song is the last we shall twine!
Go, sleep with the sunshine of Fame on thy slumbers,
　　Till touch'd by some hand less unworthy than mine;
If the pulse of the patriot, soldier, or lover,
　　Have throbb'd at our lay, 'tis thy glory alone;

11

I was *but* as the wind, passing heedlessly over,
    And all the wild sweetness I wak'd was thy own.

If some of Moore's work seems artificial and laboured, these short lyrics of his, when sung, are certainly "unmatched in their music, their delicacy, and their pathos;" and, amongst European lyrists, Moore has often been named along with Burns and Beranger.   With reference to him, as a song-writer, Shelley humbly avowed himself "proud to acknowledge his inferiority;" and Byron wrote:—"Moore has a peculiarity of talent, or rather talents—poetry, music, voice, all his own; and an expression in each which never was, nor will be, possessed by another."   And of the Melodies he enthusiastically declared that to him they were "worth all the epics that ever were composed."   Rogers quaintly said—that Moore was born "with a rose in his lips and a nightingale singing on the top of the bed!"

The following lyrics are taken from his "Ballads, Songs, &c.:"—

WHEN MIDST THE GAY I MEET.

When midst the gay I meet
    That gentle smile of thine,
Though still on me it turns most sweet,
    I scarce can call it mine:
But when to me alone
    Your secret tears you show,
Oh, then I feel those tears my own,
    And claim them while they flow.
Then still with bright looks bless
    The gay, the cold, the free;
Give smiles to those who love you less,
    But keep your tears for me.

The snow on Jura's steep
    Can smile in many a beam,

Yet still in chains of coldness sleep,
  How bright soe'er it seem.
But, when some deep-felt ray,
  Whose touch is fire, appears,
Oh, then the smile is warm'd away,
  And, melting, turns to tears.
Then still with bright looks bless
  The gay, the cold, the free;
Give smiles to those who love you less,
  But keep your tears for me.

WHEN TWILIGHT DEWS.

When twilight dews are falling soft
  Upon the rosy sea, love,
I watch the star, whose beam so oft
  Has lighted me to thee, love.
And thou too, on that orb so dear,
  Dost often gaze at even,
And think, though lost for ever here,
  Thou'lt yet be mine in heaven.

There's not a garden walk I tread,
  There's not a flow'r I see, love,
But brings to mind some hope that's fled,
  Some joy that's gone with thee, love.
And still I wish that hour was near,
  When, friends and foes forgiven,
The pains, the ills we've wept through here,
  May turn to smiles in heaven.

THE DREAM OF HOME.

Who has not felt how sadly sweet
  The dream of home, the dream of home,
Steals o'er the heart, too soon to fleet,
  When far o'er sea or land we roam?
Sunlight more soft may o'er us fall,
  To greener shores our bark may come;

But far more bright, more dear than all,
    That dream of home, that dream of home.

Ask of the sailor youth when far
    His light bark bounds o'er ocean's foam,
What charms him most, when ev'ning's star
    Smiles o'er the wave? to dream of home.
Fond thoughts of absent friends and loves
    At that sweet hour around him come;
His heart's best joy where'er he roves,
    That dream of home, that dream of home.

THEY TELL ME THOU'RT THE FAVOUR'D GUEST.

They tell me thou'rt the favour'd guest
    Of every fair and brilliant throng;
No wit like thine to wake the jest,
    No voice like thine to breathe the song;
And none could guess, so gay thou art,
That thou and I are far apart.

Alas! alas! how diff'rent flows
    With thee and me the time away!
Not that I wish thee sad—heav'n knows—
    Still if thou can'st, be light and gay;
I only know, that without thee
The sun himself is dark to me.

Do I thus haste to hall and bower,
    Among the proud and gay to shine?
Or deck my hair with gem and flower,
    To flatter other eyes than thine?
Ah, no, with me love's smiles are past,
Thou hadst the first, thou hadst the last.

THE FANCY FAIR.

Come, maids and youths, for here we sell
    All wondrous things of earth and air;
Whatever wild romancers tell,
    Or poets sing, or lovers swear,
    You'll find at this our Fancy Fair.

Here eyes are made like stars to shine,
　　And kept, for years, in such repair,
That ev'n when turn'd of thirty-nine,
　　They'll hardly look the worse for wear,
　　If bought at this our Fancy Fair.

We've lots of tears for bards to show'r,
　　And hearts that such ill-usage bear,
That, though they're broken ev'ry hour,
　　They'll still, in rhyme, fresh breaking bear,
　　If purchas'd at our Fancy Fair.

As fashions change in ev'ry thing,
　　We've goods to suit each season's air,
Eternal friendships for the spring,
　　And endless loves for summer wear,—
　　All sold at this our Fancy Fair.

We've reputations white as snow,
　　That long will last, if us'd with care,
Nay, safe through all life's journey go,
　　If pack'd and mark'd as " brittle ware,"—
　　Just purchas'd at the Fancy Fair.

BEAUTY AND SONG.

Down in yon summer vale,
　　Where the rill flows,
Thus said a Nightingale
　　To his lov'd Rose:—
" Though rich the pleasures
Of song's sweet measures,
Vain were its melody,
Rose, without thee."

Then from the green recess
　　Of her night-bow'r,
Beaming with bashfulness,
　　Spoke the bright flow'r:—
" Though morn should lend her
Its sunniest splendour,

What would the Rose be,
Unsung by thee?"

Thus still let Song attend
    Woman's bright way;
Thus still let woman lend
    Light to the lay.
Like stars, through heaven's sea,
Floating in harmony,
Beauty shall glide along,
Circled by Song.

OH, DO NOT LOOK SO BRIGHT AND BLEST.

Oh, do not look so bright and blest,
    For still there comes a fear,
When brow like thine looks happiest,
    That grief is then most near.
There lurks a dread in all delight,
    A shadow near each ray,
That warns us then to fear their flight,
    When most we wish their stay.
Then look not thou so bright and blest,
    For ah! there comes a fear,
When brow like thine looks happiest,
    That grief is then most near.

Why is it thus that fairest things
    The soonest fleet and die?—
That when most light is on their wings,
    They're then but spread to fly!
And, sadder still, the pain will stay—
    The bliss no more appears;
As rainbows take their light away,
    And leave us but the tears!
Then look not thou so bright and blest,
    For ah! there comes a fear,
When brow like thine looks happiest,
    That grief is then most near.

He was undoubtedly the greatest vocal lyrist of his age; "of all song-writers," said Professor Wilson, "that ever warbled, or chanted, or sung, the best, in our estimation, is verily none other than Thomas Moore." Lord John Russell's estimate of Moore was:—"Of English lyrical poets he is surely the first." Stopford A. Brooke writes:—"He had a slight, pretty, rarely true, lyrical power, but all the songs have this one excellence, they are truly things to be sung;" and Professor Henry Morley, in the same strain, adds: "As a lyric poet Moore was above all things a musician—one of the best writers we have ever had of *words for music*." He has been called—

"The *poet* of all circles, and the *darlint* of his own."

On the best of the *Irish Melodies*, and of the *National Songs*, Moore's lasting fame will doubtless rest. He himself has recorded this, as his own belief, in these memorable words:—"My fame, whatever it is, has been acquired by touching the harp of my country, and is, in fact, no more than the echo of the harp."

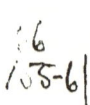

CHAPTER XI.

MOORE'S BEARING IN SOCIETY—PERSONAL APPEARANCE—THE BURNING OF BYRON'S AUTOBIOGRAPHY—THE EPICUREAN.

Of Moore's bearing, when moving in the highest circles, Lord Byron, who was a competent judge of such matters, says:—"In society he is gentlemanly, gentle, and altogether more pleasing than any individual with whom I am acquainted."

Mr. S. C. Hall describes him as graceful, small, and

slim in figure, "his upturned eyes and eloquent features giving force to the music that accompanied the songs, or rather, to the songs that accompanied the music. . . .

I recall him at this moment—his small form and intellectual face, rich in expression, and that expression the sweetest, the most gentle, and the kindliest. He had still, in age, the same bright and clear eye, the same gracious smile, the same suave and winning manner, I had noticed as the attributes of his comparative youth; a forehead not remarkably broad or high, but singularly impressive, firm, and full, with the organs of music and gaiety large, and those of benevolence and veneration greatly preponderating."

Leigh Hunt, writing of him in the prime of life, says: —"His forehead is bony and full of character, with 'bumps' of wit large and radiant enough to transport a phrenologist. His eyes are as dark and as fine as you would wish to see under a set of vine leaves; his mouth generous and good-humoured, with dimples."

Jeffrey writes of "the buoyancy of his spirits and the inward light of his mind," and declares him to be "the sweetest-blooded, warmest-hearted, happiest, hopefullest creature that ever set fortune at defiance."

Scott, in his own diary, also gives the following account of the differences and resemblances between himself and Moore:—"Nov. 22, 1825.—Moore. I saw Moore (for the first time I may say, this season). We had, indeed, met in public twenty years ago. There is a manly frankness, with perfect ease and good breeding about him which is delightful. Not the least touch of the poet or the pedant. . . . His countenance is plain, but the expression is very animated, especially in speaking or singing, so that it is far more interesting than the finest features could have rendered it. I was aware that

Byron had often spoken, both in private society and in his journal, of Moore and myself in the same breath, and with the same sort of regard; so I was curious to see what there could be in common betwixt us, Moore having lived so much in the gay world, I in the country, and with people of business, and sometimes with politicians; Moore a scholar, I none; he a musician and artist, I without knowledge of a note; he a democrat, I an aristocrat; with many other points of difference; besides his being an Irishman, I a Scotchman, and both tolerably national. Yet there is a point of resemblance, and a strong one. We are both good-humoured fellows, who rather seek to enjoy what is going forward than to maintain our dignity as Lions."

A few years later on, Willis thus sketches his appearance:—"I called on Moore with a letter of introduction, and met him at the door of his lodgings; I knew him instantly from the pictures I had seen of him, but was surprised at the diminutiveness of his person. He is much below the middle size, and with his white hat and long chocolate frock-coat, was far from prepossessing in his appearance. With this material disadvantage, however, his address is gentlemanlike to a very marked degree; and I should think no one could see Moore without conceiving a strong liking for him. As I was to meet him at dinner, I did not detain him."

This dinner was at Lady Blessington's. Willis had arrived but a few minutes when " ' Mr. Moore,' cried the footman at the bottom of the staircase; 'Mr. Moore,' cried the footman at the top; and with his glass at his eye, stumbling over an ottoman, between his near-sightedness and the darkness of the room, enter the poet. Half a glance tells you that he is at home on a carpet. Sliding his feet up to Lady Blessington (of whom he was

a lover when she was sixteen,[1] and to whom some of the
sweetest of his songs were written), he made his compli-
ments with a gaiety and an ease, combined with a kind
of worshipping deference, that was worthy of a prime
minister at the court of love. With the gentlemen, all
of whom he knew, he had the frank, merry manner of a
confident favourite, and he was greeted like one. He
went from one to the other, straining back his head to
look up at them (for singularly enough, every gentleman
in the room was six feet and upward), and to every one
he said something which from any one else would have
seemed peculiarly felicitous, but which fell from his lips
as if his breath were not more spontaneous."

Although much of his time was devoted to society,
Moore displayed an incredible amount of industry. He
might seem a butterfly, when dining out, but he was a
bee at home, and got through a great amount of work.

His *Memoirs of Captain Rock* appeared in 1824, written
after a tour in Ireland with the Marquis of Lansdowne.

It is a one-sided, rhapsodical melange, severely commenting upon the Government of Ireland by England, from
Pope Adrian's time downward. The memoirs purport to
be written by Captain Rock himself, who is thus made
the mouth-piece through which Moore, in a fanciful style,
pours the parti-coloured rose-water, rather than revolutionary, viols of his wrath on the oppressors of his country,
and on sundry enactments, which have, since that time,
been altogether removed from the statute-book.

This year Lord Byron died, and thus the existence,
and the intended publication of his memoirs, which he
had intrusted to Moore for that purpose, came to be
known.

---

[1] We do not happen to know Mr. Willis' authority for this statement, nor
have we seen any allusion to it elsewhere.—A. J. S

In 1821, Moore had sold the copyright to Murray for two thousand guineas. Byron's relatives, taking alarm, implored Moore to allow the MS. to be destroyed; to which course he consented, and, after arrangements were made accordingly, it was burned in the presence of witnesses. That Moore acquiesced in this course from a sense of honour, there could be no question; as he, on receiving advances from Longmans, actually repaid the sum which he had received from Murray, both principal and interest. The MS. memoirs had been openly handed about, and lent to ladies; and Lord John Russell stated that the whole of the objectionable passages did not amount to more than three or four pages; and also that Moore had Byron's permission to alter or leave out anything at discretion, or could, easily, have neutralized what he might deem wrong or unfair, in a foot-note. This, the mysterious destruction of Byron's MS. memoirs, is perhaps the most notable event in the latter part of Moore's life.

"As to the manuscript itself," says Lord John Russell, "having read the greater part of it, if not the whole, I should say that three or four pages of it were too gross and indelicate for publication; that the rest, with few exceptions, contained little traces of Lord Byron's genius, and no interesting details of his life. His early youth in Greece, and his sensibility to the scenes around him, when resting on a rock in the swimming excursions he took from the Piraeus, were strikingly described. But, on the whole, the world is no loser, by the sacrifice made of the memoirs of this great poet."

The following entries are taken from Moore's DIARY:—

Bowood, 24th Oct., 1824. — At breakfast "Bowles mentioned that at some celebration at Reading school, when the patrons or governors of it (beer and brandy merchants) were to be welcomed with a Latin address, the boy appointed to the task thus bespoke them '*Salvete, hospites* c̆elebeerimi,' and then turning to the others, '*Salvete, hospites* c̆elebrandi.'"

29th Oct. 1824.—At Bowood, Lord Lansdowne mentioned "a ship having been once cast away at Petersburgh, laden with the newest fashions from France, and all the fish that were caught for several days were dressed out on the different dresses, veils, caps, &c. &c. !!!"

Aug. 16, 1825.—Walking with Rogers, "mentioned Sheridan saying, when there was some proposal to lay a tax upon milestones, that it was unconstitutional, as they were a race that could not meet to remonstrate."

17th Oct., 1825 (of Mrs. Moore).—"Dear, generous girl, there never was anything like her for warmheartedness and devotion."

Moore visited Scotland in October, 1825, and was delighted with Scott at Abbotsford, with Jeffrey, with Edinburgh, and with the kind reception everywhere accorded to him.

In October, 1825, his *Life of Sheridan* appeared — a work industriously compiled and pleasantly written; also his *Evenings in Greece*, from which we take the following song:—

> "Who comes so gracefully
>   Gliding along,
> While the blue rivulet
>   Sleeps to her song;
> Song, richly vying
> With the faint sighing
> Which swans, in dying,
>   Sweetly prolong?"

> So sung the shepherd-boy
>   By the stream's side,

Watching that fairy boat
  Down the flood glide,
Like a bird winging,
Through the waves bringing
That Syren, singing
  To the hush'd tide.

"Stay," said the shepherd-boy,
  "Fairy-boat, stay,
Linger, sweet minstrelsy,
  Linger, a day."
But vain his pleading,
Past him, unheeding,
Song and boat, speeding,
  Glided away.

So to our youthful eyes
  Joy and hope shone;
So, while we gaz'd on them,
  Fast they flew on;—
Like flow'rs, declining
Ev'n in the twining,
One moment shining,
  And, the next, gone!

His journal contains some quaint stories and interesting allusions, a few of which we transcribe:—

Sept. 21, 1826.—"Quoted à *propos* of Selina Locke's eyes, the saying of a Spanish poet to a girl, 'Lend me your eyes for to-night; I want to kill a man.'"

Oct. 25, 1826.—"At Miss White's, while Head was describing the use of the lasso in catching men as well as animals, Luttrell said the first syllable of it had caught many a man."

26th Oct., 1826.—"Some one had said of Sharpe's very dark complexion that he looked as if the dye of his old trade (hat-making) had got engrained into his face. 'Yes (said Luttrell), darkness that may be *felt*.'"

13th June, 1827.—"On some one saying, 'Well, you see ——'s predictions have come true.' 'Indeed!' said Plunket, 'I always knew he was a *bore*, but I didn't know he was an *augur*.'"

From an entry, we find that on June 30, 1827, Boyle Farm Fete was celebrated — an event which furnished material for a poem which appeared four years after.

2d July, 1827.—"Lord Lansdowne mentioned a letter, he had from Ireland, speaking of the 'claw of an act,' evidently thinking that *clause* was plural."

10th July, 1827.—"Byron's mother, a vulgar, violent woman; it was she who instilled into him a dislike for Lord Carlisle, with whom she was continually at war on the subject of Byron's bringing up. Made a racket whenever she came to Glennies; and the other boys used to say, 'Byron, your mother's a fool.' 'I know it,' was his answer."

11th Aug., 1827.—Barnes of the *Times* agreed to give £400 a year for occasional contributions, squibs, &c.

19th Aug., 1827.—"Took Bessy to hear mass at Wardour; the first time she ever saw Catholic service performed. The music as usual (when it is so good) raised me to the skies, but the gaudy ceremonies and the gesticulations of the mass shocked my simple-minded Bessy, and even the music, much as she feels it, could not reconcile her to the gold garments of the priest." (Mrs. Moore was a Protestant, and their children were all baptized by Church of England clergymen.)

27th Oct., 1827.—"In talking of dogs, a case mentioned, where a man in going to bathe left his clothes in the care of his dog, but on his returning out of the water the dog, not knowing him, would not give them up again."

"Dunning once being asked how he contrived to get through his business, answered, 'I do a little; a little does itself; and the rest is undone."

In 1827 *The Epicurean* was published, illustrated with vignettes on steel after Turner. It is a romance founded on Egyptian mythology, and is the most highly finished, artistic, and imaginative of his prose writings.

He at first intended to write it in verse, and indeed began it in that form; but left it as an unfinished fragment, called "Alciphron," which appeared appended to the prose tale.

Alciphron was an Epicurean philosopher converted to Christianity, A.D. 257, by a young Egyptian maiden with whom he fell in love, but who suffered martyrdom in that year. On her death, he betook himself to the desert. During the persecution under Dioclesian, his sufferings for the faith were most exemplary, and being at length, at an advanced age, condemned to hard labour for refusing to comply with an imperial edict, he died at the brass mines of Palestine, A.D. 297. There was found, after his death, a small metal mirror, like those used in the ceremonies of Isis, suspended around his neck.

THE TEMPLE OF THE MOON.

(FROM "THE EPICUREAN.")

The rising of the moon, slow and majestic, as if conscious of the honours that awaited her upon earth, was welcomed with a loud acclaim from every eminence, where multitudes stood watching for her first light. And seldom had that light risen upon a more beautiful scene. The city of Memphis—still grand, though no longer the unrivalled Memphis, that had borne away from Thebes the crown of supremacy, and worn it undisputed through ages—now softened by the mild moonlight that harmonized with her decline, shone forth among her lakes, her pyramids, and her shrines, like one of those dreams of human glory that must ere long pass away. Even already ruin was visible around her. The sands of the Libyan desert were gaining upon her like a sea; and there, among solitary columns and sphinxes, already half sunk from sight, Time seemed to stand waiting, till all that now flourished around him should fall beneath his desolating hand like the rest.

On the waters all was gaiety and life. As far as eye could reach, the lights of innumerable boats were seen studding, like rubies, the surface of the stream. Vessels of every kind—from the light coracle, built for shooting down the cataracts, to the large yacht that glides slowly to the sound of flutes—all were afloat for this sacred festival, filled with crowds of the young and the gay, not only from Memphis and Babylon, but from cities still farther removed from the festal scene.

As I approached the island I could see, glittering through the trees on the bank, the lamps of the pilgrims hastening to the ceremony. Landing in the direction which those lights pointed out, I soon joined the crowd; and, passing through a long alley of sphinxes, whose spangling marble gleamed out from the dark sycamores around them, reached in a short time the grand vestibule of the temple, where I found the ceremonies of the evening already commenced.

In this vast hall, which was surrounded by a double range of columns, and lay open overhead to the stars of heaven, I saw a group of young maidens, moving in a sort of measured step, between walk and dance, round a small shrine, upon which stood one of those sacred birds, that, on account of the variegated colour of their wings, are dedicated to the worship of the moon. The vestibule was dimly lighted—there being but one lamp of naphtha hung on each of the great pillars that encircled it. But, having taken my station beside one of those pillars, I had a clear view of the young dancers, as in succession they passed me.

The drapery of all was white as snow; and each wore loosely, beneath the bosom, a dark blue zone, or bandelet, studded, like the skies at midnight, with small silver stars. Through their dark locks was wreathed the white lily of the Nile—that sacred flower being accounted no less welcome to the moon than the golden blossoms of the bean-flower are known to be to the sun. As they passed under the lamp, a gleam of light flashed from their bosoms, which, I could perceive, was the reflection of a small mirror, that, in the manner of the women of the East, each of the dancers wore beneath her left shoulder.

There was no music to regulate their steps; but, as they gracefully went round the bird on the shrine, some to the beat of the castanet, some to the shrill ring of a sistrum—which they held uplifted in the attitude of their own divine Isis—continued harmoniously to time the cadence of their feet; while others, at every step, shook a small chain of silver, whose sound, mingling with those of the castanets and sistrums, produced a wild, but not unpleasing harmony.

They seemed all lovely; but there was one—whose face the light had not yet reached, so downcast she held it—who attracted, and, at length, riveted all my looks and thoughts. I know not why, but there was a something in those half-seen features—a charm in the very shadow that hung over their imagined beauty—which took my fancy more than all the outshining loveliness of her companions. So enchained was I by this coy mystery, that her alone, of all the group, could I either see or think of—her alone I watched, as, with the same downcast brow, she glided gently and aërially round the altar, as if her presence, like that of a spirit, was something to be felt, not seen.

Suddenly, while I gazed, the loud crash of a thousand cymbals was heard;—the massy gates of the temple flew open, as if by magic, and a flood of radiance from the illuminated aisle filled the whole vestibule; while, at the same instant, as if the light and the sound were borne together, a peal of rich harmony came mingling with the radiance.

It was then—by that light, which shone full upon the young maiden's features, as, starting at the sudden blaze, she raised her eyes to the portal, and as quickly let fall their lids again —it was then I beheld, what even my own ardent imagination, in its most vivid dreams of beauty, had never pictured.

12

Not Psyche herself, when pausing on the threshold of heaven, while its first glories fell on her dazzled lids, could have looked more purely beautiful, or blushed with a more innocent shame. Often as I had felt the power of looks, none had ever entered into my soul so deeply. It was a new feeling—a new sense— coming as suddenly upon me as that radiance into the vestibule, and, at once, filling my whole being;—and had that bright vision but lingered another moment before my eyes I should in my transport have wholly forgotten who I was and where, and thrown myself, in prostrate adoration, at her feet.

But scarcely had that gush of harmony been heard, when the sacred bird, which had, till now, been standing motionless as an image, spread wide his wings, and flew into the temple; while his graceful young worshippers, with a fleetness like his own, followed—and she, who had left a dream in my heart never to be forgotten, vanished along with the rest. As she went rapidly past the pillar against which I leaned, the ivy that encircled it caught in her drapery, and disengaged some ornament, which fell to the ground. It was the small mirror which I had seen shining on her bosom. Hastily and tremulously I picked it up, and hurried to restore it; but she was already lost to my eyes in the crowd.

In vain did I try to follow;—the aisles were already filled and numbers of eager pilgrims pressed towards the portal. But the servants of the temple denied all further entrance, and still, as I presented myself, their white wands barred the way. Perplexed and irritated amid that crowd of faces, regarding all as enemies that impeded my progress, I stood on tiptoe, gazing into the busy aisles, and with a heart beating as I caught, from time to time, a glimpse of some spangled zone, or lotus wreath, which led me to fancy that I had discovered the fair object of my search. But it was all in vain;—in every direction files of sacred nymphs were moving, but nowhere could I discover her whom alone I sought.

In this state of breathless agitation did I stand for some time—bewildered with the confusion of faces and lights, as well as with the clouds of incense that rolled around me— till, fevered and impatient, I could endure it no longer. Forcing my way out of the vestibule into the cool air, I hurried back through the alley of sphinxes to the shore, and flung myself into my boat.

EXTRACT FROM

ALCIPHRON.

'Mong stars that came out one by one,
The young moon—like the Roman mother
    Among her living jewels—shone.
"Oh that from yonder orbs," I thought,
    " Pure and eternal as they are,
There could to earth some power be brought,
Some charm, with their own essence fraught,
    To make man deathless as a star;
And open to his vast desires
    A course, as boundless and sublime
As that which waits those comet-fires,
    That burn and roam throughout all time!"

While thoughts like these absorb'd my mind,
    That weariness which earthly bliss,
However sweet, still leaves behind,
    As if to show how earthly 'tis,
Came lulling o'er me, and I laid
    My limbs at that fair statue's base—
That miracle, which Art hath made
    Of all the choice of Nature's grace—
To which so oft I've knelt and sworn,
    That, could a living maid like her
Unto this wondering world be born,
    I would, myself, turn worshipper.

Sleep came then o'er me—and I seem'd
    To be transported far away
To a bleak desert plain, where gleam'd
    One single, melancholy ray,
Throughout that darkness dimly shed
    From a small taper in the hand

Of one, who, pale as are the dead,
  Before me took his spectral stand,
And said, while, awfully, a smile
  Came o'er the wanness of his cheek—
"Go, and beside the sacred Nile
  You'll find th' Eternal life you seek."

Soon as he spoke these words, the hue
Of death o'er all his features grew,
Like the pale morning, when o'er night
She gains the victory, full of light;
While the small torch he held became
A glory in his hand, whose flame
Brighten'd the desert suddenly,
  Even to the far horizon's line—
Along whose level I could see
  Gardens and groves, that seem'd to shine,
As if then o'er them freshly play'd
A vernal rainbow's rich cascade;
And music floated everywhere
Circling, as 'twere itself the air,
And spirits, on whose wings the hue
Of heaven still linger'd, round me flew,
Till from all sides such splendours broke,
That, with the excess of light, I woke!
  .   .   .   .

The rising of the Moon, calm, slow,
  And beautiful, as if she came
Fresh from the Elysian bowers below,
  Was, with a loud and sweet acclaim,
Welcom'd from every breezy height,
Where crowds stood waiting for her light.
And well might they who view'd the scene
  Then lit up all around them, say,
That never yet had Nature been
  Caught sleeping in a lovelier ray,
Or rivall'd her own noontide face,
With purer show of moonlight grace.

Memphis—still grand, though not the same
  Unrivall'd Memphis, that could seize
From ancient Thebes the crown of Fame,
  And wear it bright through centuries—
Now, in the moonshine, that came down
Like a last smile upon that crown,—
Memphis, still grand, among her lakes,
  Her pyramids and shrines of fire,
Rose, like a vision, that half breaks
On one who, dreaming still, awakes,
  To music from some midnight choir:
While to the west—where gradual sinks
  In the red sands, from Libya roll'd,
Some mighty column, or fair sphynx,
  That stood in kingly courts, of old—
It seem'd as, 'mid the pomps that shone
Thus gaily round him, Time look'd on,
Waiting till all, now bright and blest,
Should sink beneath him like the rest.

No sooner had the setting sun
Proclaim'd the festal rite begun,
And, 'mid their idol's fullest beams,
  The Egyptian world was all afloat,
Than I, who live upon these streams,
  Like a young Nile-bird, turn'd my boat
To the fair island, on whose shores,
Through leafy palms and sycamores,
Already shone the moving lights
Of pilgrims hastening to the rites.
While, far around, like ruby sparks
Upon the water, lighted barks,
Of every form and kind—from those
  That down Syene's cataract shoots,
To the grand, gilded barge, that rows
  To tambour's beat and breath of flutes,
And wears at night, in words of flame,
On the rich prow, its master's name;—

All were alive, and made this sea
   Of cities busy as a hill
Of summer ants, caught suddenly
   In the overflowing of a rill.

Landed upon the isle, I soon
   Through marble alleys and small groves
   Of that mysterious palm she loves,
Reach'd the fair Temple of the Moon;
And there—as slowly through the last
Dim-lighted vestibule I pass'd—
Between the porphyry pillars, twin'd
   With palm and ivy, I could see
A band of youthful maidens wind,
   In measur'd walk, half dancingly,
Round a small shrine, on which was plac'd
   That bird, whose plumes of black and white
Were in their hue, by Nature trac'd,
   A type of the moon's shadow'd light.

In drapery, like woven snow,
These nymphs were clad; and each, below
The rounded bosom, loosely wore
   A dark blue zone, or bandelet,
With little silver stars all o'er,
   As are the skies at midnight, set,
While in their tresses, braided through,
   Sparkled that flower of Egypt's lakes,
The silvery lotus, in whose hue
   As much delight the young Moon takes,
As doth the Day-God to behold
The lofty bean-flower's buds of gold.
And, as they gracefully went round
   The worshipp'd bird, some to the beat
Of castanets, some to the sound
   Of the shrill sistrum tim'd their feet;
While others, at each step they took,
A tinkling chain of silver shook.

They seem'd all fair—but there was one
On whom the light had not yet shone,
Or shone but partly—so downcast
She held her brow as slow she past.
And yet to me, there seem'd to dwell
  A charm about that unseen face—
A something in the shade that fell
  Over that brow's imagin'd grace,
Which won me more than all the best
Outshining beauties of the rest.
And *her* alone my eyes could see,
Enchain'd by this sweet mystery;
And her alone I watch'd, as round
She glided o'er that marble ground,
Stirring not more th' unconscious air
Than if a Spirit were moving there.
Till suddenly, wide open flew
The Temple's folding gates, and threw
A splendour from within, a flood
Of glory, where these maidens stood.
While, with that light—as if the same
Rich source gave birth to both—there came
A swell of harmony, as grand
As e'er was born of voice and hand,
Filling the gorgeous aisles around
With luxury of light and sound.

Then was it, by the flash that blaz'd
  Full o'er her features—oh 'twas then,
As startingly her eyes she rais'd,
  But quick let fall their lids again,
I saw—not Psyche's self, when first
  Upon the threshold of the skies
She paus'd, while heaven's glory burst
  Newly upon her downcast eyes,
Could look more beautiful, or blush
  With holier shame, than did this maid,
Whom now I saw, in all that gush

Of splendour from the aisles, display'd.
Never—though well thou know'st how much
    I've felt the sway of Beauty's star—
Never did her bright influence touch
    My soul into its depths so far;
And had that vision linger'd there
    One minute more, I should have flown,
Forgetful *who* I was and where,
        And, at her feet in worship thrown,
        Proffer'd my soul through life her own.

But, scarcely had that burst of light
And music broke on ear and sight,
Than up the aisle the bird took wing,
    As if on heavenly mission sent,
While after him, with graceful spring,
    Like some unearthly creatures, meant
        To live in that mix'd element
    Of light and song, the young maids went;
And she, who in my heart had thrown
A spark to burn for life, was flown.

In vain I tried to follow;—bands
    Of reverend chanters fill'd the aisle:
Where'er I sought to pass, their wands
    Motion'd me back, while many a file
Of sacred nymphs—but ah, not they
Whom my eyes look'd for—throng'd the way.
Perplex'd, impatient, 'mid this crowd
Of faces, lights—the o'erwhelming cloud
Of incense round me, and my blood
Full of its new-born fire—I stood,
Nor mov'd, nor breath'd, but when I caught
    A glimpse of some blue, spangled zone,
Or wreath of lotus, which I thought,
    Like those she wore at distance shone.

But no, 'twas vain—hour after hour,
    Till my heart's throbbing turn'd to pain,

And my strain'd eyesight lost its power,
　I sought her thus, but all in vain.
At length, hot—wilder'd—in despair,
I rush'd into the cool night-air,
And, hurrying (though with many a look
Back to the busy Temple), took
My way along the moonlight shore,
And sprung into my boat once more.

CHAPTER XII.

POLITICAL ODES—LIFE OF BYRON—SUMMER FETE—PENSION—
LATTER WORKS.

In 1828 Moore published "Odes on Cash, Corn, and
Catholics," full of quaint hints and pointed allusions to
the political topics of the day, which made his bright
sallies of wit immensely popular at the time. Here is a
verse which our readers might almost fancy was written
by Hood :—

> "Now, Dantzic wheat before you floats—
> 　Now, Jesuits from California—
> Now Ceres, link'd with Titus *Oats*,
> 　Comes dancing through the Porta *Cornea*,[1]

In *The Periwinkles and the Locusts, a Salmagundian
Hymn*, founded on a sentence from Rabelais' story of
Panurge, he thus hits at the financing of the govern-
ment :—

> "The Salmagundian ones were rich,
> 　Or *thought* they were—no matter which—
> For, every year, the Revenue
> From their Periwinkles larger grew !

[1] The Horn Gate, through which the ancients supposed all true dreams to
pass.

And their rulers, skill'd in all the trick
And legerdemain of arithmetic,
Knew how to place 1, 2, 3, 4,
   5, 6, 7, 8, and 9 and 10,
Such various ways—behind, before,
That they made a unit seem a score
   And proved themselves most wealthy men!

" So, on they went, a prosperous crew,
   The people wise, the rulers clever—
And God help those like me and you
Who dared to doubt (as some now do)
That the Periwinkle Revenue
   Would thus go flourishing on for ever."

We cull the following amusing entries from his
DIARY:—

Breakfasting at Rogers', May 22, 1828.—"Luttrell's
idea of the English climate,—'On a fine day, like looking
up a chimney; on a rainy day, like looking down it.'"

27th May, 1828.—"Breakfasted at Rogers'. Anecdote
of the Disputatious Man:—'Why, it is as plain as that
two and two make four.' 'But I deny *that* too; for 2
and 2 make twenty-two.'"

June 6, 1828.—"Talking of figurative oratory, mentioned the barrister before Lord Ellenborough. 'My
lord, I appear before you in the character of an advo-
cate from the city of London; the city of London herself
appears before you as a suppliant for justice. My lord, it
is written in the book of nature—' 'What book?' says
Lord E. 'The book of nature.' 'Name the page,' says
Lord E., holding his pen uplifted, as if to note the page
down."

6th July, 1828.—"*Apropos* of loss of friends, somebody
was saying the other day, before Morgan, the great calcu-
lator of lives, that they had lost so many friends (men-

tioning the number) in a certain space of time, upon which Morgan, coolly taking down a book from his office shelf, and looking into it, said, 'So you ought, sir, and three more.'"

Aug. 11, 1828.—"Anecdote of the Rival Shoemakers. —One of them putting up over his shop, '*Mens consciâ recti*,' and the other instantly mounting, 'Men's and Women's conscia recti.'"

July 5th, 1829.—"Rogers mentioned a clever thing said by Lord Dudley, on some Vienna lady remarking impudently to him, 'What wretchedly bad French you all speak in London!' 'It is true, Madame,' he answered, 'we have not enjoyed the advantage of having the French twice in our capital.'"   (6)

21st Sept., 1829.—"Crocker told the following anecdote:—Fenelon, who had often teazed Richelieu (and ineffectually, it would seem) for subscriptions to charitable undertakings, was one day telling him that he had just seen his picture. 'And did you ask it for a subscription?' said Richelieu sneeringly. 'No, I saw there was no chance,' replied the other; 'it was so like you.'"

5th Oct., 1829.—Dining at Murray's, "Charles Lamb, sitting next some chattering women at dinner; observing he didn't attend to her, 'You don't seem,' said the lady, 'to be at all the better for what I have been saying to you.' 'No, ma'am,' he answered, 'but this gentleman at the other side of me must, for it all came in at the one ear and went out at the other.'

"Bannister's melancholy at finding himself sixty-five, exactly the number of his own house.—Looking up at the plate on the door, and soliloquizing, 'Ay, you needn't tell me, I know it; you told me the same thing yesterday.'"

16th Dec., 1829.—Bowood. "A Russian mentioned, at

dinner, an anecdote of a Swiss and a Brabanter talking together, and the latter reproaching the Swiss with fighting for money, while he (the Brabanter) fought for honour. 'The fact is,' answered the Swiss drily, 'we each of us fight for what each most wants'"

20th Dec., 1829.—Dining at Murray's, the host told of "a man recounting his feats in shooting, and appealing to Murray, who had been out with him, and his saying, 'What he hit is history; what he missed is mystery— a double joke, taking it as *his*-story and *my*-story.'"

Jan. 4–7, 1830.—At Bowood. "Dean Ogle, a very absent man, has been known more than once at a strange table, where there happened not to be a very good dinner, to burst out with, 'Dear me, what a very bad dinner! I am so sorry not to have given you a better,' &c. &c., thinking himself at home."

Jan. 4–7, 1830.—At Bowood. "Story of a sick man telling his symptoms (which appeared to himself, of course, dreadful), to a medical friend, who, at each new item of the disorder, exclaimed, 'Charming!' 'Delightful!' 'Pray go on!' and when he had finished, said with the utmost pleasure, 'Do you know, my dear sir, you have got a complaint which has been supposed for some time to be extinct!'"

26th Feb., 1830.—"At Lord Lansdowne's, Charles Kemble told a story of an "Irishman mulcted in £5 for beating a fellow, and saying, 'What, five pounds! Well' (turning to the patient), 'wait till I get you in Limerick, where *bating* is *cheap*, and I'll take it out of you.'"

4th May, 1830.—Evening at the Duchess Cannizzaro's. —"Lord Dudley, upon being asked whether he had read some new novel of Scott's, said, 'Why, I am ashamed to say I have not; but I have hopes it will soon *blow over*.'"

In 1830 he edited *The Letters and Journals of Lord*

Byron, with Notices of his Life. This work, which appeared
in two quarto volumes, compiled from Byron's journals
and such materials as he could subsequently procure, is
interesting, but too copious, and, as might be expected,
partial and lenient in its criticism.

Moore's biographical works, although industriously
compiled, are somewhat faulty and diffuse, but they
all abound in sparkling passages; his notices of Lord
Byron are generally written with taste and modesty,
and in very pure and unaffected English. As an editor,
however, in this instance, he admits far too much trivial
matter, and his judgment is considerably biassed by
friendship. Yet Lord Macaulay has characterized it as a
lucid narrative "deserving to be classed amongst the best
specimens of English prose which any age has produced."
For this biography, which was transferred from Longmans to Murray, he ultimately obtained £4870.

Of a visit to Ireland he writes, 29th Sept. 1830:—
"Altogether our visit has been a most happy one. My
mother and Nell had known little of my excellent Bessy
but through my report of her, it being now fifteen years
since they had (for a very few weeks, and living in
separate houses) any opportunity of knowing her. They
have now, however, had her with them as one of themselves, and the result has been what I never could doubt
it would be. Her devoted attention to my mother, her
affection to dear Nell, all was in the best spirit of amiable-
ness and good sense. Being better able to see, than
I could, all the little things, in the way of comfort, that
my poor mother's establishment wants, she has, in the
nicest and most delicate way, procured them, and made a
few pounds do wonders in this way. The two boys,
too, have been a great delight to my mother. Young
Mulvaney has painted a picture of her for me, with Tom

leaning on her lap; and Lover has done a very successful portrait of dear Russell, taking his idea of the attitude, &c., from my song of 'Love is a Hunter Boy.'"

In Oct. 1830, he was invited on a visit to Watson Taylor's to meet the Duchess of Kent and our Queen, then the young Princess Victoria. Of the meeting, he writes:—"The duchess sung a duet or two with the Princess Victoria, and several pretty German songs by herself. One or two by Weber and Hummel particularly pretty, and her manner of singing just what a lady's ought to be. No attempt at bravura or graces, but all simplicity and expression. I also sung several songs, with which her R. H. was pleased to be pleased. Evidently very fond of music, and would have gone on singing much longer, if there had not been rather premature preparations for bed. . . . After breakfast the duchess expressed a wish for a little more music, and she and the princess and myself sung a good deal. The duchess sung over, three or four times, with me 'Go where Glory Waits Thee,' pronouncing the words very prettily, and altogether singing it more to my taste than any one I ever found. Repeated also her pretty German songs, and very graciously promised me copies of them, having intimated how much she should like to have copies of those songs I had sung for her."

Nov. 1830 (Prowses and Corry dining with Moore).— "Henry Bushe's account of his place, to the Sinecure Committee, that he was 'Resident Surveyor, with perpetual leave of absence.' 'Don't you do any work for it?' 'Nothing but receive my salary four times a year.' 'Do you receive that yourself?' 'No, by deputy.'"

17th Dec. 1830.—"Went to take leave of Rogers, who sends by me to Bessy a large-paper copy of his most beautiful book, *Italy*, the getting up of which has cost him

£5000. Told me of a squabble he has had with the
publisher of it, who, in trying to justify himself for
some departure from his original agreement, complained
rather imprudenly of the large sum of ready-money he
had been obliged to lay out upon it. 'As to that,' said
Rogers, 'I shall remove that cause of complaint instantly.
'Bring me your account.' The account was brought;
something not much short of £1500. 'There,' said
Rogers, writing a cheque for the whole sum, 'I shall
leave you nothing more to say upon that ground.' 'Had
I been a *poor* author' (added Rogers, after telling me
these circumstances), 'I should have been his slave for
life.' "

17th Dec. 1830.—"Brougham mentioned to-day that,
on the Princess of Wales' coming over to England, it was
a matter of discussion among a party, where Lady
Charlotte Lindsay was, what *one* word of English, Her
Royal Highness (who was totally ignorant of the language)
should be first taught to speak. The whole company
agreed that 'yes' was the most useful word, except
Lady Charlotte, who suggested that 'no' was twice as
useful, as it often stood for 'yes.' This story, Brougham
said, he once made use of in court, in commenting on the
manner in which a witness had said 'no.' "

In 1831 was published his *Life of Lord Edward Fitzgerald;* followed by *The Summer Fête,* a poem, celebrating
an entertainment which had been given at Boyle Farm
in 1827.

Boyle Farm was the seat of Lord Henry Fitzgerald,
and the fête had been given by five noblemen, who sub-
scribed four or five hundred pounds each towards it. The
arrangements were all in the best taste. The beauty
and élite of the gay world was assembled. Four hundred
and fifty sat down to dinner in a tent on the lawn, and

fifty to the royal table in the conservatory. Minstrels sang and played; barcarolles were heard dying away. Madame Vestris, Fanny Ayton, and others, skimming about as dominoes in gondolas, sang Moore's song, 'Oh, Come to Me when Daylight Sets.' The June evening was delicious, and, as soon as it grew dark the groves were all lighted up with coloured lamps in quaint devices. There were grottos and lakes, and the lights reflected in the water gave the whole an oriental or fairy-like aspect.

Mrs. Norton was one of those who had been present, and, to her, Moore dedicated this poem suggested by the scene. It is interspersed with songs and trios. We quote from it the following lines:—

"Now in his Palace of the West,
    Sinking to slumber, the bright Day,
Like a tir'd monarch fann'd to rest,
    Mid the cool airs of Evening lay;
While round his couch's golden rim
    The gaudy clouds, like courtiers, crept—
Struggling each other's light to dim,
    And catch his last smile e'er he slept.
How gay, as o'er the gliding Thames
    The golden eve its lustre pour'd,
Shone out the high-born knights and dames
    Now group'd around that festal board;
A living mass of plumes and flowers,
As though they'd robb'd both birds and bowers—
A peopled rainbow, swarming through
With habitants of every hue;
While, as the sparkling juice of France
High in the crystal brimmers flow'd,
    Each sunset ray that mix'd by chance
With the wine's sparkles, show'd
    How sunbeams may be taught to dance."

.   .   .   .   .

" Here shone a garden—lamps all o'er,
  As though the Spirits of the Air
Had tak'n it in their heads to pour
  A shower of summer meteors there;—
While here a lighted shrubb'ry led
  To a small lake that sleeping lay,
Cradled in foliage, but, o'er-head,
  Open to heaven's sweet breath and ray;
While round its rim there burning stood
  Lamps, with young flowers beside them bedded,
That shrunk from such warm neighbourhood;
  And, looking bashful in the flood,
  Blush'd to behold themselves so wedded.

" Hither, to this embower'd retreat,
  Fit but for nights so still and sweet;
Nights, such as Eden's calm recall
In its first lonely hour, when all
  So silent is, below, on high,
  That if a star falls down the sky,
You almost think you hear it fall—
Hither, to this recess, a few,
  To shun the dancers' wild'ring noise,
And give an hour, ere night-time flew,
  To Music's more ethereal joys,
Came with their voices—ready all
As Echo, waiting for a call—
In hymn or ballad, dirge or glee,
To weave their mingling minstrelsy.

" And, first, a dark-ey'd nymph, array'd—
Like her, whom Art hath deathless made,
Bright Mona Lisa—with that braid
Of hair across the brow, and one
Small gem that in the centre shone—
With face, too, in its form resembling
  Da Vinci's Beauties—the dark eyes,
Now lucid, as through crystal trembling,
  Now soft, as if suffus'd with sighs—
13

Her lute, that hung beside her, took,
And, bending o'er it with shy look,
More beautiful, in shadow thus,
Than when with life most luminous,
Pass'd her light finger o'er the chords,
And sung to them these mournful words:—

"SONG.

"Bring hither, bring thy lute, while day is dying—
Here will I lay me, and list to thy song;
Should tones of other days mix with its sighing,
Tones of a light heart, now banish'd so long,
Chase them away—they bring but pain,
And let thy theme be woe again.

"Sing on, thou mournful lute—day is fast going,
Soon will its light from thy chords die away;
One little gleam in the west is still glowing,
When that hath vanish'd, farewell to thy lay.
Mark, how it fades!—see, it is fled!
Now, sweet lute, be thou, too, dead.

  •   •   •   •   •   •

"SONG.

"Who'll buy?—'tis Folly's shop, who'll buy?—
We've toys to suit all ranks and ages;
Besides our usual fools' supply,
We've lots of playthings, too, for sages.
For reasoners, here's a juggler's cup,
That fullest seems when nothing's in it;
And nine-pins set, like systems, up,
To be knock'd down the following minute.
Who'll buy?—'tis Folly's shop, who'll buy?

"Gay caps we here of foolscap make,
For bards to wear in dog-day weather;
Or bards, the bells, alone may take,
And leave to wits the cap and feather.

Tetotums we've for patriots got,
    Who court the mob with antics humble;
Like theirs, the patriot's dizzy lot,
    A glorious spin, and then—a tumble.
              Who'll buy, &c. &c.

"Here, wealthy misers to inter,
    We've shrouds of neat post-obit paper;
While, for their heirs, we've *quick*silver,
    That, fast as they can wish, will caper.
For aldermen we've dials true,
    That tell no hour but that of dinner;
For courtly parsons sermons new,
    That suit alike both saint and sinner.
              Who'll buy, &c. &c.

"No time we've now to name our terms,
    But, whatsoe'er the whims that seize you,
This oldest of all mortal firms,
    Folly and Co., will try to please you.
Or, should you wish a darker hue
    Of goods than *we* can recommend you,
Why then (as we with lawyers do)
    To Knaver's shop next door we'll send you.
              Who'll buy, &c. &c."

In his diary we find the following entries:—

15th Feb., 1831 (in Dublin).—"Some conversation with old Peter Burrows. Agreed with me in opinion that O'Connell had done more harm to the cause of liberty in Ireland than its real friends could repair within the next half century; and mentioned what Grattan had said of him—that 'He was a bad subject, and a worse rebel.' This is admirable; true to the life, and in Grattan's happiest manner. The lurking appreciation of a *good* rebel which it implies is full of humour."

20th Feb., 1831 (of Lady Lansdowne).—"Had a long conversation with her, and came away (as I always do)

more and more impressed with the excellent qualities of
her mind and heart; even her very faults are but the
selvage of fine and sound virtues."

"On the 28th (March, 1831), Bessy went with me to
dine at Lacock, and was much delighted with her visit,
from which we returned home next day.   Lady E. whispered me, on our arrival, 'I take for granted there is
nobody dying in your neighbourhood, or we should not
have had Mrs. Moore's company to-day.'   It is true that
she is never half so happy as when helping those who
want assistance, or comforting those who are afflicted."

28th April, 1831 (at Rogers').—"A curious conversation after dinner from my saying that 'after all, it was in
high life one met the best society;' Rogers violently opposing me; he, too, of all men, who (as I took care to
tell him) had throughout the greater part of his life
shown practically that he agreed with me, by confining
himself almost exclusively to this class of society.   It is,
indeed, the power which these great people have of commanding, among other luxuries, the presence of such men
as he is, at their tables, that sets their circle (taking all its
advantages into account) indisputably above all others in
the way of *society*.—Said, with some bitterness, that, on
the contrary, the high class were the vulgarest people one
met.   Vulgar enough, God knows! some of them are;
vulgar in *mind*, which is the worst sort of vulgarity.   But,
to say nothing of women, *where*, in any rank or station of
life, could one find *men* better worth living with, whether
for manners, information, or any other of the qualities
that render society agreeable, than such persons as Lords
Holland, Grey, Carlisle, Lansdowne, Cowper, King, Melbourne, Carnarvon, John Russell, Dudley, Normanby,
Morpeth, Mahon, and numbers of others that I can speak
of from personal knowledge?"

15th June, 1831.—"In writing to Sydney Smith, to-day, sending him Crabbe's address, which he wanted, I said that 'I was sorry he had gone away so soon from Ellis' the other night, as I had improved (*i.e.* my singing) afterwards, and he was one of the few I always wished to do my *best* for.' In answer to this, received the following flattering note from him, written, evidently, under the impression that I had been annoyed by his going away:—

"'My Dear Moore,—By the beard of the prelate of Canterbury, by the cassock of the prelate of York, by the breakfasts of Rogers, by Luttrell's love of side-dishes, I swear that I had rather hear you sing than any person I ever heard in my life, male or female. For what is your singing but beautiful poetry floating in fine music and guided by exquisite feeling? Call me Dissenter, say that my cassock is ill put on, that I know not the delicacies of decimation, and confound the greater and smaller tithes; but do not think or say that I am insensible to your music. The truth is, that I took a solemn oath to Mrs. Beauclerk to be there by ten, and set off, to prevent perjury, at eleven; but was seized with a violent pain in my stomach by the way, and went to bed.—Yours ever, my dear Moore, very sincerely, SYDNEY SMITH.'"

17th June, 1831.—"Met Bishop, at Power's, to arrange about my music. Mentioned what some of the fine ladies of the Bazaar had told me of the trouble some of their customers had given in looking over different things and not buying any; and that they were sure some of the tradesmen they had themselves plagued in this way.had come there expressly to turn the tables on them. Bishop remarked that this would tell very well in a farce, and so it would."

18th June, 1831.—"Walked with Sydney Smith; told me his age; turned sixty. Asked me how I felt about dying. Answered that if my mind was but at ease about the comfort of those I left behind, I should leave the world without much regret, having passed a very happy life, and enjoyed (as much, perhaps, as ever man did yet) all that is enjoyable in it; the only single thing I have had to complain of being want of money. I could therefore die with the same words that Jortin died, 'I have had enough of everything.' "

17th Nov., 1831.—"Left Rogers's with Campbell, who told me, as we walked along, the friendly service which Rogers had just done him by consenting to advance £500; which Campbell wants at this moment to purchase a share in the new (Metropolitan) magazine of which he is editor, the opportunity, if let slip now, being wholly lost to him. Campbell had offered as security an estate, worth between four and five thousand pounds, which he has in Scotland, but Rogers had very generously said that he did not want security; Campbell, however, was resolved to give it. These are noble things of Rogers, and he does more of such things than the world has any notion of."

To this entry in Moore's diary Lord John Russell appends the following foot-note:—"Not only more than the world has any notion of, but more than any one else could have done. Being himself an author, he was able to guess the difficulties of men of letters, and to assist them, not only with his ready purse, but with his powerful influence and his judicious advice." In this particular instance, however, Campbell afterwards found that the speculation would not be to his advantage, and returned the money.

Nov. 3d–9th, 1831.—"Saw my 'Lord Edward' announced as one of the articles in the *Quarterly*—to be abused, of course; and this, so immediately after my dinings and junketings with both editor and publisher!

Having occasion to write to Murray, sent him the following squib:—

THOUGHTS ON EDITORS.

EDITUR ET EDIT.

No, editors don't care a button
    What false and faithless things they do;
They'll let you come and cut their mutton,
    And then they'll have a cut at you.

With Barnes I oft my dinner took,
    Nay, met even Horace Twiss to please him;
Yet Mr. Barnes traduced my book,
    For which may his own devils seize him!

With Doctor Bowring I drank tea,
    Nor of his cakes consumed a particle;
And yet th' ungrateful LL.D.
    Let fly at me next week an article.

John Wilson gave me suppers hot,
    With bards of fame like Hogg and Packwood,
A dose of black strap then I got,
    And after a still worse of *Blackwood.*

Alas! and must I close the list
    With thee, my Lockhart, of the *Quarterly,*
So kind, with bumper in thy fist,—
    With pen, so *very* gruff and tartarly.

Now in thy parlour feasting me,
    Now scribbling at me from thy garret,—
Till, 'twixt the two, in doubt I be
    Which sourest is, thy wit or claret."

27th March, 1832.—"Breakfasted at Rogers'. Proctor told of Charles Lamb saying to ——, in his odd, stammering way, on ——'s making some remark, 'Johnson has said worse things than that;' then, after a short pause, 'and *better.'*

"Barnes at Longman's told a similar saying of his—
'You have no mock modesty about *you*, nor real either.'"

30th March, 1832.—"Van Buren, the American am-
bassador said, 'If there is anything which rank and
station cannot do in England, I have not found it out.'
He then added (what struck me a good deal, both as
coming from a republican and as agreeing perfectly with
my own opinion), 'But still I must say that rank and
station in England deserves (as far as *society* goes) the
value set upon it; for I have found that the higher one
rises in the atmosphere the purer the tone of society is.'
Told him how much this coincided with the whole of my
own experience; I was glad to be backed in my opinion
by such an authority as his, coming, as he did, free from
all our little prepossessions and ambitions, and being in
this respect so much more qualified to form an impartial
judgment.   He expressed, at the same time, strong dis-
gust at the perpetual struggle, towards this higher region,
that was visible in those below it; all trying to get above
their own sphere, and sacrificing comfort and temper in
the ineffectual effort.   I agreed with him, and said it was
like the exercise of the tread-mill; perpetual climbing
without ever mounting.   It was, indeed, the absence of
this sort of ambitious effort that gave the upper classes
so much more repose of manner, and made them, accordingly, so much better company."

Moore was repeatedly and earnestly urged to stand as
a member for Parliament.   The people of Limerick even
pledged themselves to purchase and present him with an
estate, worth about £400 a year, if he would comply with
their requisition.   O'Connell used his influence in the
same direction, and deputations waited upon him, but all
to no purpose.   Moore stated his reasons for declining
the intended honour in the following sensible and manly

letter, of which William Curran wrote, "I join most heartily with you in your admiration of Moore's address. It breathes the dignity of the bard, and the spirit of the gentleman, the latter rather a novelty of late here."

"Sloperton Cottage, Nov. 8th, 1832.

"Gentlemen,—I have to acknowledge, with every feeling of respect and gratitude, the requisition so numerously signed which I have this day had the honour of receiving from you. Already had I been in a great degree prepared for such a call by a correspondence in which I have been engaged by one of your fellow-citizens, and which, though but preliminary to the decisive step which has now been taken, had put me fully in possession of the kind feelings entertained towards me by the greater portion of the enlightened electors of your city.

"To know that even a thought of selecting me as their representative had once entered into the contemplation of persons like yourselves, so well qualified by a zealous sense of the value of liberty to judge of the requisites of those to whom such a trust should be confided, would in itself have been a source of pride and gratification to my mind; you may judge, therefore, what are my feelings on receiving so signal a proof, both in the cordial and unsought requisition which has this morning reached me, and in those further proceedings which I understand you meditate, that the honour you did me in selecting my name from among the many offered to you was no light or transient compliment, but that you deliberately think me worthy of being the representative of your interests in the great crisis, as well for England as for Ireland, which is now approaching.

"But, gentlemen, rarely in this life can so high and bright a position as that in which your offer now places me be enjoyed without its opposing shadow; and in proportion to the pleasure, the triumph, which I cannot but feel at this manifestation of your opinion,—placing, as it does, within my reach a post of honour which I have so often in the ambition of my young days sighed for,—in proportion to my deep and thorough sense of the distinction you would thus confer upon me, is the pain with which I am compelled reluctantly to declare that I cannot accept it. The truth, plainly told, is, that my circumstances render such an appropriation of my time impossible: not even for a single session could I devote myself to the duties of Parliament without incurring considerable embarrassment. To the labour of the day, in short, am I indebted for my daily support; and though it is by being content with this lot that I have been able to preserve that independence of mind which has now so honourably and, I may be allowed to boast, in so many quarters won for me the confidence of my fellow-countrymen, it is not the less an insuperable impediment to the acceptance of the high honour you offer me.

"I am not unaware, as I have already intimated, that, in your strong and generous desire to remove this only obstacle which you know opposed itself to my compliance with your wishes, you have set on foot a national subscription for the purpose, as you yourselves express it, of providing me with the qualification necessary for a member of the House of Commons. This proof of your earnestness in the cause I feel, both on public and private grounds, most sensibly. But, however honourable I might deem such a gift after the performance of services in Parliament, I see objections to it which to me are insurmountable. Were I obliged to choose which should be my direct paymaster, the Government or the People, I should say without hesitation the People; but I prefer holding on my free course, humble as it is, unpurchased by either; nor shall I the less continue, as far as my limited sphere of action extends, to devote such powers as God has gifted me with, to that cause which has always been uppermost in my heart, which was my first inspiration and shall be my last,—the cause of Irish freedom.—I have the honour to be, gentlemen, your faithful and devoted servant, ˙   THOMAS MOORE."

The following epigram was called forth by the project for making Moore member for Limerick:—

" When Limerick, in idle whim,
    Moore as her member lately courted,
' The boys,' for form's sake, ask'd of him,
    To state what party he supported.

" When, thus, his answer promptly ran
    (Now give the wit his mead of glory),
' I'm of no party, as a man,—
    But as a poet, *am-a-tory.*' "

Gerald, who was one of the deputation from Limerick, thus describes his visit to Sloperton, the previous year, in a letter dated March 31, 1833, and addressed to a fair Quaker friend:—"We drove away until we came to a cottage—a cottage of gentility, with two gateways and pretty grounds about it; and we alighted and knocked at the hall-door; and there was dead silence, and we whispered one another; and my nerves thrilled as the wind rustled in the creeping shrubs that graced the retreat of Moore. . . . The door opened, and a young woman appeared. 'Is Mr. Moore at home?' 'I'll see, sir. What name shall I say, sir?' Well, not to be too particular, we were shown upstairs, where we found the nightingale in his cage; in honester language, and more to the purpose, we found our hero in his study, a table before him covered with books and papers, a drawer half-opened and stuffed with letters, a piano also open at a little distance; and the thief himself, a little man, but full of spirits, with eyes, hands, feet, and frame for ever in motion, looking as if it would be a feat for him to sit for three minutes quiet in his chair. I am no great observer of proportions, but he seemed to me to be a neat-made little fellow, tidily buttoned up, young as fifteen at heart, though with hair that reminded me of 'Alps in the sunset;' not handsome, perhaps, but something in the whole *cut* of him that pleased me; finished as an actor, but without an actor's affectation; easy as a gentleman, but without *some* gentlemen's formality.   In a word, as people say when they find their brains begin to run aground at the fag-end of a magnificent period, we found him a hospitable, warm-hearted Irishman, as pleasant as could be, himself, and disposed to make others so. And is this enough?   And need I tell you the day was spent delightfully, chiefly in listening to his innumerable jests and admirable stories, and beautiful similes—beautiful and original as those he throws into his songs—and anecdotes that would make the Danes laugh? and how we did all we could, I believe, to get him to stand for Limerick; and how we called again the day after, and walked with him about his little garden; and how he told us he always wrote walking; and how we came in again and took luncheon; and how I was near forgetting that it was Friday (which you know I am rather apt to do in pleasant company); and how he walked with us through the fields, and wished us good-bye, and left us to do as well as we could without him?"

At this time he chiefly adhered to prose, and only occasionally wrote verse, in the shape of political squils or satires, for *The Times* or the *Morning Chronicle*, for which service he was paid at the rate of about £400 a year. These biting epigrams derived their point from current events long passed away, and, consequently, many of them seem, comparatively, flat and uninteresting.   Here, however, is a perennial:—

TRANSLATION FROM THE GULL LANGUAGE.

'Twas grav'd on the Stone of Destiny,
In letters four, and letters three;
And ne'er did the King of the Gulls go by
But those awful letters scar'd his eye;

For he knew that a Prophet Voice had said,
" As long as those words by man were read,
The ancient race of the Gulls should ne'er
One hour of peace or plenty share."
But years on years successive flew,
And the letters still more legible grew,—
At top, a T, an H, an E,
And underneath, D. E. B. T.

Some thought them Hebrew,—such as Jews,
More skill'd in Scrip than Scripture, use;
While some surmis'd 'twas an ancient way
Of keeping accounts, (well known in the day
Of the fam'd Didlerius Jeremias,
Who had thereto a wonderful bias,)
And prov'd in books most learnedly boring,
'Twas called the Pon*tick* way of scoring.

Howe'er this be, there never were yet
Seven letters of the alphabet,
That 'twixt them form'd so grim a spell,
Or scar'd a Land of Gulls so well,
As did this awful riddle-me-ree
Of T. H. E. D. E. B. T.

　　　.　　.　　.　　.　　.

Hark !—it is struggling Freedom's cry;
Help, help, ye nations, or I die;
'Tis freedom's fight, and, on the field
Where I expire, *your* doom is seal'd."
The Gull-King hears the awakening call,
He hath summon'd his Peers and Patriots all,
And he asks, "Ye noble Gulls, shall we
Stand basely by at the fall of the Free,
Nor utter a curse, nor deal a blow?"
And they answer, with voice of thunder, " No."

Out fly their flashing swords in the air!—
But,—why do they rest suspended there?
What sudden blight, what baleful charm,
Hath chill'd each eye, and check'd each arm?

Alas! some withering hand hath thrown
The veil from off that fatal stone,
And pointing now, with sapless finger,
Showeth where dark those letters linger,—
Letters four, and letters three,
T. H. E.   D. E. B. T.

At sight thereof, each lifted brand
Powerless falls from every hand;
In vain the Patriot knits his brow,–
Even talk, his staple, fails him now.
In vain the King like a hero treads,
His Lords of the Treasury shake their heads;
And to all his talk of "brave and free,"
No answer getteth His Majesty
But "T. H. E.   D. E. B. T."

In short, the whole Gull nation feels
They're fairly spell-bound, neck and heels;
And so, in the face of the laughing world,
Must e'en sit down, with banners furl'd,
Adjourning all their dreams sublime
Of glory and war to—some other time.

In 1833 followed *Travels of an Irish Gentleman in
Search of a Religion,* a perfectly serious and earnest book,
in defence of the Roman Catholic system.   These imagi-
nary travels were published anonymously, but were always
known to have been written by Moore.   The poetical translations from the fathers, such as the renderings from the
homilies of St. Basil and St. Chrysostom, instead of being
grave and severe in style, as one might expect, read very
much as if they might have appeared in the *Loves of the
Angels.*   Of the work it has been said:—"There is a vast
amount of erudition displayed in its pages; and, remem-
bering how slow and painstaking a workman Moore
declared himself to be, it must, one would suppose, have
been the work of years.   The author's object is to prove,

from the writings of the early fathers and other evidence, that the peculiar dogmas and discipline and practice of the Church of Rome date from the apostolic age, or at least from the first centuries of the Christian era, and are consequently true. This the writer does, at least, entirely to his own satisfaction; which is generally the case, we believe, with controversial writers. The book concludes with the following words, addressed to the Catholic Church, which his after-life proves to have been earnest and sincere:—'In the shadow of thy sacred mysteries let my soul henceforth repose, remote alike from the infidel who scoffs at their darkness, and the rash believer who would pry into its recesses.' "

His journal at this period is enlivened by the following entries:—

6th Feb. 1833 (at Bowood).—"Talking of the bread they were now about to make from sawdust, Sydney said, people would soon have *sprigs* coming out of them. Young ladies, in dressing for a ball, would say, 'Mamma, I'm beginning to sprout.'"

6th Feby., 1833.—"On Fontenelle saying that he flattered himself that he had a good heart, some one replied, 'Yes, my dear Fontenelle, you have as good a heart as can be made out of brains.'"

13th Mar. 1833.—(Moore says of Sydney Smith):— "Sydney is, in his way, inimitable; and, as a conversational wit, beats all the men I have ever met. Curran's fancy went much higher, but also much *lower*. Sydney, in his gayest flights, though boisterous, is never vulgar."

31st March, 1833. (Dining at Lansdowne House.)— "Luttrell mentioned rather an amusing quaintness he had read somewhere lately. In speaking of some young man just come of age, it was said, 'he had nothing to do, and a great deal of money to do it *with*.'"

26th May, 1833.—(Sir Robert Peel characterized Moore as) "one who has done honour to the literature of his country by his genius, and has upheld its character by a high spirit of integrity and independence."

14th Nov. 1833.—(Dining at Longmans',) "Sydney Smith, in talking of the fun he had had in the early times of the *Edinburgh Review*, mentioned an article on Ritson, which he and Brougham had written together; and one instance of their joint contribution which he gave me was as follows:—'We take for granted' (wrote Brougham), 'that Mr. Ritson supposes Providence to have had some share in producing him—though for what inscrutable purposes (added Sydney) we profess ourselves unable to conjecture.'"

20th April, 1834.—"A beautiful present from Mr. Costello, of a cup formed out of the calabash-nut, which he brought some years ago for me from Bermuda; taken from the tree which is there shown as one I used to sit under, while writing my poems. The cup very handsomely and tastefully mounted, and Bessy all delight about it."

June 12, 1834.—Brabant "mentioned in the course of our conversation that Sir Astley Cooper had in *one* year made £24,000."

12th Aug., 1834.—"Went (from Miss Costello's) to the Hollands, where I found a scene that would rather have alarmed, I think, a Tory of the full-dress school. There was the Chancellor in his black frockcoat, black cravat; while upon the sofa lay stretched the Prime Minister, also in frock and boots, and with his legs cocked up on one of Lady Holland's fine chairs. Beside him sat Lord Holland, and at some distance from this group was my Lady herself, seated at a table with Talleyrand, and occupying him in conversation to divert his attention from the ministerial confab at the sofa. Joined these two, being the first time that I was ever regularly introduced to Talleyrand."

Sept. 16, 1834.—Sydney Smith, "talking of the bad effects of late hours, and saying of some distinguished diner-out, that there would be on his tomb 'He dined late'—'and died early,' rejoined Luttrell."

In the middle of Dec., 1834, Moore was saddened by the death of his sister Kate.

The *History of Ireland* (4 vols. 12mo) appeared in 1835, and was written for Lardner's *Cabinet Cyclopedia.* It embraced a long period, from the earliest king to the latest chief. It is admitted to be a very important work, and, of its kind, is thought to be his best. It is certainly an interesting and careful production, though by no means an impartial one.

In 1835 he published *The Fudges in England,* a volume of humorous sallies, the wit, polish, and sparkle of which are decidedly better of their kind, than the sentimental songs which he still occasionally wrote. From this volume we quote the following "Letter:"—

FROM LARRY O'BRANIGAN, IN ENGLAND, TO HIS WIFE JUDY, AT MULLINAFAD.

Dear Judy, I sind you this bit of a letther,
By mail-coach conveyance—for want of a betther—
To tell you what luck in this world I have had
Since I left the sweet cabin, at Mullinafad.
Och, Judy, that night!—when the pig which we meant
To dry-nurse, in the parlour, to pay off the rent,
Julianna, the craythur—that name was the death of her[1]—

[1] The Irish peasantry are very fond of giving fine names to their pigs. I have heard of one instance in which a couple of young pigs were named, at their birth, Abelard and Heloise. In Scotland, a farmer, near Dumfries, called a pig "Maud," because it always acted as if it had received an invitation to "come into the garden!"

14

Gave us the shlip and we saw the last breath of her!
And *there* were the childher, six innocent sowls,
For their nate little play-fellow tuning up howls;
While yourself, my dear Judy (though grievin's a folly),
Stud over Julianna's remains, melancholy—
Cryin', half for the craythur, and half for the money,
"Arrah, why did ye die till we'd sowl'd you, my honey?"

But God's will be done!—and then, faith, sure enough,
As the pig was desaiced, 'twas high time to be off.
So we gother'd up all the poor duds we could catch,
Lock'd the owld cabin-door, put the kay in the thatch,
Then tuk laave of each other's sweet lips in the dark,
And set off, like the Christians turn'd out of the Ark;
The six childher with you, my dear Judy, ochone!
And poor I wid myself, left condolin' alone.

How I came to this England, o'er say and o'er lands,
And what cruel hard walkin' I've had on my hands,
Is, at this present writin', too tadious to speak,
So I'll mintion it all in a postscript, next week:—
Only starv'd I was, surely, as thin as a lath,
Till I came to an up-and-down place they call Bath,
Where, as luck was, I manag'd to make a meal's meat,
By dhraggin owld ladies all day through the street—
Which their docthors (who pocket, like fun, the pound
        starlins,)
Have brought into fashion to plase the owld darlins.
Div'l a boy in all Bath, though *I* say it, could carry
The grannies up hill half so handy as Larry;
And the higher they liv'd, like owld crows, in the air,
The more *I* was wanted to lug them up there.

But luck has two handles, dear Judy, they say,
And mine has *both* handles put on the wrong way.
For, pondherin', one morn, on a drame I'd just had
Of yourself and the babbies, at Mullinafad,
Och, there came o'er my sinses so plasin' a flutther,
That I spilt an owld Countess right clane in the gutther,

Muff, feathers and all!—the descint was most awful,
And—what was still worse, faith—I knew 'twas unlawful:
For, though, with mere *women*, no very great evil,
T' upset an owld *Countess* in Bath is the divil!
So, liftin' the chair, with herself safe upon it,
(For nothin' about her was *kilt*, but her bonnet,)
Without even mentionin' "By your lave, ma'am,"
I tuk to my heels and—here, Judy, I am!

What's the name of this town I can't say very well,
But you're heart sure will jump when you hear what befell
Your own beautiful Larry, the very first day,
(And a Sunday it was, shinin' out mighty gay,)
When his brogues to this city of luck found their way.
Bein' hungry, God help me, and happenin to stop,
Just to dine on the shmell of a pasthry-cook's shop,
I saw, in the window, a large printed paper,
And read there a name, och! that made my heart caper—
Though printed it was in some quare A B C,
That might bother a schoolmasther, let alone *me*.
By gor, you'd have laugh'd, Judy, could you've but listen'd,
As, doubtin', I cried, "Why it *is!*—no, it *isn't:*"

But it *was*, after all—for, by spellin' quite slow,
First I made out "Rev. Mortimer"—then a great "O;"
And, at last, by hard readin' and rackin' my skull again,
Out it came, nate as imported, "O'Mulligan!"

Up I jump'd, like a sky-lark, my jewel, at that name,—
Div'l a doubt on my mind, but it *must* be the same.
"Masther Murthagh, himself," says I, "all the world over!
My own fosther-brother—by jinks, I'm in clover.
Though *there*, in the play-bill, he figures so grand,
One wet-nurse it was brought us *both* up by hand,
And he'll not let me shtarve in the inemy's land!"

Well, to make a long hishtory short, niver doubt
But I manag'd, in no time, to find the lad out;
And the joy of the meetin' bethuxt him and me,
Such a pair of owld cumrogues—was charmin' to see.

Nor is Murthagh less plas'd with th' evint than *I* am,
As he just then was wanting a Valley-de-sham;
And, for *dressin'* a gintleman, one way or t'other,
Your nate Irish lad is beyant every other.

But now, Judy, comes the quare part of the case;
And, in throth, it's the only drawback on my place,
'Twas Murthagh's ill luck to be cross'd, as you know,
With an awkward mishfortune some short time ago;
That's to say, he turn'd Protestant—*why*, I can't larn;
But, of coorse, he knew best, an' it's not *my* consarn.
All I know is, we both were good Cath'lics, at nurse,
And myself am so still—nather betther nor worse.
Well, our bargain was all right and tight in a jiffey,
And lads more contint never yet left the Liffey,
When Murthagh—or Mortimer, as he's *now* christen'd,
His *name* being convarted, at laist, if *he* isn't—
Lookin' sly at me (faith, 'twas divartin' to see)
" *Of coorse*, you're a Protestant, Larry," says he.
Upon which says myself, wid a wink just as shly,
" Is't a Protestant?—oh yes, *I am*, sir, says I;—
And there the chat ended, and div'l a more word
Controvarsial between us has since then occurr'd.

What Murthagh could mane, and, in troth, Judy dear,
What *I myself* meant, doesn't seem mighty clear;
But the thruth is, though still for the Owld Light a stickler,
I was just then too shtarv'd to be over partic'lar:—
And, God knows, between us, a comic'ler pair
Of twin Protestants couldn't be seen *any* where.

Next Tuesday (as towld in the play-bills I mintion'd,
Address'd to the loyal and godly intintion'd,)
His rivirence, my master, comes forward to preach,—
Myself doesn't know whether sarmon or speech,
But it's all one to him, he's a dead hand at each;
Like us, Paddys, in gin'ral, whose skill in orations
Quite bothers the blarney of all other nations.

But, whisht!—there's his Rivirence, shoutin' out "Larry,"
And sorra a word more will this small paper carry;
So, here, Judy, ends my short bit of a letther,
Which, faix, I'd have made a much bigger and betther,
But div'l a one Post-office hole in this town
Fit to swallow a dacent siz'd billy-dux down.
So good luck to the childer!—tell Molly, I love her;
Kiss Oonagh's sweet mouth, and kiss Katty all over—
Not forgettin' the mark of the red currant whiskey
She got at the fair when yourself was so frisky.
The heavens be your bed!—I will write, when I can again,
Yours to the world's end,

LARRY O'BRANIGAN.

To revert to his DIARY—

20th Feby., 1835.—At Rogers' met Wordsworth, who "spoke of the immense time it took him to write even the shortest copy of verses,—sometimes whole weeks employed in shaping two or three lines, before he can satisfy himself with their structure. Attributed much of this to the unmanageableness of the English as a poetical language: contrasted it with the Italian in this respect, and repeated a stanza of Tasso to show how naturally the words fell into music of themselves. . . . Thought, however, that, on the whole, there were advantages in having a rugged language to deal with; as in struggling with words one was led to give birth to and dwell upon thoughts, while, on the contrary, an easy and mellifluous language was apt to tempt, by its facility, into negligence, and to lead the poet to substitute music for thought."

28th March, 1835.—Breakfasted in the morning at Rogers', to meet the new poet, Mr. Taylor (Sir Henry Taylor), the author of *Van Artevelde:* our company, besides, being Sydney Smith and Southey. Van Arte-velde, a tall, handsome young fellow. Conversation

chiefly about the profits booksellers make of us scribblers.
I remember Peter Pindar saying, one of the few times I
ever met him, that the booksellers drank their wine in
the manner of the heroes in the Hall of Odin, 'out of
authors' skulls.'"

13th Aug. 1835 (in Dublin).—"Drove about a little
in Mrs. Meara's car, accompanied by Hume, and put in
practice what I had long been contemplating—a visit to
No. 12 Aungier Street, the house in which I was born.
On accosting the man who stood at the door, and asking
whether he was the owner of the house, he looked
rather gruffly and suspiciously at me, and answered 'Yes;'
but the moment I mentioned who I was, adding that
it was the house I was born in, and that I wished to be
permitted to look through the rooms, his countenance
brightened up with the most cordial feeling, and seizing
me by the hand he pulled me along to the small room
behind the shop (where we used to breakfast in old times),
exclaiming to his wife (who was sitting there), 'Here
Sir Thomas Moore, who was born in this house, come to
ask us to let him see the rooms; and it's proud I am
to have him under the old roof.' He then, without
delay, and entering at once into my feelings, led me
through every part of the house, beginning with the
small old yard and its appurtenances, then the little dark
kitchen where I used to have my bread and milk in the
morning before I went to school; from thence to the
front and back drawing-rooms, the former looking more
large and respectable than I could have expected, and
the latter, with its little closet, where I remember such
gay supper-parties, both room and closet fuller than
they could well hold, and Joe Kelly and Wesley Doyle
singing away together so sweetly. The bed-rooms and
garrets were next visited, and the only material alteration

I observed in them was the removal of the wooden partition by which a little corner was separated off from the back bed-room (in which the two apprentices slept) to form a bed-room for me. The many thoughts that came rushing upon me in thus visiting, for the first time since our family left it, the house in which I passed the first nineteen or twenty years of my life, may be more easily conceived than told; and I must say, that if a man had been got up specially to conduct me through such a scene, it could not have been done with more tact, sympathy, and intelligent feeling than it was by this plain, honest grocer; for, as I remarked to Hume as we entered the shop, 'only think, a grocer's still.' When we returned to the drawing-room, there was the wife with a decanter of port, and glasses on the table, begging us to take some refreshment, and I with great pleasure drank her and her good husband's health. When I say that the shop is still a grocer's, I must add, for the honour of old times, that it has a good deal gone down in the world since then, and is of a much inferior grade of grocery to that of my poor father, who, by the way, was himself one of nature's gentlemen, having all the repose and good breeding of manner by which the true gentleman in all classes is distinguished.

"Went, with all my recollections of the old shop about me, to the grand dinner at the Park."

On this visit to Ireland, in Aug., 1835, Moore received quite an ovation—a right royal reception from all classes of the community — from the Lord Lieutenant downwards.

This year (1835), during Lord Melbourne's administration, a pension of £300 a year was bestowed upon him for his literary merits.

Lord Lansdowne, in communicating the fact to Moore

on August 22d, kindly wrote—that, although regretting the smallness of the sum at their disposal, the pension only represented merit, and was "due from any government, but much more from one, some of the members of which are proud to think themselves your friends."

Moore scribbled a few lines to his sweet Bessy to inform her of this good news. She wrote in reply:—

"Sloperton, Tuesday Night.

"My dearest Tom,—Can it *really* be true that you have a pension of £300 a year? Mrs., Mr., two Misses, and young Lougman were here to-day, and tell me it is really the case, and that they have seen it in two papers. Should it turn out true, I know not how we can be thankful enough to those who gave it, or to a Higher Power. . . . If the story is true of the £300, pray give dear Ellen twenty pounds, and insist on her drinking five pounds worth of wine *yearly*, to be paid out of the £300 a year. . . . Three hundred a year—how delightful! But I have my fears that it is only a castle in the air. I am sure I shall dream of it; and so I will get to bed, that I may have this pleasure *at least;* for I expect the morning will throw down my castle."

"Wednesday Morning.

"Is it true? I am in a fever of hope and anxiety, and feel very oddly. No one to talk to but sweet Buss, who says, 'Now Papa will not have to work so hard, and will be able to go out a little.' . . .

"*N.B.*—If this good news be true, it will make a great difference in my *eating*. I shall then indulge in butter to potatoes. *Mind* you do not tell this piece of gluttony to any one."

The following discriminating passage on Moore's politics, we transcribe, from *Chambers' Papers for the People*, as it very nearly hits the mark:—

"Turning from Moore the poet to Moore the politician, there is not much to remark upon ; neither certainly is there place for two opinions. Moore wrote politics at times—pointed, bitter, rankling politics—but he was really at heart no politician. There was no earnestness in what he did in this way, and it was early and abundantly evident from his alternate eulogies and vituperation of democratic institutions, that he had no firmly-based convictions. His love for Ireland was a sentiment only: it never rose to the dignity of a passion. Not one of his patriotic songs breathes the fiery energy, the martyr zeal, the heroic hate and love, which pulsate in the veins of men who ardently sympathize with a people really oppressed, or presumed to be so.

" But let us hasten to say, that if there was little of the hero or martyr, there was nothing of the renegade or traitor about Thomas Moore.

" The pension of three hundred a year obtained for him of the crown by his influential friends was not the reward of baseness or of political tergiversation. It was the prize and reward of his eminence as a writer, and his varied social accomplishments. If he did not feel strongly, he at all events felt honestly; and although he had no mission to evoke the lightning of the national spirit, and hurl its consuming fire at the men who, had they possessed the power, would have riveted the bondage of his people, he could and did soothe their angry paroxysms with lulling words of praise and hope, and, transforming their terribly real, physical, and moral griefs and ills into picturesque and sentimental sorrows, awakened a languid admiration, and a passing sympathy for a nation which could boast such beautiful music, and whose woes were so agreeably, so charmingly sung.

" Liberal opinions, Moore supported by tongue and pen, but then they were fashionable within a sufficiently-extensive circle of notabilities, and had nothing of the coarseness and downrightness of vulgar Radicalism about them. The political idiosyncrasy of Moore is developed in the same essential aspect in his memoir of Lord Edward Fitzgerald as in his national songs. There is nothing impassioned, nothing which hurries the pulse or kindles the eye—but a graceful regret, a carefully-guarded appreciation of the acts and motives of that unfortunate and misguided nobleman run throughout. Moore was what men call a fair-weather politician—which means, not that storms do not frequently surround them, but that by a prudent forethought, a happy avoidance of prematurely committing themselves, they contrive to make fair weather for themselves, however dark and tempestuous may be the time to other and less sagacious men, and who, when their sun does at last shine, come out with extreme effulgence and brilliancy.

"Moore, therefore, as a politician, was quite unexceptionable, though not eminent. He was at once a pensioned and unpurchased, and, we verily believe, unpurchasable partisan; an honest, sincere, and very mild patriot; a faithful, and at the same time prudent and circumspect lover of his country, its people, and its faith. There are very high-sounding names in the list of political celebrities, of whom it would be well if such real, though not highly-flattering, praise could be truly spoken."

He wrote little else, after this period, beyond an occasional trifle in verse for the periodicals, and the prefaces, with a few additions, to a collected edition of his poetical works, issued by the Longmans (1840–42) in ten volumes. In these *Prefaces*, Moore sometimes assigns erroneous dates to events or poems—for example, to the poem written on the fete at *Boyle Farm*. His memory, alas! was failing. Such slips, on his part, quite explain and account for the pardonable mistakes which are frequently to be met with in many biographical notices of the poet.

The remaining years of his life may be partially bridged, by the following selection of interesting passages from his DIARY:—

April 7, 1837.—"Rogers very agreeable. Mentioned, the Duke of Wellington saying to some enthusiastic woman who was talking in raptures about 'glories of a

victory,' 'I should so like to witness a victory!' &c. &c.,
'My dear Madame, a victory is the greatest tragedy in
the world except one—and that is a defeat.'"

This humane feeling, fostered by experience, accords
with an entry, made eight years before, relating to the
duke, and which was as follows:—"Murray mentioned
that he heard yesterday Dr. Hume describe circumstances
connected with the Duke of Wellington after the battle
of Waterloo; his going to bed, covered with dust as he
was, having stript himself, and lying then on his back,
talking to Hume of the friends he had lost that day.
There is such a one gone, and such a one; and then,
'There is poor Ponsonby. I have some hopes that his
body will be found, and have despatched an orderly to
search for it.' He then, Hume said, burst into tears as
he lay, and said, 'I have never lost a battle, but to win
one, thus, is paying hard for it.'"

12th April, 1837.—(Of the Duke of Wellington's despatches, then recently published, Moore writes):—"Those
most interesting despatches—full of traits of thoughtful-
ness, modesty, consideration for others, patience under
misrepresentation, and all, in short (combined with the
vast things he was then accomplishing and preparing),
that goes to make the character of a great man, as well
as of a great and fortunate soldier."

27th April, 1837.—(Shiel related of the Irish barrister
Keller, who was Moore's godfather, that), "To some
judge, an old friend of Keller's, a steady, solemn fellow,
who had succeeded as much in his profession as Keller
had failed, he said one day, 'In opposition to all the laws
of natural philosophy, you have *risen* by your *gravity*,
while I have *sunk* by my *levity*.'"

22d Nov., 1837.—"Read a story of Lover's for the
party in the evening."

The following letter, addressed to Thomas Longman, jun., shows Moore's accurate estimate of his own work:—

"Nov. 23, 1837.

"Dear Tom,—With respect to what you say about *Lalla Rookh* being the 'cream of copyrights,' perhaps it may, in a *property* sense; but I am strongly inclined to think, that, in a race into future times (if anything of mine could pretend to such a run), those little ponies, the *Melodies*, will beat the mare *Lalla*, hollow. As to the other things being 'unproductive,' why, it is to *make* them productive that the edition is contemplated. What have *Madoc, Joan of Arc*, &c., been *producing* all this time?—Yours, my dear Tom, very truly, THOMAS MOORE."

On 10th March, 1838, "met Mr. Luttrell at breakfast, at Mr. Rogers'. Talked of Irishmen's unwillingness to pay ready money, their notions of the *ready* being always a bill at sixty-one days' date. Somebody saying that one would think every Irishman was born sixty-one days too late, from their being always that space of time behind the rest of the world; and Luttrell described the process of purchasing a horse between one Irish gentleman and another: Price sixty pounds, for which you have no occasion to pay down cash—*only commit your thoughts to paper.'*"

19th May, 1838.—"Breakfasted with Rogers. Story of the lady who wrote to Talleyrand informing him, in high-flown terms of grief, of the death of her husband, and expecting an eloquent letter of condolence in return; his answer only, 'Hélas, Madame, votre affectioné, &c., Talleyrand.' In less than a year another letter from the same lady informed him of her having married again; to which he returned an answer in the same laconic style:— 'Oh, oh, Madame! Votre affectioné, &c., Talleyrand.'"

21st Nov., 1838.—"Dined at Bentley's. The company all the very *haut ton* of the literature of the day—Jerdan,

Ainsworth, Lover, Luttrell, Dickens, Barham, Moran, and Campbell."

16th June, 1839.—"Rogers, alluding to Moore's numerous engagements, said that, whenever he is asked 'Where Mr. Moore is?' he always answers, 'He is at this moment in three different places.'"

19th Feby., 1840.—When arranging to place his son Tom at the university, he was told by one of the authorities that the exhibition coming to him from the Charter House would be, on an average, about £100 a year, and it was coolly added, "To that you would have to give him, from yourself, only £150 a year." "That," remarks Moore, "is the *half* of the *only* income (my pension) that ever I possess without working hard for it; ay, and sharing my earnings all the time with almost everybody related to me. If I had thought but of 'living like a *gentleman*' (as those colonels and tutors style it), what would have become of my dear father and mother, of my sweet sister Nell, of my admirable Bessy's mother?"

Aug. 2, 1840 (in London). . . . "In passing through Brompton, showed them the house which Bessy and I occupied on our marriage, and where, at a breakfast we gave a few months after, I introduced her to Lady Donegall, Miss Godfrey, Rogers, Corry, and one or two other very old friends."

From entries, July 1-6, 1841, we find his son Tom drawing bills on him, one for £112, and within a week another for £100. He accepted them, but did not know how they were to be met. Moore's memory, from this time (1842), exhibits more frequent signs of decay, and his diary is painfully marked with the difficulties and distress which were brought upon him by the thoughtlessness of one son, and the premature decay of the other.

12th Nov., 1841.—"A note from Sydney Smith asking

me to breakfast with him to-morrow: 'Dear Moore,—I
have a breakfast of philosophers to-morrow at ten *punc-
tually.* Muffins and metaphysics; crumpets and contradic-
tion. Will you come?' Wrote him an excuse, telling
him of my engagement at the State Paper Office, and
saying that, though his breakfast would be very agreeable,
it would 'take a large slice of a reign out of me.' "

19th Nov., 1841 (An ominous entry).—"After returning from the State Paper Office yesterday I was seized
with a giddiness, during which the room seemed to turn
round with me. The cause of this, I have no doubt, is
my having kept my head down over those papers for so
many successive days, and so many hours each day. This
morning, however, I held the paper in my hand and sat
upright."

Troubles gathered around him; and tidings reached
him that, " In the indulgence of careless habits, young
Thomas Moore got into debt; and that in a thoughtless
moment he had resolved to sell his commission."

11th and 12th Jany., 1842.—" To say nothing of the
anxiety and grief caused by it, how on earth am I to
meet the additional expenses which the return of both
boys will now entail, while still I am in debt, too, for
most of the money which their first outfit, passage, &c.,
required? I am still willing, and, thank God, able to
work; but the power comes slower, and the effort is
therefore more wearing."

On 18th March, 1842, we have another melancholy
symptomatic entry: "Dined at Mrs. Cunliffe's. Company
large enough, but (strange to say) quite a blank in my
memory; whether through *their* fault or *mine*, I know
not. I have heard of a '*tabula rasa*,' but a whole dinner
table thus suddenly erased from one's memory is a new
phenomenon."

March 12, 1842.—(On Hume kindly accommodating him and enabling him to provide for a bill drawn on him by his son Russell, Moore makes the following entry): "Was delighted to have to tell my dear Bessy that all had been arranged so comfortably. Couldn't help ruminating a little on the essential difference there is between useful and merely ornamental friends. But one mustn't grumble; both are good in their different ways."

13th March, 1842.—"Breakfasted with Rogers. Company Everett (the American minister), Lord Mahon, Milnes, Luttrell, &c. &c. Talking of Lady Holland's crowded dinners, and her bidding people constantly 'to make room,' Luttrell said, 'It must certainly be *made*, for it does not exist.' . . . Rogers' theory is that the close packing of Lady Holland's dinners is one of the secrets of their conversableness and agreeableness, and perhaps he is right."

The following announcement of an honour conferred upon Moore by the King of Prussia appeared in the *Prussian State Gazette*:—"Berlin, June 1, 1842. His Majesty has been pleased to found a special class of the order '*pour le mérite*,' to be conferred on persons who have distinguished themselves in the sciences and arts. The numbers of the members of the German nation is fixed at thirty. To enhance the splendour of the order it will also be conferred on eminent foreigners, the number of whom is not fixed, but is never to exceed that of the German members. Among the foreign members in the class of science (including, it seems, Belles Lettres) are Michael Faraday, Sir John Herschel, members of the Royal Society of London, and Mr. Thomas Moore."

An odd anecdote illustrative of Moore's increasing and widely-spread fame may here be given. He was surprised one day at receiving from Sweden an offer to be elected a knight of the ancient Order of St. Joachim. This distinction, it was announced in the missive, which purported to come from the chancellor of the order, was tendered as a mark of the admiration entertained by the honourable fraternity for his very charming poetry. Moore was puzzled—mystified. He had never before heard of the Order of St. Joachim, and vehemently suspected some kind friend of seeking to play him a malicious trick. St. Joachim! Might it not turn out to be St. Joke'm? He, however, stealthily inquired amongst persons versed in knightly orders, and was informed that there really was a Swedish knighthood of the name mentioned, and that several presentable persons had belonged to it. Still, after due deliberation, he resolved to decline the generously-proffered honour. It was too hazardous. Sir Joke'm Moore! He was a man to face the battery of a three-decker cheerfully rather than risk the possibility of such a sobriquet as that!

On June 5, 1843, he could not remember where he had promised to dine. In the exigence, he recollected that Rogers told him he was to dine at home and alone, so sauntered down to St. James Place, about a quarter past seven. Just as he was passing Burdett's, Mrs. Otway Cave's carriage stopped at the door, and, as he recognized and handed her out, she asked, "Where are you going?" "To dine with Rogers," said Moore; "if he is at home." "You had better far stop here," she replied, "for I see dinner is on the table." So Moore turned in with her and found himself most heartily welcomed, there being but one other guest, an old acquaintance of his own. From the Burdetts he went by appointment to join the Russells; and, after that, to the Polish Fancy Ball—not reaching home till between two and three in the morning! Under this date we also find the following entry in his DIARY. "Some one mentioned to-day that Charles Napier,[1] in writing to a friend the night before his late victory at Meanee, said, 'If I survive I shall soon be with those I love; if I fall, I shall be with those I *have* loved.'"

Sydney Smith often laughed at Moore for his "occasional absences," and the following letter alludes to them:—

"August 7, 1843.

"Dear Moore,—The following articles have been found in your room and forwarded by the Great Western. A right-hand glove, an odd stocking, a sheet of music paper, a missal, several letters,—apparently from ladies,—an Elegy on Phelim O'Neil. There is also a bottle of eau de Cologne. What a careless mortal you are!—God bless you."

In reply, Moore scribbled off the following droll lines:—

"Rev. Sir,—Having duly received by the post
Your list of the articles missing and lost
By a certain small poet, well known on the road,
Who has lately set up at your flowery abode,
We have balanced what Hume calls ' the tottle o' the whole,'
(Making all due allowance for what the bard stole),
And, hoping th' inclosed will be found quite correct,
Have the honour, Rev. Sir, to be—
                                    Yours with respect.
Left behind, a kid glove that once made a pair,
An odd stocking, whose fellow is—heaven knows where;

    .   .   .   .

Such was all that, on diligent search we can find
Which the bard, so mis-called, in his flight left behind;
While, thief as he is, he took slyly away
Rich treasures to last him for many a day.

---

[1] The late General Sir Charles Napier.

15

Recollections unnumbered of sunny Combe-Florey;
Its cradle of hills, where it slumbers in glory;
Its Sydney himself, and the countless bright things
Which his tongue or his pen from the deep-shining springs
Of wisdom and wit ever flowingly brings.
Such being, on both sides, the 'tottle' amount,
We shall leave to your Rev'rence to settle th' account."

30th and 31st Dec. — On the last day of the year (1843), he wrote:—"A strange life mine; but the best as well as the pleasantest part of it lies *at home*. I told my dear Bessy this morning—that while I stood at my study window looking out at her, as she crossed the field, I sent a blessing after her. 'Thank you, bird,' she replied, 'that's better than money;' and so it is. 'Bird' is a pet name she gave me in our younger days, and was suggested by Hamlet's words, 'Hillo, ho, ho, boy! come, bird, come;' being the call, it seems, which falconers use to their hawk in the air, when they would have him come down to them."

8th to 10th Feb., 1844.—"Have been laid up, all this time, more with the consequences of influenza than that disease itself, the violent coughing having strained me so much that I found it necessary to send for Norman to Bath; at least, my dear Bessy, in her anxiety, thought it necessary, though at an expense of £10, which was the amount of his fee. Such is her noble nature; sparing of all unnecessary expenditure, but on great occasions, whether of use, honest pride, or generosity, ready to the last farthing."

Sept. 10, 1844.—(At Hobhouse's, he found the following scrap, in an old book, and thought it worth preserving):—"There was a Spanish doctor who had a fancy that Spanish, Italian, and French were spoken in Paradise: that God Almighty commanded in Spanish, the Tempter persuaded in Italian, and Adam begged pardon in French."

In July, 1845, he notes a good hit, made in the House of Commons:—" One night, a blustering orator having triumphantly, as he thought, exclaimed, 'I am the guardian of my own honour,' Sir Boyle Roche quietly settled the orator, by saying, 'I wish the honourable gentleman joy on his sinecure appointment.'"

Here is another House of Commons scene, as given by Moore:—

"*Government side.*—'Mr. Speaker, have we laws, or have we *not* laws? If we *have* laws, to what purpose were those laws made, unless they are *obeyed?*'

"*Opposition side.*—'Mr. Speaker, did that gentleman speak to the purpose or *not* to the purpose, and if he did *not* speak to the purpose, to what purpose did he speak?'"

July, 1845.—"One night when John Kemble was performing, at some country theatre, one of his most favourite parts, he was much interrupted, from time to time, by the squalling of a young child in one of the galleries. At length, angered by this rival performance, Kemble walked with solemn step to the front of the stage, and, addressing the audience in his most tragic tones, said, 'Ladies and gentlemen, unless the play is stopped, the child cannot possibly go on.' The effect on the audience of this earnest interference in favour of the child may be easily conceived."

"July, 1845 (Moore writes):—"I don't know where I found the following, but there is a homely sort of philosophy in it that rather takes my fancy:

" 'This world's a good world to live in,
    To lend, and to spend, and to give in;
    But to beg, or to borrow, or ask for one's own,
    'Tis the very worst world that ever was known.'"

Thus, Moore, we have seen, began his literary career when a youth of twenty-one, and was received into the first London society. His fame increased till 1823, and was then at its height, when he published *The Loves of the Angels.* For the next thirty years, "he wrote occasionally; but, adding nothing to his fame, he lived upon the glory of his youth."

CHAPTER XIII.

LATTER YEARS AND DEATH.

Moore's latter years were clouded by domestic grief, his children having all died before him. In 1846 the poet made this sad entry in his diary, "The last of our five children is gone, and we are left desolate and alone; not a single relative have I now left in the world." His father had died in 1825, his mother in 1832, and his sister Nell in 1846; and his children had dropped off one after another,—three of them in youth, and two grown up to manhood. Here, we may, shortly, enumerate them:—

Moore's eldest daughter, Ann Jane Barbara, died in 1817, at the age of five. His second daughter, Anastatia Mary, died in 1829, at the age of nearly seventeen. A third daughter, Ovilia Byron, lived only a few months. John Russell Moore, the second son, died in 1842 at the age of nineteen. He was a cadet in the East India Company's service.

The last surviving of Moore's children was his eldest son, Thomas Lansdowne Parr Moore. He died, as we have seen, in 1846, in his eight-and-twentieth year. He held a commission in India, and breaking down there, through the climate and excesses, he entered the French service in Algiers—got worse, and died of consumption in the hospital of Mostorganem. The wildness of this son, and his melancholy end, told fearfully on the mind and strength of the poet.

On one occasion, long before and already alluded to, when Moore was visiting his mother in Dublin, accompanied by his wife and children, Samuel Lover, who was always a great favourite with the delightful, cheery, old grandmother, was invited to her house on the very day that the interesting party arrived. He was struck by the beauty of the boy Russell, and painted a charming miniature portrait of him as a gift to the child's mother. In it, he caught, with great felicity, the bright expression and great resemblance that the boy bore to his father. In a letter to Mrs. Hall, Lover says:—

"You ask me to give you some description of Russell Moore. You know how hard, or, rather, how impossible it is for words to give any notion of lineaments.

"All children's faces are, to a certain extent, round; but Russell's might have been remarked for roundness, even among children—nose, though *retroussé*, nicely defined about the nostril, a pretty mouth, well marked eyebrows, and dark brown eyes of remarkable beauty, with a certain expression of archness that reminded one of his father—you remember what brilliant and vivacious eyes *his* were,—in short, Russell Moore's face would have been a good model for a painter who wanted a suggestion for a little Cupid."

This picture relates to spring days. Now, with Moore, it was the sere and yellow leaf. Of this period Lord John Russell says:—"The death of his only remaining child, and his last and most beloved sister, deeply affected the health, crushed the spirits, and impaired the mind of Moore. An illness of an alarming nature shook his frame, and for a long time made him incapable of any exertion. When he recovered he was a different man. His memory was perpetually at fault, and nothing seemed to rest on his mind. He made engagements to dinners and parties, but usually forgot half of them. When he did appear, his gay flow of spirits, happy application of humorous stories, and constant and congenial ease were all wanting. The brilliant hues of his varied conversation had failed, and the strong powers of his intellect had manifestly sunk. There was something peculiarly sad in the change. It is not unusual to observe the faculties grow weaker with age; and, in the retirement of a man's own home, there may be 'no unpleasing melancholy' in the task of watching such a decline. But when, in the midst of the gay and the convivial, the wit appeared without his gaiety, and the guest without his conviviality,—when the fine fancy appeared not so much sobered as saddened,—it was a cheerless sight.

"Happily for Moore and his partner they had a certain income, derived from the bounty of the sovereign, which flowed on in a stream, not exuberant indeed, but perpetual. On this income, Mrs. Moore regulated her expenses, and regulated them so as to incur no debts."

Worn down by mental overwork, by the claims of society, and by grief over "faded flowers,"

'When friendships decay,
And, from Love's shining circle, the gems drop away,"

he was now fast breaking up. His memory failed rapidly; he stooped and looked old; and, in 1848—as in the cases of Swift, Scott, and Southey—mental imbecility gradually set in, caused by softening of the brain.

In 1850, Mrs. Moore received a pension of £100 a year, in consideration of her husband's literary services; and no wife ever deserved recognition more than she for *her own* sweet sake. She was in every respect a true and model wife. Moore's loss of memory was in his case, perhaps, a blessing, "bestowing a calm," as William Howitt remarks, "on his closing period, which otherwise could not have existed." Of this period, S. C. Hall writes: —"Two years and two months Moore may be said to have lain on his death-bed—dying all that weary time. His mind became obliterated; restorations to reason being only occasional and very partial. His disease was softening of the brain. Sometimes he knew and recognized his 'Bessy.' During the whole of that sad period, she was never for an hour out of his room. She told us that, when intelligence was at all active, he would ask her to read the Bible, but his great delight was to hear her sing; that his frequent desire was for a hymn, 'Come to Jesus,' in the refrain of which he always joined, and which he often asked her to sing for him a second time. Almost his last words—and they were frequently repeated—were, 'Lean upon God, Bessy; lean upon God!'"

Of Mrs. Moore, Mrs. Hall writes:—"I never knew anyone with such active and genial affections as Moore, except his wife. Her nature was quite as sympathetic as that of her husband; and while her reverence for that husband amounted to devotion, she watched over him as a mother watches over a tender and beloved child. It was the most wonderful blending of admiration, duty, and lovingness I ever witnessed or could fancy. At times, even then, though, as her husband tenderly said, she had wept her eyes away, crying for her children, she looked radiantly beautiful. . . . Imagination, thought, memory were worn out. At last—at last—she knew it; the greatest trial of her sorely tried life had come. Her idol whom she worshipped with perfect enthusiasm—he of whose genius she was so proud, to become what he was—still tender and gentle, but mindless as an infant. She could not bear anyone to see him in that state; day and night, night and day, for months and months, she *alone* ministered to him; at his desire, frequently singing for him scraps of hymns. We can easily imagine how the perpetual watching and waiting preyed on a constitution already enfeebled by sorrows, which it had been her chief care to prevent *his* feeling in their intensity. She was ever at her post. The sick-room was the heart of the house; the life-blood beat there, more and more feebly, but still it beat; and then there was no longer need for watching: the end came—the end here!"

" His last days," says Lord John Russell, " were peaceful and happy; his domestic sorrows, his literary triumphs, seem to have faded away alike into a calm repose. He retained to his last moments a pious submission to God, and a grateful sense of the kindness of her whose tender office it was to watch over his decline." His frame grew weaker and weaker, and he died at Sloperton Cottage, his home for more than thirty years, on the 26th of February, 1852, aged seventy-two years and nine months, and was buried in the churchyard of Bromham, Bedfordshire, within view of his own house, and by the side of two of his children;—the one, his daughter Anastasia Mary, the other, his son John Russell Moore, the god-son of Lord John Russell."

Only two persons from a distance, of all the many with whom he had mingled in the years of his youth and fame, stood by his grave when he was laid to rest—one of them a clergyman and the other one of the Messrs. Longmans, his publishers, who had been, in truth, his life-long and substantial friends.

Of Thomas Moore, Samuel Carter Hall thus writes:— "Let it be inscribed on his tomb, that ever, amid privations and temptations, the allurements of grandeur and the suggestions of poverty, he preserved his self-respect; bequeathing no property, but leaving no debts; having had no testimonial of acknowledgment or reward; seeking none, nay avoiding any; making many his debtors for intense delight, and acknowledging himself paid by 'the poet's meed, the tribute of a smile;' never truckling to power; labouring ardently and honestly for his political faith, but never lending to party that which was meant for mankind; proud, and rightly proud, of his self-obtained position; but neither scorning nor slighting the humble race from which he sprung."

CHAPTER XIV.

MOORE'S MEMOIRS—OPINIONS AS TO HIS CHARACTER—MRS. MOORE.

Lord John Russell generously negotiated, for the publication of Moore's *Memoirs, Journal and Correspondence*, with the Longmans, who brought them out in eight volumes (1852–56) and under Lord John's own editorial supervision, in accordance with the desire of the poet.

The editing was executed without sufficient care. The arrangement of the matter was not satisfactory, and much of it might, according to those well able to judge, have been omitted with advantage. Although set with sparkling gems, it was too long spun out, and was, on the whole, heavy reading; nor did it convey so pleasant an impression of the poet as "Mr. Burke's brighter and briefer biography."

With the £3000 obtained for the work, an annuity was purchased for Mrs. Moore, equal to the whole income which she and her husband had enjoyed during the latter years of his life. The journal embraces the period between 1818 and 1847. From it we have given a sprinkling of quotations, chiefly anecdotes, racy drolleries, or witty sayings. Mrs. Moore survived her husband until 1865, and generously presented the poet's valuable library to the Royal Irish Academy. She died at Sloperton Cottage, on the 4th of September, aged sixty-eight.

It must be admitted, that too much of Moore's time was frittered away amongst the mob of those who were merely titled people. We do not, of course, refer to the Russells, Lansdownes, and Hollands, where, on equal terms with these able men, he also met Byron, Jeffrey, Sydney Smith, Campbell, Rogers, Brougham, and the like.

Moore's life may be summed up as "an untiring pursuit of poetry, prose, and fashionable society." Byron said, "Tommy dearly loved a lord;" and his journals continually evince his vanity in this respect, although it was, essentially, of a very harmless and kindly sort. Besides, most certainly, in Moore's case, it was the aristocracy that courted him; while he ever maintained his thorough independence both of spirit and action, and chiefly valued his titled friends for their own intrinsic, personal worth.

William Howitt, who knew him, also wrote, "It is as useless to wish Moore anything but what he was, as to wish a butterfly a bee, or that a moth should not fly into a candle. It was his nature; and the pleasure of being

caressed, flattered, and admired by titled people must be
purchased at any cost. Neither poverty nor sorrow could
restrain him from this dear enjoyment. We find him at
one moment overwhelmed by some death or distress
amongst his nearest relatives or in the very bosom of his
family. News arrives that a son is ill in a far-off land,
or a daughter is dead at home. In the very next entry
in his diary he has rushed away with his grief into some
fashionable concert, where he sings and breaks down in
tears. . . . He goes into the charmed, glittering ring
to forget his trouble, and leaves poor, desolate Mrs.
Moore solitarily at home to remember it.

"At another time you find him invited to dine with
some great people, but he has not a penny in his pocket;
Bessy, however, has scraped together a pound or two out
of the housekeeping cash, and lets him have it, and he is
off.

"And yet this strange little fairy was a most affection-
ate husband, son, and brother. We find him and his
wife at one time staying at Lord Moira's for a week beyond the time that they should have left, because they
had not money enough to give to the servants. Thus,
night after night, season after season, he is the flattered
and laughing centre of the most brilliant circles of lords
and ladies, while he and his wife, in the daytime, are at
their wits' end to find the means of meeting the demands
of their humble *ménage*. He is joking and carolling like
a lark, while his thoughts are, at every pause, running on
how that confounded bill is to be taken up. All the
time, his wife is sitting solitarily at home pondering on
the same thing, and cannot call on her friends because it
would necessitate the hire of a coach."

In extenuation, it has been said, that Moore wished to
keep himself before the people who could purchase his

expensive quarto volumes, and that Mrs. Moore acquiesced in what was thus for their mutual benefit.

However, it must be admitted that Moore was a spendthrift to the end of his days. His writings brought him £30,000, and he had nothing to leave to his wife—his sole survivor—but his DIARY in MS.

Owing chiefly, perhaps, to her good sense, they always lived in houses of low rents; and, of these, only two were residences of long duration—the one, Mayfield Cottage, near the river Dove, in Derbyshire; and the other, Sloperton Cottage, in Wiltshire.

But we find him borrowing a large house of Lord Lansdowne, at Richmond, one summer; borrowing his friend's carriages, and giving great dinners and fêtes champêtres; so that it is easy to see how the money went.

Amidst all this, he was attached to his family, a faithful, kind, and generous friend; he habitually wrote to his mother twice a week; and when he got £3000 for *Lalla Rookh*, he left £2000 in the hands of his publishers, directing the interest (£100 a year) to be handed to his parents, to whom he was devotedly attached, and this sum was paid them while they lived, even when he himself was often sorely pressed for money. Nor did he by his extravagance ever involve them in any expense.

"Moore," says Lord John Russell, very justly, "was imbued throughout his life with an attachment to the principles of liberty; and he naturally adopted the principles of that party which contended for religious liberty and political reform. His taste for educated and refined society led him into the company of the aristocratic classes in London. Among these, he was understood, appreciated, and admired. The more eminent of all political parties were charmed by his poetry, struck with his wit, and attached by the playful negligence of his conversation.

A man who was courted and esteemed by Lord Lansdowne, Mr. Canning, Sir Robert Peel, Mr. Rogers, the Rev. Sydney Smith, Sir Walter Scott, and Lord Byron, must have had social as well as literary merits of no common order. . . .

"Moore's domestic life gave scope to the best parts of his character. His beautiful wife, faultless in conduct, a fond mother, a lively companion, devoted in her attachment, always ready—perhaps too ready, to sacrifice her own domestic enjoyments that he might be admired and known, was a treasure of inestimable value to his happiness. I have said that perhaps she was too ready to sacrifice herself, because it would have been better for Mr. Moore if he had not yielded so much to the attractions of society, however dazzling and however tempting. Yet those who imagine that he passed the greater part of his time in London are greatly in error. The London days are minutely recorded; the Sloperton months are passed over in a few lines. Except when he went to Bowood, or some other house in the neighbourhood, the words 'read and wrote' comprise the events of week after week of literary labour and domestic affection.

"Those days of intellectual society, and patient labour, have alike passed away. The breakfasts with Rogers, the dinners at Holland House, the evenings when beautiful women and grave judges listened in rapture to his song, have passed away. The days when a canto of *Childe Harold*, the *Excursion* of Wordsworth, the *Curse of Kehama* of Southey, and the *Lalla Rookh* of Moore, burst in rapid succession upon the world are gone. But the world will not forget that brilliant period; and while poetry has charms for mankind, the *Melodies* of Moore will survive."

As to his religion, "That God is Love," wrote Lord John Russell, "was the summary of his belief; that a man should love his neighbour as himself seems to have been the rule of his life." The Earl of Carlisle, when inaugurating the statue of the poet, bore testimony to his moral and social worth "in all the holy relations of life." Lord O'Hagan, on the same occasion said, "he was the idol of his household." And Dr. Parr, in bequeathing him a ring, put his opinion in this form, "To one who stands high in my estimation for original genius, for his exquisite sensibility, for his independent spirit, and incorruptible integrity." It is quite evident that all who knew him loved him; however, as Professor Morley observes, "He loved his mother and his wife, but dining out did not deepen his character."

Much that was indelicate in his earlier writings, he lived to regret; and, as he advanced in life, he breathed a purer and serener atmosphere. Sydney Smith described Moore as "a gentleman of small stature, but full of genius, and a steady friend of all that is honourable and just." And Sir Walter Scott wrote, "It would be a delightful addition to life, if Thomas Moore had a cottage within two miles of me."

Lord John Russell, who was his intimate and attached friend, closes the *Memoirs, Journal and Correspondence of Thomas Moore*, which he edited, with the following tribute:—"Those who have enjoyed the brilliancy of his wit, and heard the enchantments of his song, will never forget the charms of his society. The world, so long as it can be moved by sympathy and exalted by fancy, will not willingly let die the tender strains, and the patriotic fires, of a true poet."

Mrs. Hall, when she visited Mrs. Moore, about six months after the poet's death, specially noticed her kind ministrations to the poor villagers; her going upstairs and unlocking the library door to sweep and dust it herself, for she never invited or permitted any one to enter it; and how she watched over the "Tara ivy" on the poet's terrace walk, and the roses on which he had looked, or from which he had gathered a blossom! She was still the same good kindly soul who, in other years, had made a shift to do with one servant in order to enable Moore to assist his mother; and who had sold her jewels to pay the debts of her son who had died, so that no stain of dishonour might rest on his memory.

After speaking of Mrs. Moore sitting for hours alone in the library, Mrs. Hall goes on to say, "It often seemed to me strange how the last great sorrow had tided over all others—all except one. The eldest son, Tom, was known to have died in Africa; they had received confirmatory letters and all his 'things' long ago, but *she* retained fragments of broken hope that he would yet return. One particular evening, we had been sitting still and silent a long time, when suddenly the garden gate was thrown open; her pale cheek flushed, she started up and looked out, then sank into a chair. 'What was it, dear?' I inquired. 'You will think it a weakness,' she said, 'or perhaps insanity, but I have never quite believed in our son's death, and I seldom hear the garden gate opened at an unusual hour without a hope that it is my boy.'" What a touching picture!

CHAPTER XV.

MOORE'S POPULARITY—HIS CENTENARY—ORATION AND ODES
ON THAT OCCASION.

There are translations of the following verses, in various
European languages, so admirably rendered that it would
be hard for a person, who did not already know, to guess
which version was the original:—

LITTLE MAN AND LITTLE SOUL.

A BALLAD.

There was a little Man, and he had a little Soul,
And he said, "Little Soul, let us try, try, try,
    Whether it's within our reach
    To make up a little Speech,
Just between little you and little I, I, I,
    Just between little you and little I!"

    Then said his little Soul,
    Peeping from her little hole,
"I protest, little Man, you are stout, stout, stout,
    But if it's not uncivil,
    Pray tell me what the devil
Must our little, little speech be about, bout, bout,
    Must our little, little speech be about?"

    The little Man look'd big
    With th' assistance of his wig,
And he call'd his little Soul to order, order, order,
    Till she fear'd he'd make her jog in
    To jail, like Thomas Croggan,
(As she wasn't duke or earl) to reward her, ward her, ward her,
    As she wasn't duke or earl, to reward her.

    The little Man then spoke,
    "Little Soul, it is no joke,

For as sure as J—cky F—ll—r loves a sup, sup, sup,
    I will tell the Prince and People
    What I think of Church and Steeple,
And my little patent plan to prop them up, up, up,
  And my little patent plan to prop them up."

      Away then cheek by jowl,
      Little Man and little Soul
Went and spoke their little speech to a tittle, tittle, tittle,
      And the world all declare
      That this priggish little pair
Never yet in all their lives look'd so little, little, little,
  Never yet in all their lives look'd so little!

It may be noticed, that amongst the numerous testimonials to the merits of *Lalla Rookh*, there was one pridefully recorded by the author, that must have compensated *him* a thousand-fold for the coarse remark of Hazlitt, that Moore ought not to have published *Lalla Rookh* even for three thousand guineas. Its chief incidents were represented by *tableaux vivans* at the Château-Royal, Berlin, in 1822, by the imperial and royal personages whose names appear in the following extract from a printed French programme of the entertainments :—

"Faladin, Grand Nasir, - - .- Comte Haach Maréchale de Cour.

Aliris, Roi de Bucharie, - - S. A. I. Le Grand Duc Nicholas de Russie.

Lalla Roûkh, - - - - - - S. A. I. La Grande Duchesse.

Arungzebed, le Grand Mogul, S. A. R. Le Prince Guillaume (Frère du Roi).

Abdallah, Père d'Aliris, - - S. A. R. Le Duc de Cumberland.

La Reine, son épouse, - - - S. A. R. La Princesse Louise de Radzivil."

Some portions of the scenery were magnificent, especially the gate of Eden, with its crystal bar, and occasional glimpses of splendour jetting through and falling upon the repentant Peri. At the close of the entertainments,

16

Son Altesse Impériale la Grande Duchesse, afterwards Empress of all the Russias,[1] made, it is said, the following speech:—"Is it, then, all over? Are we now at the close of all that has given us so much delight? And lives there no poet who will impart to others and to future times some notion of the happiness we have enjoyed this evening?" In answer to this irresistible appeal one of the actors, the poetical Baron de la Motte Fouqué, stepped gallantly forward, and vowed that _he_ would give the poem to the world in a German dress. On hearing which the Empress Lalla Rookh "graciously smiled." This story rests for its authority on the preface to Monsieur Le Baron de la Motte Fouqué's translation.

Of Moore, Lord O'Hagan said:—"Whilst he lived, he had, probably, a wider popularity than any man of his day; and, since his death, that popularity has been indefinitely diffused, with the ever-widening expansion of the races which speak the tongue of England.

"I visited the British Museum lately, and, looking through its great folio catalogue, I found sixty-four pages devoted exclusively to various editions, in various languages, of the works of Moore—surely an impressive proof of his large approval by the world."

Many sumptuous editions of Moore's works have been called for, especially of the _Irish Melodies_, and of _Lalla Rookh_. The former, with 161 designs from an Irish pencil—that of Daniel Maclise—engraved on steel, was published by Longmans, in 1845, imperial 8vo, at £3, 3s., in boards. Two hundred proof copies were published at double that price; and twenty-five copies, India proofs in a folio, were issued at £31, 10s. each!

And _Lalla Rookh_, beautifully printed in large 8vo,

---

[1] Alexandra Feodorowna, wife of Nicholas I.

illustrated by sixty-nine exquisite wood engravings from designs by John Tenniel, was published in 1861.

Finden's Illustrated Beauties of Moore, in Imperial 4to, appeared in 1849, at £3, 3s. and £5, 5s. per copy. This was followed by *Poetry and Pictures from Moore*, the illustrations engraved from original designs after Stothard, Maclise, and sixteen other artists.

Recent editions of *Moore's Poems* have been issued both by Messrs. Routledge, and Messrs. Warne.

A *Biography of Moore*, by H. R. Montgomery, was published in 1860. There is also a *Biography* by Burke. Much information may be gleaned from Moore's own prefaces; and biographical notices have been prefixed to various subsequent editions of the poet's works; those by Dr. John Francis Waller and Mr. William Michael Rossetti are specially noteworthy. Moore's *Hitherto Uncollected Writings*, edited by R. H. Shepherd, appeared in London in 1877.

Mr. S. C. Hall, shortly before Moore's Centenary, published *A Memory of Thomas Moore*, with whom he was acquainted so long ago as 1821. This he issued in order to aid in collecting funds for the placing of a memorial window, looking towards the *west*, in Bromham Church. This stained-glass window represents the "Last Judgment," and was unveiled by Mr. Hall on Saturday, 13th Sept., 1879. From Mr. Hall's brochure, we have already made several quotations.

A portrait-bust of Moore is placed in the National Portrait Gallery.

The celebration of the hundredth anniversary of the birth of Moore took place in Dublin (and elsewhere) on Wednesday, the 28th day of May, 1879, and, as an expression of popular admiration and gratitude for the poet's works, was a decided success. The Exhibition

Palace was thrown open and filled with enthusiastic crowds of all classes. Lord O'Hagan delivered an oration, and the Rev. Charles Edward Tisdall, D.D., Chancellor of Christ Church Cathedral, read the beautiful Centenary Ode, composed for the occasion by Denis Florence M'Carthy, rendering it with great dramatic power; the *Melodies* were sung with thrilling effect by some of the leading singers of the day; an interesting collection of relics of the poet was displayed to view, and excited the eager curiosity of thousands; and a ball at the Mansion House, one of the most brilliant seen in Dublin for many a day, wound up the day's proceedings. On all hands, the festival was admitted to have been worthy of Moore.

In his oration on this occasion, Lord O'Hagan said:— " Moore clung to Ireland with an intense and unchanging affection, which is testified by every act of his life and every page of his writings; and all who, now or hereafter, may cherish true attachment to her, whatever may be their honest varieties of sentiment, will find in him— when they have eliminated all they can disapprove in his dealings with temporary struggles and the passions they aroused—an Irishman with whose love for Ireland and constant desire to promote her welfare they can have cordial sympathy. According to his conception of her interests and his own duty, he was staunch to her, in periods of the worst discouragement as in those of the highest hope; and he refused, for her sake, to falsify his convictions, when he might have gained place and power by giving even silent countenance to public action of which he disapproved. For these things, he should command the respect of men of every creed and party. But, by the majority of Irishmen, he is entitled to be regarded with a far warmer feeling; and of that feeling,

even in this mixed assembly, one who cherishes it deeply
will not be forbidden to speak. I speak of it as referring
to an event long past—as an Englishman might speak of
Runnymede, or a Scotchman of Bannockburn. During
the long struggle for emancipation, he never failed or
faltered for an hour, in urging the claims of the Catholics
of Ireland. By playful wit, by pungent sarcasm, by
vehement invective—with all the energy of his soul and
all the resources of his genius—he pressed them on a
reluctant legislature and a hostile people. And the influence he exerted was incalculable. Circles, into which
political agitation could never break, opened freely to
the pleadings of the poet. The same melodious voice,
which roused the Irish millions to remember they had a
country, and rely on themselves for their own political
salvation, resounded in the halls and saloons of the British
aristocracy, dispelling prejudice and denouncing wrong,
with a power and sweetness which touched many a heart,
and awakened many a conscience theretofore hardened
against the cold appeals of justice. The strife is over, and
the victory achieved. We are fast forgetting the en-
venomed hatreds and cruel struggles of other days. We
will yet learn, with God's blessing, to trust each other
and love each other, as if they had never been. But, in
the prosperous harmony of a better time, the enfranchised
masses of the Irish people can never be such ingrates as
to forget the noble service they owed, in their hour of
trial, to the courage and the faithfulness of Thomas Moore.
And if his patriotism be undeniable, can any one doubt
of the independence and consistency which, in the view
of Lord Charlemont, made his character complete. I
venture to say, that no man, of whom we have authentic
record, was more distinguished by those high qualities.
He was placed in circumstances most adverse to the cul-

tivation of them. He was poor. He had to procure, by
continuous effort, the ordinary comforts of existence.
He moved amongst the wealthy and the great, many of
whom had strong attachment to him, and would have
been happy to supply his wants. He had faculties of
brain and pen, invaluable to any party which could have
procured the use of them. He loved his relatives, with a
devoted affection which might have prompted any sacrifice to elevate them and advance their interests. Briefly,
he had the amplest opportunities of commanding a profit-
able dependence, and the strongest temptations to employ
them. And he could have done so, without any flagrant
impropriety, or any forfeiture of the world's esteem. But
he refused. He endured his poverty, and preserved his
honour. He lived and died a self-relying, self-abnegating,
self-respecting man, and left to posterity an example of
independence—seldom more needed than at the present
hour—which, so far as I know, has not had many paral-
lels. . . .

"But, much more was wanting, for the safety and the
honour of our dear old music. It needed some one
who could clothe it in fitting words, and commend it to
popular acceptance. It needed a gifted man to interpret
the spirit and character of Ireland—her fancy and her
feeling—her sorrows and her hopes. It needed that the
'inarticulate poetry' of sound should find verbal expression, and that the strains which had floated down through
the ages—so sweet, so various, so marvellously expressing, in their pathos and their mirthfulness, the changeful
phases of the Irish nature—should at last be 'married to
immortal verse.' The hour came—and the man. The
concurrence was singular, as it was fortunate. The
harpers had met, and Bunting was preparing his collections, whilst Moore was practising on the broken harpsi-

chord which his father had taken in discharge of a trifling debt. Occasion, and capacity to use it, are the conditions of success in human affairs. He discovered his faculty for music and his vocation as a poet; and the melodies he learned to love induced him to exercise the one, and to pursue the other, until he became for Ireland, in Shelley's famous words—

"'The sweetest lyrist of her saddest wrong.'

In the earliest advertisement of the *Melodies*, Moore said —that, if Burns had been an Irishman, 'his heart would have been proud of such music, and he would have made it immortal.' He had not then tested his own powers, and could scarcely have anticipated that he himself was destined to give it immortality. But we may fairly apply his words to his accomplished work. Petrie recognized the fact, that the finest of our airs obtained their first appreciation in later days, less from a sense of their intrinsic merit than from their union with lyrics which seized on the popular attention; and thus it was that Moore saved them from degradation, and made them a present service and a possession for all time to his country and his race. Very long ago, in words too old to be remembered, I said that he did for us what we wanted, and no one had done before him. Exquisitely organized in soul and sense, he gathered up the fragments of our melodies, associated them with songs, such as had not been heard in latter days, and made them 'joys for ever' to his country and the world. Those songs have resounded wherever the English tongue—destined, as it seems, to become the dominant language of mankind— is borne by the millions who utter it throughout the earth. They are resounding still beneath the eastern suns, and amidst Canadian snows. — in the forests of the West, and at the antipodes, where young empires begin their conquering progress. The same sweet words, coupled with the same old music, have been heard throughout Christendom, and far beyond it—have been sung by the Frenchman and the Russian, the Persian and the Pole—and thus have the name, and the history, and the genius of our land been made familiar to distant nations, and we all have been exalted by claiming, as our own, one of the greatest lyrists of modern times."

In illustration of the honours paid to his memory by those who are far away, we quote the concluding stanzas from a centenary ode written by T. D. Sullivan, and recited, at the celebration of the Tom Moore Literary Club, in San Francisco:—

> " Oh, Tara's hill may waste away,
>   The Shannon's source may fail,
>   The mingled waters cease to play
>   Through fair Avoca's vale;
> ' Loved Arranmore' may fade from sight,
>   But you will still endure
>   In Irish hearts, fresh, warm, and bright,
>   Enchanting songs of Moore!

> " Yea, even if our ancient race
>   In time should cease to be,
>   And if our dear old native place
>   Should sink into the sea—
>   The world would save from out the wave,
>   And hold the prize secure,
>   The harp you strung, the songs you sung,
>   Our own immortal Moore!"

Scribner's Monthly Magazine, for July, contained the following fine tribute by Richard Henry Stoddard:—

THOMAS MOORE.

(MAY 28, 1879.)

A lord of lyric song was born
  A hundred years ago to-day;
Loved of that race that long has worn
  The shamrock for the bay!

He sung of wine, and sung of flowers,
  Of woman's smile, and woman's tear,—
Light songs, that suit our lighter hours,
  But oh, how bright and dear!

Who will may build the epic verse,
  And, Atlas-like, its weight sustain;
Or solemn tragedies rehearse
  In high, heroic strain.

So be it. But when all is done,
  The heart demands for happy days
The lyrics of Anacreon,
  And Sappho's tender lays.

Soft souls with these are satisfied;
  He loved them, but exacted more,—
For his the lash that Horace plied,
  The sword Harmodius wore!

Where art thou, Brian, and thy knights,
  So dreaded by the flying Dane?
And thou, Con, of the Hundred Fights?
  Your spirits are not slain!

Strike for us, as ye did of yore,
  Be with us,—we shall conquer still,
Though Irish kings are crowned no more
  On Tara's holy hill!

Perhaps he was not hero born,
  Like those he sung—Heaven only knows;

He had the rose without the thorn,
    But he deserved the rose!

For underneath its odorous light
    His heart was warm, his soul was strong;
He kept his love of country bright,
    And sung her sweetest song!

Therefore her sons have gathered here
    To honour him, as few before,
And blazon on his hundredth year
    The fame of Thomas Moore!

And the following admirable poem was read at the Boston centenary of the Bard of Erin by Dr. Oliver Wendell Holmes, the well-known "Autocrat of the Breakfast-table."

THOMAS MOORE.

Enchanter of Erin, whose magic has bound us,
    Thy wand for one moment we fondly would claim,
Entranced while it summons the phantoms around us
    That blush into life at the sound of thy name.
The tell-tales of memory wake from their slumbers,
    I hear the old song with its tender refrain,
What passion lies hid in those honey-voiced numbers,
    What perfume of youth in each exquisite strain!
The home of my childhood comes back as a vision—
    Hark! hark! a soft chord from its song-haunted room,
'Tis a morning of May, when the air is elysian,
    The syringa in bud and the lilac in bloom;
We are clustered around the "Clementi" piano—
    There were six of us then, there are two of us now—
She is singing, the girl with the silver soprano,
    How "the Lord of the Valley" was false to his vow.
"Let Erin remember" the echoes are calling,
    Through "the Vale of Avoca" the waters are rolled,
"The Exile" laments while the night dews are falling,
    "The Morning of Life" dawns again as of old.

But, ah! those warm love songs of fresh adolescence
  Around us such raptures celestial they flung,
That it seemed as if Paradise breathed its quintessence
  Through the seraph-toned lips of the maiden that sung.
Long hushed are the chords that my boyhood enchanted,
  As when the smooth wave by the angel was stirred,
Yet still with their music is memory haunted,
  And oft in my dreams are their melodies heard;
I feel like the priest to his altar returning;
  The crowd that was kneeling no longer is there;
The flame has died down, but the brands are still burning,
  And sandal and cinnamon sweeten the air.

The veil, for her bridal, young Summer is weaving
  In her azure-domed hall with its tapestried floor,
And spring, the last tear-drops of May-dew, is leaving
  On the daisy of Burns and the shamrock of Moore.
How like, how unlike, as we view them together,
  The song of the minstrels, whose record we scan,
One fresh as the breeze blowing over the heather,
  One sweet as the breath from Odalisque's fan;
Ah! passion can glow mid a palace's splendour;
  The cage does not alter the song of the bird,
And the curtain of silk has known whispers as tender
  As ever the blossoming hawthorn has heard.
No fear lest the step of the soft-slippered graces
  Should fright the young loves from their warm little nest,
For the heart of a Queen, under jewels and laces,
  Beats time with the pulse in the peasant girl's breast.
Thrice welcome each gift of kind nature's bestowing,
  Her fountain heeds little the goblet we hold;
Alike, when its musical waters are flowing,
  The shell from the seaside, the chalice of gold.
The twins of the lyre to her voices had listened,
  Both laid their best gifts upon Liberty's shrine;
For Cœla's loved minstrel the holly wreath glistened;
  For Erin's the rose and the myrtle entwine—
And while the fresh blossoms of Summer are braided,
  For the sea-girdled, stream-silvered, lake-jewelled isle,

While her mantle of verdure is woven unfaded,
   While Shannon and Liffey shall dimple and smile.
The land where the staff of St. Patrick was planted,
   Where the shamrock grows green from the cliffs to the
      shore,
The land of fair maidens and heroes undaunted,
   Shall wreath her bright harp with the garlands of Moore.

The following fine-toned and beautiful ode by Denis
Florence M'Carthy, which was read by Dr. Tisdall at
the Dublin Moore Centenary, and to which allusion has
already been made, we deem a fitting conclusion for this
volume :—

CENTENARY ODE.

TO THE MEMORY OF THOMAS MOORE.

Joy to Ierné, joy,
   This day a deathless crown is won,
   Her Child of Song, her glorious son,
Her Minstrel Boy,
Attains his century of fame,
   Completes the time-allotted zone,
And proudly with the world's acclaim
   Ascends the Lyric Throne.

Yes, joy to her whose path so long,
   Slow journeying to her realm of rest
   O'er many a rugged mountain's crest,
He charmed with his enchanting song,
Like his own princess in the tale,
   When he who had her way beguiled
   Through many a bleak and desert wild
Until she reached Cashmere's bright vale
Had ceased those notes to play and sing
   To which her heart responsive swelled,
   She looking up in him beheld
Her minstrel lover and her king—
So Erin now, her journey well-nigh o'er,
Enraptured sees her minstrel king in Moore.

And round that throne whose light to-day
  O'er all the world is cast,
In words though weak, in hues though faint,
Congenial Fancy rise and paint
  The spirits of the past
Who here their homage pay—
  Those who his youthful Muse inspired,
  Those who his early genius fired
To emulate their lay :—
And as in some phantasmal glass
Let the immortal spirits pass,
Let each renew the inspiring strain,
And fire the poet's soul again.

  First there comes from classic Greece,
  Beaming love and breathing peace,
  With her pure sweet smiling face,
  The glory of the Æolian race,
  Beauteous Sappho, violet-crowned,
  Shedding joy and rapture round :—
  In her hand a harp she bears,
  Parent of celestial airs—,
  Love leaps trembling from each wire,
  Every chord a string of fire :—
  How the poet's heart doth beat,
  How his lips the notes repeat,
  Till in rapture borne along,
  The Sapphic lute, the lyrist's song
  Blend in one delicious strain,
  Never to divide again.

  And beside the Æolian Queen
  Great Alcæus' form is seen,
  He takes up in voice more strong
  The dying cadence of the song,
  And on loud-resounding strings,
  Hurls his wrath on tyrant kings :—
  Like to incandescent coal
  On the poet's kindred soul

Fall these words of living flame,
Till their songs become the same,—
The same hate of slavery's night,
The same love of freedom's light,
Scorning aught that stops its way,
Come the black cloud whence it may,
Lift alike the inspirèd song
And the liquid notes prolong.

Carolling a livelier measure
Comes the Teian Bard of Pleasure,
Round his brow where joy reposes
Radiant Love enwreaths his roses,
Rapture in his verse is ringing,
Soft persuasion in his singing:—
'Twas the same melodious ditty
Moved Polycrates to pity,
Made that tyrant heart surrender
Captive to a tone so tender:
To the younger bard inclining,
Round his brow the roses twining,
First the wreath in red wine steeping,
He his cithern to his keeping
Yields, its glorious fate foreseeing,
From her chains a nation freeing,
Fetters new around it flinging
In the flowers of his own singing.

But who is this that from the misty cloud
  Of immemorial years,
Wrapped in the vesture of his vaporous shroud
  With solemn step appears?
His head with oak-leaves and with ivy crowned
  Lets fall its silken snow,
While the white billows of his beard unbound
  Athwart his bosom flow:—
Who is this venerable form
Whose hands, prelusive of the storm

Across his harp-strings play—
That harp which trembling in his hand
Impatient waits its lord's command
To pour the impassioned lay?
Who is it comes with reverential hail
  · To greet the Bard who sang his country best?
'Tis Ossian—primal Poet of the Gael—
The Homer of the West.

He sings the heroic tales of old
  When Ireland yet was free,
Of many a fight and foray bold,
  And raid beyond the sea.

Of all the famous deeds of Fin,
  And all the wiles of Maev,
Now thunders 'mid the battle's din,
  Now sobs beside the wave.

That wave empurpled by the sword
  The hero used too well,
When great Cuchullin held the ford,
  And fair Ferdiah fell.

And now his prophet eye is cast
  As o'er a boundless plain,
He sees the future as the past,
  And blends them in his strain.

The Red-Branch Knights their flags unfold
  When danger's front appears,
The Sun-burst breaks through clouds of gold
  To glorify their spears.

But ah! a darker hour drew nigh,
  The hour of Erin's woe,
When she, though destined not to die
  Lay prostrate 'neath the foe.

When broke were all the arms she bore,
  And bravely bore in vain,

Till even her harp could sound no more
    Beneath the victor's chain.

Ah! dire constraint, ah! cruel wrong,
    To fetter thus its chord,
But well they knew that Ireland's song
    Was keener than her sword.

That song would pierce where swords would fail,
    And o'er the battle's din,
The sweet sad music of the Gael
    A peaceful victory win.

Long was the trance, but sweet and low
    The harp breathed out again
Its speechless wail, its wordless woe
    In Carolan's witching strain.

Until at last the gift of words
    Denied to it so long,
Poured o'er the now enfranchised chords
    The articulate light of song.

Poured the bright light from genius won
    That woke the harp's wild lays—
Even as that statue which the sun
    Made vocal with his rays.

Thus Ossian in disparted dream
    Outpoured the varied lay,
But now in one united stream
    His rapture finds its way:—

"Yes, in thy hands, illustrious son,
    The harp shall speak once more,
Its sweet lament shall rippling run
    From listening shore to shore.

"Till mighty lands that lie unknown
    Far in the fabled West,

And giant isles of verdure thrown
Upon the South Sea's breast,

"And plains where rushing rivers flow—
Fit emblems of the free—
Shall learn to know of Ireland's woe,
And Ireland's weal through thee."

'Twas thus he sang,
And while tumultuous plaudits rang
From the immortal throng,
In the younger minstrel's hand
He placed the emblem of the land—
The harp of Irish song.

Oh! what dulcet notes are heard,
Never bird
Soaring through the sunny air
Like a prayer
Borne by angels' hands on high
So entranced the listening sky
As his song—
Soft, pathetic, joyous, strong,
Rising now in rapid flight
Out of sight
Like a lark in its own light,
Now descending low and sweet
To our feet,
Till the odours of the grass
With the light notes as they pass
Blend and meet.
All that Erin's memory guards
In her heart,
Deeds of heroes, songs of bards,
Have their part.
Brian's glories reappear,
Fionualla's song we hear,
Tara's walls resound again
With a more inspirèd strain,

17

Rival rivers meet and join,
Stately Shannon blends with Boyne,
While on high the storm-winds cease
Heralding the arch of peace.

And all the bright creations fair
    That 'neath his master-hand awake,
Some in tears and some in smiles,
Like Nea in the summer isles,
    Or Kathleen by the lonely lake,
Round his radiant throne repair:
Nay, his own Peri of the air
    Now no more disconsolate,
    Gives in at Fame's celestial gate
His passport to the skies—
    The gift to Heaven most dear,
    His country's tear.
From every lip the glad refrain doth rise,
"Joy, ever joy, his glorious task is done,
The gates are passed and Fame's bright heaven is won!"

Ah! yes, the work, the glorious work is done,
And Erin crowns to-day her brightest son,
Around his brow entwines the victor bay,
And lives herself immortal in his lay—
Leads him with honour to her highest place,
For he had borne his more-than-mother's name
Proudly along the Olympic lists of fame
When mighty athletes struggled in the race.
Byron, the swift-souled spirit, in his pride
Paused to cheer on the rival by his side,
    And Lycidas so long
Lost in the light of his own dazzling song,
Although himself unseen,
Gave the bright wreath that might his own have been
To him whom mid the mountain shepherd throng,
The minstrels of the isles,
    When Adonais died so fair and young,
Ierné sent from out her green defiles

"The sweetest lyrist of her saddest wrong,
And love taught grief to fall like music from his tongue."—
And he who sang of Poland's kindred woes,
And Hope's delicious dream,
And all the mighty minstrels who arose
In that auroral gleam
That o'er our age a blaze of glory threw
Which Shakspere's only knew—
Some from their hidden haunts remote,
Like him the lonely hermit of the hills,
Whose song like some great organ note
The whole horizon fills,
Or the great Master, he whose magic hand,
Wielding the wand from which such wonder flows,
Transformed the lineaments of a rugged land,
And left the Thistle lovely as the Rose.
Oh! in a concert of such minstrelsy,
In such a glorious company,
What pride for Ireland's harp to sound,
For Ireland's son to share,
What pride to see him glory-crowned,
And hear amid the dazzling gleam
Upon the rapt and ravished air
Her harp still sound supreme!

Glory to Moore, eternal be the glory
   That here we crown and consecrate to-day,
Glory to Moore, for he has sung our story
   In strains whose sweetness ne'er can pass away.

Glory to Moore, for he has sighed our sorrow
   In such a wail of melody divine,
That even from grief a passing joy we borrow,
   And linger long o'er each lamenting line.

Glory to Moore, that in his songs of gladness
   (Which neither change nor time can e'er destroy)
Though mingled oft with some faint sigh of sadness,
   He sings his country's rapture and its joy.

What wit like his flings out electric flashes
   That make the numbers sparkle as they run—
Wit that revives dull history's Dead-sea ashes,
   And makes the ripe fruit glisten in the sun?

What fancy full of loveliness and lightness
   Has spread like his as at some dazzling feast,
The fruits and flowers, the beauty and the brightness,
   And all the golden glories of the East?

Perpetual blooms his bower of summer roses,
   No winter comes to turn his green leaves sere,
Beside his song-stream where the swan reposes
   The bulbul sings as by the Bendemeer.

But back returning from his flight with Peris,
   Above his native fields he sings his best,
Like to the lark whose rapture never wearies,
   When poised in air he singeth o'er his nest.

And so we rank him with the great departed,
   The kings of song who rule us from their urns,
The souls inspired, the natures noble hearted,
   And place him proudly by the side of Burns.

And as not only by the Calton Mountain
   Is Scotland's bard remembered and revered,
But wheresoe'er, like some o'erflowing fountain,
   Its hardy race a prosperous path has cleared,

There, 'mid the roar of newly rising cities,
   His glorious name is heard on every tongue,
There to the music of immortal ditties,
   His lays of love, his patriot songs are sung;

So not alone beside that Bay of beauty
   That guards the portals of his native town,
Where like two watchful sentinels on duty,
   Howth and Killiney from their heights look down.

But wheresoe'er the exiled race hath drifted,
  By what far sea, what mighty stream beside,
There shall to-day the poet's name be lifted,
  And Moore proclaimed its glory and its pride.

There shall his name be held in fond memento,
  There shall his songs resound for evermore,
Whether beside the golden Sacramento,
  Or where Niagara's thunder shakes the shore;—

For all that's bright indeed must fade and perish,
  And all that's sweet when sweetest not endure,
Before the world shall cease to love and cherish
  The wit and song, the name and fame of MOORE.

BOOKS OF PERMANENT INTEREST,

PUBLISHED BY

HARPER & BROTHERS, NEW YORK.

☞ HARPER & BROTHERS *will send any of the following works by mail, postage prepaid, to any part of the United States, on receipt of the price.*

Deshler's Afternoons with the Poets.

Afternoons with the Poets. By C. D. DESHLER. Post 8vo, Cloth, $1 75.

Bayne's Lessons from My Masters.

Lessons from My Masters: Carlyle, Tennyson, and Ruskin. By PETER BAYNE, M.A., LL.D. 12mo, Cloth, $1 75.

Symonds's Greek Poets.

Studies of the Greek Poets. By JOHN ADDINGTON SYMONDS. 2 vols., square 16mo, Cloth, $3 50.

Symonds's Southern Europe.

Sketches and Studies in Southern Europe. By JOHN ADDINGTON SYMONDS. 2 vols., square 16mo, Cloth, $4 00.

Mahaffy's Greek Literature.

A History of Classical Greek Literature. By the Rev. J. P. MAHAFFY, M.A., Trinity College, Dublin, Author of "Social Life in Greece." 2 vols., 12mo, Cloth, $4 00.

Miss Mitford's Life and Letters.

The Life of Mary Russell Mitford, Author of " Our Village," &c., told by Herself in Letters to her Friends. With Anecdotes and Sketches of her most celebrated Contemporaries. Edited by the Rev. A. G. K. L'ESTRANGE. 2 vols., 12mo, Cloth, $3 50.

Miss Mitford's Recollections.

Recollections of a Literary Life; or, Books, Places, and People. By MARY RUSSELL MITFORD. 12mo, Cloth, $1 50.

Beattie's Life and Letters of Thomas Campbell.

Life and Letters of Thomas Campbell. Edited by W. BEATTIE, M.D. With an Introductory Letter by WASHINGTON IRVING. 2 vols., 12mo, Cloth, $3 00.

Leigh Hunt's Autobiography.

Autobiography of Leigh Hunt, with Reminiscences of Friends and Contemporaries. 2 vols., 12mo, Cloth, $3 00.

Leigh Hunt's Men, Women, and Books.

Men, Women, and Books. A Selection of Sketches, Essays, and Critical Memoirs from his Uncollected Prose Writings. By LEIGH HUNT. 2 vols., 12mo, Cloth, $3 00; Half Calf, $6 50.

Carleton's Farm Legends.

Farm Legends. By WILL CARLETON. Illustrated. Square 8vo, Ornamental Cloth, $2 00; Gilt Edges, $2 50.

Carleton's Farm Ballads.

Farm Ballads. By WILL CARLETON. Illustrated. Square 8vo, Ornamental Cloth, $2 00; Gilt Edges, $2 50.

Seymour's Self-Made Men.

Self-Made Men. By CHARLES C. B. SEYMOUR. Many Portraits. 12mo, Cloth, $1 75.

The Bazar Book of Decorum.

The Bazar Book of Decorum. The Care of the Person, Manners, Etiquette, and Ceremonials. 16mo, Cloth, $1 00.

The Bazar Book of the Household.

The Bazar Book of the Household. Marriage, Establishment, Servants, Housekeeping, Children, Home Life, Company. 16mo, Cloth, $1 00.

The Bazar Book of Health.

The Bazar Book of Health. The Dwelling, the Nursery, the Bedroom, the Dining-Room, the Parlor, the Library, the Kitchen, the Sick-Room. 16mo, Cloth, $1 00.

Countess Guiccioli's Lord Byron.

My Recollections of Lord Byron; and those of Eye-Witnesses of his Life. By the Countess GUICCIOLI. Translated by HUBERT E. H. JERNINGHAM. With a Portrait. 12mo, Cloth, $1 75.

Sara Coleridge's Memoir and Letters.

Memoir and Letters of Sara Coleridge. Edited by her Daughter. With Two Portraits on Steel. Crown 8vo, Cloth, $2 50; Half Calf, $4 50.

Haweis's Music and Morals.

Music and Morals. By Rev. H. R. HAWEIS, M.A. With Illustrations and Diagrams. 12mo, Cloth, $1 75.

Lamb's Complete Works.

The Works of Charles Lamb. Comprising his Letters, Poems, Essays of Elia, Essays upon Shakspeare, Hogarth, &c., and a Sketch of his Life, with the Final Memorials, by T. NOON TALFOURD. Portrait. 2 vols., 12mo, Cloth, $3 00.

Yonge's Life of Marie Antoinette.

The Life of Marie Antoinette, Queen of France. By CHARLES DUKE YONGE. With Portrait. Crown 8vo, Cloth, $2 50.

Randolph's Domestic Life of Jefferson.

The Domestic Life of Thomas Jefferson: compiled from Family Letters and Reminiscences, by his Great-Granddaughter, SARAH N. RANDOLPH. Illustrated. Crown 8vo, Cloth, $2 50.

Whartons' Queens of Society.

The Queens of Society. By GRACE and PHILIP WHARTON. Illustrated by Charles Altamont Doyle and the Brothers Dalziel. 12mo, Cloth, $1 75.

Whartons' Wits and Beaux of Society.

The Wits and Beaux of Society. By GRACE and PHILIP WHARTON. With Illustrations from Drawings by H. Browne and Jas. Godwin. Engraved by the Brothers Dalziel. 12mo, Cloth, $1 75.

Parton's Caricature and other Comic Art.

Caricature, and other Comic Art, in all Times and Many Lands. By JAMES PARTON. With 203 Illustrations. 8vo, Cloth, Gilt Tops and Uncut Edges, $5 00; Half Calf, $7 25.

Trowbridge's Book of Gold, and other Poems.

The Book of Gold, and other Poems. By J. T. TROWBRIDGE. Illustrated. 8vo, Ornamental Covers, Gilt Edges, $2 50. (In a box.)

Bigelow's Bench and Bar.

Bench and Bar: a Complete Digest of the Wit, Humor, Asperities, and Amenities of the Law. New Edition, greatly Enlarged. By L. J. BIGELOW. Crown 8vo, Cloth, $2 00.

Clayton's Queens of Song.

Queens of Song: being Memoirs of some of the most Celebrated Female Vocalists who have performed on the Lyric Stage, from the Earliest Days of Opera to the Present Time. To which is added a Chronological List of all the Operas that have been performed in Europe. By ELLEN CREATHORNE CLAYTON. With Portraits. 8vo, Cloth, $3 00; Half Morocco, $4 75.

Green's Stray Studies from England and Italy.

Stray Studies from England and Italy. By JOHN RICHARD GREEN, M.A. Post 8vo, Cloth, $1 75.

Brougham's Autobiography.

The Life and Times of Henry, Lord Brougham. Written by Himself. 3 vols., 12mo, Cloth, in a box, $6 00.

Macready's Reminiscences.

Macready's Reminiscences, and Selections from his Diary and Letters. Edited by Sir FREDERICK POLLOCK, Bart., one of his Executors. With Portraits. Crown 8vo, Cloth, $1 50.

Castelar's Life of Lord Byron.

Life of Lord Byron, and other Sketches. By EMILIO CASTELAR. Translated by Mrs. ARTHUR ARNOLD. 12mo, Cloth, $1 50.

Castelar's Old Rome and New Italy.

Old Rome and New Italy. By EMILIO CASTELAR. Translated by Mrs. ARTHUR ARNOLD. 12mo, Cloth, $1 75.

Countess Blessington's Memoirs.

The Literary Life and Correspondence of the Countess of Blessington. Compiled and Edited by R. R. MADDEN. With Portrait. 2 vols., 12mo, Cloth, $3 00.

Haydon's Autobiography.

Life of Benjamin Robert Haydon, Historical Painter, from his Autobiography and Journals. Edited and Compiled by TOM TAYLOR, of the Inner Temple. 2 vols., 12mo, Cloth, $3 00. '

Lord Holland's Foreign Reminiscences.

Foreign Reminiscences, by Henry Richard, Lord Holland. Edited by his Son, HENRY EDWARD, LORD HOLLAND. 12mo, Cloth, $1 25.

Simms's Chevalier Bayard.

Life of the Chevalier Bayard. By W. GILMORE SIMMS. Illustrated. 12mo, Cloth, $1 50.

Holmes's Life of Mozart.

Life of Mozart, including his Correspondence. By EDWARD HOLMES. 12mo, Cloth, $1 00.

Sydney Smith's Life and Letters.

A Memoir of the Reverend Sydney Smith. By his Daughter, LADY HOLLAND. With a Selection from his Letters, Edited by Mrs. AUSTIN. 2 vols., 12mo, Cloth, $3 00; Half Calf, $6 50.

Curtis's Lotus-Eating.

Lotus-Eating. A Summer Book. By GEORGE WILLIAM CURTIS. Illustrated from designs by Kensett. 12mo, Cloth, $1 50.

Curtis's Nile Notes of a Howadji.

Nile Notes of a Howadji. By GEORGE WILLIAM CURTIS. 12mo, Cloth, $1 50.

Curtis's Prue and I.

Prue and I. By GEORGE WILLIAM CURTIS. 12mo, Cloth, $1 50.

Curtis's Howadji in Syria.

The Howadji in Syria. By GEORGE WILLIAM CURTIS. 12mo, Cloth, $1 50.

Curtis's Potiphar Papers.

The Potiphar Papers. By GEORGE WILLIAM CURTIS. Illustrated by Drawings from Hoppin. 12mo, Cloth, $1 50.

Curtis's Trumps.

Trumps. A Novel. By GEORGE WILLIAM CURTIS. Illustrated by Hoppin. 12mo, Cloth, $2 00.

Disraeli's Amenities of Literature.

Amenities of Literature; consisting of Sketches and Characters of English Literature. By I. DISRAELI, D.C.L., F.S.A. 2 vols., 12mo, Cloth, $2 50.

Howitt's Homes and Haunts of the British Poets.

Homes and Haunts of the British Poets. By WILLIAM HOWITT. Illustrated. 2 vols., 12mo, Cloth, $3 50.

Forney's Anecdotes of Public Men.

Anecdotes of Public Men. By JOHN W. FORNEY. 12mo, Cloth, $2 00.

Cox's Why We Laugh.

Why We Laugh. By SAMUEL S. COX. 12mo, Cloth, $1 50.

Smiles's Character.

Character. By SAMUEL SMILES. 12mo, Cloth, $1 00.

Smiles's Self-Help.

Self-Help; with Illustrations of Character, Conduct, and Perseverance. By SAMUEL SMILES. New Edition, Revised and Enlarged. 12mo, Cloth, $1 00.

Smiles's Thrift.

Thrift. By SAMUEL SMILES. 12mo, Cloth, $1 00.

Smiles's Life of a Scotch Naturalist.

Life of a Scotch Naturalist: Thomas Edward, Associate of the Linnæan Society. By SAMUEL SMILES. Portrait and Illustrations. 12mo, Cloth, $1 50.

Smiles's Lives of the Stephensons.

The Life of George Stephenson, and his Son, Robert Stephenson; comprising, also, a History of the Invention and Introduction of the Railway Locomotive. By SAMUEL SMILES. With Portraits and numerous Illustrations. 8vo, Cloth, $3 00.

Smiles's Robert Dick.

Robert Dick, Baker, of Thurso; Geologist and Botanist. By SAMUEL SMILES, LL.D. With a Portrait and numerous Illustrations. 12mo, Cloth, $1 50.

Pardoe's Louis the Fourteenth.

Louis the Fourteenth and the Court of France in the Seventeenth Century. By Miss JULIA PARDOE. Illustrated. 2 vols., 12mo, Cloth, $4 00.

Moore's Life of Byron.

Letters and Journals of Lord Byron. With Notices of his Life. By THOMAS MOORE. 2 vols., 8vo, Cloth, $4 00; Sheep, $5 00; Half Calf, $8 50.

GEORGE ELIOT'S WORKS.

ADAM BEDE. A Novel. Illustrated. 12mo, Cloth, $1 25.

DANIEL DERONDA. A Novel. 2 vols., 12mo, Cloth, $2 50.

IMPRESSIONS OF THEOPHRASTUS SUCH. 12mo, Cloth, $1 25.

FELIX HOLT, THE RADICAL. A Novel. Illustrated. 12mo, Cloth, $1 25.

MIDDLEMARCH. A Novel. 2 vols., 12mo, Cloth, $2 50.

ROMOLA. A Novel. Illustrated. 12mo, Cloth, $1 25.

SCENES OF CLERICAL LIFE, and SILAS MARNER, The Weaver of Raveloe. Illustrated. 12mo, Cloth, $1 25.

THE MILL ON THE FLOSS. A Novel. Illustrated. 12mo, Cloth. $1 25.

HARPER & BROTHERS *also publish Cheaper Editions* of GEORGE ELIOT'S WORKS, as follows:

DANIEL DERONDA. 8vo, Paper, 50 cents.—IMPRESSIONS OF THEOPHRASTUS SUCH. 4to, Paper, 10 cents. — FELIX HOLT. 8vo, Paper, 50 cents.—THE MILL ON THE FLOSS. 8vo, Paper, 50 cents.—MIDDLEMARCH. 8vo, Paper, 75 cents; Cloth, $1 25.—ROMOLA. 8vo, Paper, 50 cents.—SCENES OF CLERICAL LIFE. 8vo, Paper, 50 cents. (Also, in 3 vols., 32mo, Paper, AMOS BARTON, MR. GILFIL'S LOVE STORY, JANET'S REPENTANCE, 20 cents each.)—SILAS MARNER. 12mo, Cloth, 75 cents. — BROTHER JACOB; THE LIFTED VEIL. 32mo, Paper, 20 cents.

PUBLISHED BY HARPER & BROTHERS, NEW YORK.

☞ *Any of the above works will be sent by mail, postage prepaid, to any part of the United States, on receipt of the price.*

W. M. THACKERAY'S WORKS.

HARPER'S POPULAR EDITION.

8vo, Paper.

NOVELS: Denis Duval. Illustrated. 25 cents. — Henry Esmond. 50 cents.—Henry Esmond, and Lovel the Widower. Illustrated. 60 cents.—Lovel the Widower. 20 cents.—Pendennis. Illustrated. 75 cents.—The Adventures of Philip. Illustrated. 60 cents.—The Great Hoggarty Diamond. 20 cents.—The Newcomes. Illustrated. 90 cents.—The Virginians. Illustrated. 90 cents.—Vanity Fair. Illustrated. 80 cents.

HENRY ESMOND, 4to, Paper, 15 cents.

HARPER'S HOUSEHOLD EDITION.

12mo, Cloth.

NOVELS: Vanity Fair.—Pendennis.—The Newcomes.—The Virginians. — Adventures of Philip. — Henry Esmond, and Lovel the Widower. Illustrated. Six volumes, 12mo, Cloth, $1 25 per volume.

MISCELLANEOUS WRITINGS: Barry Lyndon, Hoggarty Diamond, &c.— Paris and Irish Sketch Books, &c.—Book of Snobs, Sketches, &c.—Four Georges, English Humorists, Roundabout Papers, &c. —Catherine, Christmas Books, &c. Illustrated. Five volumes, 12mo, Cloth, $1 25 per volume.

Complete Sets (11 *vols*), $12 00.

PUBLISHED BY HARPER & BROTHERS, NEW YORK.

☞ HARPER & BROTHERS *will send any of the above volumes by mail, postage prepaid, to any part of the United States, on receipt of the price.*

CHARLES LEVER'S NOVELS.

A DAY'S RIDE. A Life's Romance. Illustrated. 8vo, Paper, 40 cents.

BARRINGTON. 8vo, Paper, 40 cents.

GERALD FITZGERALD, "THE CHEVALIER." 8vo, Paper, 40 cents.

LORD KILGOBBIN. Illustrated. 8vo, Paper, 50 cents; Cloth, $1 00.

LUTTRELL OF ARRAN. 8vo, Paper, 60 cents; Cloth, $1 10.

MAURICE TIERNAY, THE SOLDIER OF FORTUNE. 8vo, Paper, 50 cents.

ONE OF THEM. 8vo, Paper, 50 cents.

ROLAND CASHEL. Illustrated. 8vo, Paper, 75 cents.

SIR BROOK FOSSBROOKE. 8vo, Paper, 50 cents.

SIR JASPER CAREW, KNT.; HIS LIFE AND EXPERIENCES. With some Account of his Over-reachings and Short-comings, now first given to the World by Himself. 8vo, Paper, 50 cents.

THAT BOY OF NORCOTT'S. Illustrated. 8vo, Paper, 25 cents.

THE BRAMLEIGHS OF BISHOP'S FOLLY. 8vo, Paper, 50 cts.

THE DALTONS; OR, THREE ROADS IN LIFE. 8vo, Paper, 75 cents.

THE DODD FAMILY ABROAD. 8vo, Paper, 60 cents.

THE FORTUNES OF GLENCORE. 8vo, Paper, 50 cents.

THE MARTINS OF CRO' MARTIN. 8vo, Paper, 60 cents.

TONY BUTLER. 8vo, Paper, 60 cents; Cloth, $1 10.

The Set Complete, 5 vols., 8vo, Cloth, $12 00.

PUBLISHED BY HARPER & BROTHERS, NEW YORK.

☞ *Any of the above works will be sent by mail, postage prepaid, to any part of the United States, on receipt of the price.*

CHARLES READE'S WORKS.

HARPER'S POPULAR EDITION.

8vo, Paper.

HARD CASH. Illustrated. 50 cents.
A WOMAN-HATER. Illustrated. 60 cents.
FOUL PLAY. 35 cents.
GRIFFITH GAUNT. Illustrated. 40 cents.
IT IS NEVER TOO LATE TO MEND. 50 cents.
LOVE ME LITTLE, LOVE ME LONG. 35 cents.
PEG WOFFINGTON, CHRISTIE JOHNSTONE, AND OTHER TALES. 50 cents.
PUT YOURSELF IN HIS PLACE. Illustrated. 50 cents.
THE CLOISTER AND THE HEARTH. 50 cents.
THE WANDERING HEIR. Illustrated. 25 cents.
WHITE LIES. 40 cents.
A HERO AND A MARTYR. With a Portrait. 15 cents.
A SIMPLETON. 35 cents.
A TERRIBLE TEMPTATION. Illustrated. 40 cents.

32mo, Paper.

THE JILT. Illustrated. 20 cents.
THE COMING MAN. 20 cents.

HARPER'S HOUSEHOLD EDITION.

Illustrated. 12mo, Cloth.

HARD CASH.	A WOMAN-HATER.
FOUL PLAY.	NEVER TOO LATE TO MEND.
WHITE LIES.	PEG WOFFINGTON, &c.
LOVE ME LITTLE, LOVE ME LONG.	PUT YOURSELF IN HIS PLACE.
GRIFFITH GAUNT.	A TERRIBLE TEMPTATION.
THE CLOISTER AND THE HEARTH.	A SIMPLETON, & THE WANDERING HEIR.

Twelve Volumes. $1 00 per vol.

Complete Sets, $10 00.

PUBLISHED BY HARPER & BROTHERS, NEW YORK.

Sent by mail, postage prepaid, on receipt of price.